continued . . .

"Riveting! *Dire Needs* hooked me from the very first page." —bestselling author Shiloh Walker

"*Dire Needs* creates an interesting new world, with lots of history and mythology. Great plot twists and turns, hot and steamy sex in the woods, and a bit of sweet thrown into the mix." —Sizzling Hot Book Reviews

"An exciting new paranormal series." —Romance Reader at Heart

"The chemistry between Rifter and Gwen sizzles." —Manga Maniac Cafe

"The first chapter was one of the best I've read in a while. . . . The instant the book begins, you know you are in for a great ride." —That's What I'm Talking About

"A fresh and sexy take on werewolves . . . a very imaginative story . . . a great read with smoking-hot scenes." —Nocturne Romance Reads

**Praise for Other
Novels by Stephanie Tyler**

"Unforgettable." —*New York Times* bestselling author Cherry Adair

"Red-hot romance. White-knuckle suspense." —*New York Times* bestselling author Lara Adrian

"Sexy and witty." —Fresh Fiction

"Stephanie Tyler is a master." —Romance Junkies

DIRE DESIRES

A NOVEL OF THE ETERNAL WOLF CLAN

STEPHANIE TYLER

A SIGNET ECLIPSE BOOK

SIGNET ECLIPSE
Published by the Penguin Group
Penguin Group (USA) Inc., 375 Hudson Street,
New York, New York 10014, USA

USA | Canada | UK | Ireland | Australia | New Zealand | India | South Africa | China

Penguin Books Ltd., Registered Offices: 80 Strand, London WC2R 0RL, England
For more information about the Penguin Group visit penguin.com.

First published by Signet Eclipse, an imprint of New American Library,
a division of Penguin Group (USA) Inc.

First Printing, July 2013

ISBN 978-0-451-24001-9

Printed in the United States of America
10 9 8 7 6 5 4 3 2 1

ALWAYS LEARNING   PEARSON

For Sharon Muha,
who is more help than she knows

. . . you know love when you see it,
you can feel its lunar strength, its brutal pull.
—"Facts About The Moon" by Dorianne Laux

Glossary

abilities: The now-immortal Dire wolves were all born with abilities, except for Rifter, who was cursed with his at birth. These abilities were looked at with fear by the Dire population at large. In fact, the Elders were once Dire wolves who were sacrificed to Hati, the creator of the Dires, because they had abilities. The abilities range from dreamwalking to communicating with the dead, and can often be seen as both a gift and a curse to the wolves trying to balance them out.

Adept: An immortal, master witch.

Brother Wolf: A Dire wolf is a dual-natured beast who lives with his Brother Wolf inside of him. These Brother Wolves are also depicted in a life-sized glyph on the Dires' backs, the glyph coming out fully after a Dire's first shift at age twenty-one. The Dires and their inner wolves have an even balance of power and a deep respect for one another. They both run the show, bowing to each other's needs and wants when necessary. This differentiates them from Weres, who, when shifted into wolf form, cannot communicate or control their wolf sides.

Catskills, NY: Place where the Dire wolves currently call home. Also home to the supernatural world of witches, vampires and other shifters who are not friendly and remain hidden; it coexists alongside the human world.

deadheads: Old Dire wolf word for vampires. Current meaning: fans who follow the Grateful Dead.

Dire wolves: (*Also see **Brother Wolf**) Dire wolves are alpha, immortal wolves who live in tandem with their Brother Wolf and take on human form to survive in the world. Dire wolves are differentiated from Weres because they cannot be killed by any means, thanks to a curse of immortality cast upon them by the Elders. When first in existence, the Dire wolves lived a long time, with an approximate one-hundred-year life span, but they were not immortal. The majority of the Dire wolf population—which was quite large, since it preceded the Were population—was killed during the Extinction, and the curse on the remaining Dire wolves with abilities was cast at that time.

However, with their gifts, immortality is exhausting for the Dires—it forces them to remain in hiding and move quite often because their human sides will not age, unlike Weres, who, although immortal in theory, can be killed and will age, albeit slowly, in their human forms.

The Dires were trained in the warrior ways. They are powerful fighters, far more powerful and violent than Weres. However, both Dires and Weres can shift at will and both are pulled by the full moon, although the Dire wolves will never fall prey to moon craze, which often happens to young Weres during their earliest shifts and can last from the age of sixteen until they are twenty-one.

Dire ghost army: These are the Dire wolves killed during the Extinction. They are raised by Seb, the master witch, through a black magic spell and are intent on harming the living Dire wolves. They then plan on spreading their destruction outward to Weres and humans.

the Elders: The Elders are a mythical group of otherworldly spirit wolves responsible for the creation of both the Dires and the Weres, and also responsible for meting out justice to both populations when necessary. One example of this was the Extinction. There were originally four Elders: Hildr, Eydis, Leifr and Meili. Hildr asked to be released from her duties (aka killed) when outvoted on an important matter concerning the Dires and their abilities rather than go against what she believed in.

the Extinction: In Norway, the Dire wolf packs committed a massacre of humans (who will later form the weretrappers) in direct opposition to orders from the Elders. The Elders killed all Dire wolves except for five Dires who were out on their Running—Harm, Rifter, Vice, Jinx and Rogue. Later the Dires discovered that another pack of non-immortal Dires in Greenland had also been saved by the Elders. Stray and Killian are immortal, since they have abilities, but the rest of their Greenland pack isn't.

fated: In the time of the Dires, their word for love was fated, so when a Dire talks about being fated, he's really talking about love.

Greenland pack: A pack of non-immortal Dires kept alive by the Elders after the Extinction so that wolves in that pack could give birth to brothers who would have abilities and thus fulfill an old prophecy.

hunters: A human antidote to the weretrappers, they're a group of humans who are on the side of good and therefore trying to weed out the bad supernaturals from the good, rather than use them or kill them at will, as the trappers do. In the supernatural world, they're seen as just as dangerous.

mating: Weres can mate with humans or Weres and sometimes with other shifter species like lion shifters. For the Dires, it's a very different story, as the old ways dictate that Dires can mate only with other Dires and it must be ceremonial. First and foremost, a mating can never happen during first-time sex. It's too dangerous to try to mate with a new wolf because shifting for the first several times is too hard and new wolves are uncontrollable. Mating happens by consent on both sides during the third time a male and female Dire lay together—that is the Dire custom because they don't encourage sex without mating. Sex for the last remaining Dires is painful, because it goes against their mating protocol. During the mating, the non-shifted male is chained and the female will shift uncontrollably at the end. Thus mating equals danger for the male—will he be able to handle his proposed female wolf? After a mating, the Dires must come before the Elders to have the mating blessed. Mating makes Dires stronger.

the old country: The Dire wolves were created by Hati during Viking times and lived primarily in Norway, with a large pack also in Greenland.

the Running: An adult Dire has a great responsibility to his pack. Even before his shift, he trains as a warrior, as Dire culture is a warrior one. Also, because the shift for a Dire requires great strength, their lives are devoted to gaining the necessary strength before they turn twenty-one. After their shift, there is an importance placed on sensuality and play. The Running happens after their first several shifts, while they are allowed to run and play apart from the packs for six months in order to see if they are truly independent and able to blend well with humans now that their wolves have emerged.

Skinwalker: There are many myths about how skinwalkers are created. The Dire wolves know that they can become skinwalkers if they commit matricide and/or patricide. Since this killing is an unnatural act, they become unnatural beings, although they remain, first and foremost, Dire wolves. A skinwalker can shift into other beings, taking on various personas for short periods of time. Some can see the future, and others are thought to be able to curse those who speak out against them. Some are seen as witch doctors, and typically, they are cast out and live alone.

Weres: (See **Dire wolves** for more differences between Weres and Dires.) Were who are newly shifted can experience moon craze, in which they become uncontrollable and therefore dangerous to themselves, their packs and the human race. Many young wolves are put down because of this. The Dire wolves will often take in moon-crazed Weres they believe have the potential to become great warriors.

werepacks: Werepacks are scattered across the United States and the rest of the world. The main pack is located in New York City, with other large packs being in Texas, California and Wisconsin. The **outlaw pack** that forms from the New York pack is now taking in rogue wolves from other packs to join their cause. They believed that if their king Linus sold out the Dires to the weretrappers, the Weres would be left alone. They are angry wolves, not very organized, and more intent on killing than following the old ways, which makes them quite dangerous. They like killing humans and have taken to selling their own kind to the weretrappers in exchange for protection. Some of them will work as bodyguards for both the witches and weretrappers.

weretrappers: A paramilitary group of humans intent on destroying Dires and Weres, as well as using Weres for their own nefarious purposes. Their purpose had evolved over the years. At first, they were formed during Viking times; they were a tight-knit group intent on keeping humans safe from wolves. During the current century, they began to realize the power they could have if they were able to harness the power of the Weres. They capture Weres and experiment with ways to keep them under their control. They also create a pact with the witches, realizing they will need more supernatural help in order to gain domination over humans. Their goal is ultimate power and world domination, and they've begun to experiment with the dark arts (aka black magic).

witches: Witches live in covens and stay among their own kind. Widely regarded with suspicion and hatred by the rest of the supernatural world, many have started allying themselves with the weretrappers for security, which will allow their race to survive.

Prologue

Two days earlier

When she dragged in with the old blanket draped over her naked shoulders, she knew she still wore the wildness in her eyes like the chill of a winter night.

She hated daytime the most. The other patients did as well, avoided the sun, hated to be pulled into the fresh air as if they were horses to be exercised in captivity. She wanted the air and exercise, no doubt, but unfettered.

She wanted the moon. The small pad of paper she'd stolen during her last therapy appointment would be in its hiding spot, showing the beginnings of many crude drawings of the orb.

In her mind's eye, it was perfect, beautiful.

She wouldn't talk about it in the sessions with the man with the glasses. For five years, others had tried and failed. He would fail as well, because Gillian had stopped listening, stopped knowing what she once was.

A daughter. Once loved, until something went wrong. She began to talk about wolves, to run in the woods alone. Naked.

That was, apparently, unacceptable. Signaled illness.

Since she continued to escape, that meant the illness was getting worse, not better. She felt it too. But she always came back voluntarily because there was no other place for her. And still, something inside her compelled her to look for others whenever the moon grew heavy—and lately, when it didn't. The past two months had been a roller coaster of emotions. This time, she knew the wildness was too much for her—it threatened to overwhelm her, suck her into its madness, never, ever to let go. Maybe one day she'd allow herself to go all the way in, see that it was for the best.

But today she returned. Last night she'd run and then she'd lain under the stars and she'd dreamed. The dreams were of another time and place— distant, beautiful—and she felt stately and wise despite the way the men looked at her when she strode in.

They shoved her to the ground unceremoniously. Checked her for weapons.

I am a weapon, the rustling in her ears told her. But the men who held her down didn't know that, and she knew better than to tell them.

After she felt the initial prick of the needle, she waited for the familiar poison to work itself through her body. Her muscles relaxed. The rustling in her ears stopped.

But in her dreams, she ran.

Chapter 1

Vice swore he heard something slam to the ground in the woods outside the Dire house right after four in the morning. He'd been out running the woods and had just showered and prepared a snack fit for a king, but his curious Brother Wolf wouldn't not let him check it out. And since he was the only one either not on his honeymoon or in a coma, he went. Left the house naked and shifted the second his foot touched grass.

The nighttime air was cool and soothing. For an hour, he ran through the brush and remnants of snow, searching for whatever it was that made the noise.

He ended up at the tree he thought of as Eydis's, since he was always drawn to it when that specific Elder called for him. Vice listened when called, because he was compelled to do so.

Still, he couldn't control what he said in front of any of them, but hey, he was immortal, so what could they really do—kill him? That would be a fucking relief.

The tree was a massive, thousand-year-old oak that had been split straight down the middle by lightning. Like the Dires themselves, it had survived centuries, still standing healthy and straight.

The tree blossomed during springtime, stayed green until the worst of winter. Even barren, the tree stood out. It was magnificent.

Now it was entirely destroyed—one half lying on the ground, the other bent and broken—and he felt sick.

It would take something powerful to do that. Or something magical. He saw a hole in the ground close by, shaped as though something— or someone—had been thrown from the heavens.

He looked at the shimmering white glow that lined the empty space and sucked in a breath. There was no way that could've happened.

He wanted to call out her name, crawl into the hollow and wait for her. . . .

She hasn't come looking for you. And she won't.

With that last thought, he gave a howl, long and loud, the most mournful one he'd ever heard his wolf make. Not since Eydis was sacrificed and was picked to be an Elder.

He'd been sixteen when that happened.

Brother Wolf circled the tree, stared at it for hours, trying to think of a way to repair it. But there wasn't one. Nothing could handle this kind of wrath and survive—no one could.

Except you.

And then something inside of him stirred that made the wolf break into a dead run toward the house.

Something he hadn't felt for six months.

Rogue was awake and at his window, staring down at him. Vice howled with approval and relief, and he saw Rogue smile a little.

He shifted quickly and took the stairs two at a time, all the while trying to tamp down his emotions so they wouldn't be too hard for Rogue to deal with. It wasn't easy. He took a deep breath, then slammed the door open, raced to Rogue and hugged the crap out of him. "Dude, you're really up."

Rogue hugged him back, didn't say anything for a long moment, and Vice was pretty sure he was crying. When they pulled away, Rogue wiped his cheeks. "You look good, wolf."

"You don't look half bad for what you've been through." Indeed, Rogue's chest still bore marks from the mare who'd held him in a supernatural coma for six months. She'd been under Seb's spell—and Seb was a powerful witch who'd once been friends with the Dires. "You know Seb's gone?"

"I heard. I knew what was happening around me. I just couldn't do shit about it," Rogue confirmed.

"Did you call Jinx?"

"Not yet. Just give me some time, all right?" Rogue said and Vice cocked his head and stared into the wolf's eyes.

Finally he said, "Gotta at least tell Rift. Gwen

will need to check you over." Although they were all alphas, Rifter was their king, and they owed him that respect.

"I'm fine. Really. Cover for me, Vice. A couple of hours and then I'll tell them. I want to shower. Clean the hell up."

How could he turn Rogue down after what he'd been through? And of course, that was what Rogue was counting on. "Yeah, all right—coupla hours but that's all. And don't tell Rifter—no need for him to have my head again."

"Deal." Rogue hugged him again and man, it was good to have Jinx's other half back. Although Vice hated to leave him, he did so out of respect, and closed the door and went downstairs.

He rounded the corner to the kitchen and found Rifter and Stray standing there.

"Hey," Vice said in what he hoped was a normal voice. Then again, he'd never been normal, and Stray and Rifter had apparently been trying to fuck themselves to death with their mates, so the last thing they cared about was how Vice sounded. And by the looks on their faces, they weren't angry at all. "I was just out running and—"

"Kate's got the wolf—the glyph," Stray interrupted him. "It's my Brother Wolf—smaller, but it's there."

"So she'll run with us under the blue moon," Rifter said with a great deal of satisfaction. "It's a good day."

Indeed it was.

When the dust had settled and the Dire ghost

army was put down, they had all been relieved. Leo Shimmin, newest head of the weretrappers, was taken down, and so was the biggest facility where the trappers experimented, along with the castle where Seb was kept.

Seb had disappeared. Vice had blown the place sky high and Jinx had done some binding spells with Kate's help.

For now the trappers were in a state of disarray—in New York, at least. In other parts of the country they were gearing up, and that's where Liam came in.

The young wolf was King of the Manhattan pack. After Linus, his father, had been killed by the trappers and the rogue Weres working for them, Liam had lain low and gained support. He'd taken Cyd and Cain as part of his pack, would take them to Manhattan with him. Those two Weres that Jinx had taken in as moon-crazed and newly shifted teenagers were a far cry from the twenty-one-year-old alpha and omega.

Liam would step up his game now, since the king of the Manhattan pack was also the king of all Weres. He would have to guide them through the upcoming assaults the trappers would no doubt try in order to get some power back.

"For the first time in a while, things are looking up," Rifter said. "Once Rogue wakes up, we'll have more reason to celebrate."

Vice nodded with a smile as was expected of him, but his mind kept wandering back to the damned oak tree. When Eydis spoke to Stray days earlier, she told him that Kate could only mate with a Dire under one condition: A life for a life, and the Elders didn't just forget about shit like that. Someone was going to pay—or else someone already had.

And now, the mating had been allowed. Vice thought about the tree and the life for a life thing and shook his head. No way. *No goddamned way.*

Chapter 2

Jinx was on the highway going much faster than necessary when Vice rang him up and started talking as soon as Jinx answered.

"Listen, two things—Kate's got Stray's glyph on her back. And Rogue's awake."

Jinx gripped the wheel tightly at the last sentence and lost his breath for a moment, until Vice prodded, "Dude, you with me?"

"Yeah, I'm here."

"He's gonna be fucked up for a while. Just gotta deal with it," Vice offered. "If I hadn't seen him, he wouldn't have called for me. He just wants a few hours."

Jinx could understand that—really, he could. But his fucking twin . . . it was like not calling himself. "So, about Kate's glyph . . ."

"Guess the Elders approved the mating."

"When have the Elders helped us, besides Gwen?" Jinx demanded.

"Kate's still here," Vice pointed out.

"The Elders didn't come down and allow it. It's a trap."

"But they didn't stop it—and they gave her Stray's wolf."

"I don't trust it. They screw us for centuries and now they're nice to us?" Jinx shook his head. "Look, they were Dires just like us, with abilities and everything. You'd think that would make them less dick-like."

"What do you want me to say? Most people in power are pricks."

"Right. So the Elders can go fuck themselves." And that's why Jinx planned on handling the shit that had come out of purgatory that needed to be put down, since he'd been the one to open purgatory in the first place. That was his ability, the one he was born with—he could see ghosts. Rogue, his twin, could see spirits. But those stuck in purgatory were somewhere between the two—crossed over to a certain point, but not all the way there. Jinx would lead them back into hell. And if Rogue got off his ass and decided to help, that would be great too, but Jinx wasn't holding his breath.

Vice changed the subject quickly. "Liam's going to fight tonight. Twins too. You'll be there?"

"I can't. I've got to hunt. Business as usual." Although it wasn't. Not by a long shot.

The Dire ghost army had actually been laid to rest because they'd been killed honorably in battle, so Jinx didn't need to worry about sending them anywhere. They were finally at peace, even though they'd died at the hands of their sons. And the Dires took pride in the fact that they'd fought and won. They'd used their warrior ways.

But Jinx and Rifter were still at odds, meaning Jinx wasn't invited back to the mansion to live. And that was fine by him. "Keep me updated."

"Will do. You know where to find us if you change your mind."

Jinx hung up and glanced at the vampire sitting next to him in the truck, the one he currently shared the penthouse with in a Dire-owned apartment building because neither supernatural being would give an inch.

"Shouldn't you go with Vice?" Jez asked.

"He doesn't need my help."

"You can't still be worried about this 'Jinx is evil' shit."

"How do you know the evil from purgatory didn't hang around me? Vice is really goddamned susceptible to being possessed without warning," Jinx told him. "If he got too close to what we're dealing with . . ."

"I get it," Jez said. Jinx was pretty sure Vice did as well, but the wolf wasn't any less pissed at him. "Rogue's awake?"

"Awake and not wanting to see anyone for a couple of hours. Fucking diva," Jinx muttered as they pulled up to the gated brick building after their four-hour drive and got a visitor's pass for the car. "Let's just do this job and I'll deal with my twin later."

When Marley, a human ghost hunter Jinx had met months earlier on another job, had called him last night and told him that she'd gone to the facility to find a ghost and ended up running from a monstrous being instead, Jinx knew right away what was hiding inside that building.

A psych facility was the perfect spot for a monster from purgatory to hide—and by monster, he knew it could be a lesser demon or something worse. If people paid more attention to those who claimed to see monsters instead of drugging them, the world would be a better place.

"Goddamned humans, always screwing themselves over," he groused.

"Your human friend gave you the lead," Jez reminded him.

"Since when are you so reasonable about them?"

"They have their uses."

"I haven't seen you feed from one."

"True."

So how *was* Jez feeding? Jinx wanted to ask but figured it was safer not knowing. He was grateful to have any help at all.

Still, he couldn't help but think about how helpful Rogue would be as well, but he was still too fragile. And probably pissed at Jinx. He wondered if his twin would keep his secret about purgatory, since none of the other Dires, or the Weres who lived with them, knew. Only Rogue and the witch Kate, who promised discretion.

He decided he couldn't worry about that. "Let's

get the wolf out first and then we'll deal with the evil later on tonight."

"While you're in, I'll get the lay of the land, so to speak. Check in with a few of the patients about what they've seen."

"How're you going to do that without a visitor's pass?" Jinx asked and Jez smiled.

"Let me worry about that, wolf."

Jez was a deadhead—aka vampire from an old order—and, if Jinx understood it correctly, Jez had been brought back from wherever vampires waited to die in order to help the Dires through their current messes. That meant he was far stronger than most vamps—the same way Dires were stronger than Weres. Jez could go out in sunlight, enjoy food. According to Jez, there were more like him, but he'd been sent specifically to help Jinx through these current battles.

There was always a goddamned battle. Always would be. But for now, he could kill two birds with one stone: grab the evil being and put him back in purgatory and save a wolf named Gillian.

He wasn't surprised a Were had been placed in a psych hospital. It had happened countless times before. He was just lucky that Marley picked up on it before she'd been run out by the monster.

Now they got out of the car, and Jez disappeared around the back of the building while Jinx went in the legal way. He showed his fake ID—it read JOSH TODD—and from there gained easy entrance. Stray had already gotten into the hospital's system and given Gillian a brother named John, and put John down on the list of visitors. Jinx figured that there would be so many people there that day wandering the grounds that breaking her out should be relatively easy.

This place was worse than the morgue and he steeled himself as he walked through, ignoring the ghosts that harangued him for attention. They flew at him like incoming missiles with deadly aim as an orderly named Ken came to guide him to Gillian's room.

Jinx kept his eyes akimbo and his fists tightened at his sides. He felt hinky here—the result of the monster, not the ghosts. Whatever it actually was, he was pretty sure it was gone now, but it was bad. Really fucking bad, since his skin crawled as if it were contaminated.

"She doesn't like to come out during the day," Ken told him.

Makes sense, Jinx mused as he nodded and the guy continued, "At least she's back."

"She never says where she's been?"

"Won't tell us, and if she tells the shrink, he can't say." Ken paused outside the locked door. "She took her pills this morning. But it's been a while since you've seen her, right?"

"I'm in the military, so I haven't been able to get home much."

"I'm not sure if you know . . . but she can get violent. I'll stay with you."

"That's not necessary," Jinx told him. "I'll be fine. But I would like to try to get her out for a walk."

Ken looked at Jinx like he belonged in the padded room as well. "She can't."

"Why?"

"She's considered too dangerous."

Jinx stopped arguing and instead looked into the small window.

Gillian had her back to the door. She was curled like a wolf on the bed, the T-shirt she wore riding up on her thighs.

"We give her clothes but she barely wears them. The nurse got her into that when she was half asleep."

The door clicked behind her and Gillian jumped up and stared at him. Jinx remained in place, more out of shock than because it was the best way to handle this wild wolf.

She was no Were—he'd known that the second he'd stepped inside. Gillian Black was a Dire, and she was weeks away from her first shift. His Brother Wolf could smell a Sister Wolf, and his wolf surged in a nearly uncontrollable frenzy. That hadn't happened to Jinx since he was newly transitioned himself.

It didn't hurt that she was gorgeous. Wild, long-limbed, brown hair tumbling over her shoulders. Golden skin and her eyes glowed nearly aqua, like the shimmering ocean that reminded him of the old country.

"Down, Brother," he murmured to himself and she cocked her head and stared at him.

He had no doubt his eyes had begun to change to the wolf's. "Gillian, I'm here to help you."

"They all say that." Her voice was raspy from underuse.

"I mean it."

Sister Wolf is confused, Brother told him.

"Who are you?" she demanded. She might not have been trained in the warrior ways, but she circled him as if ready to fight.

"I'm just like you."

"A mental patient?"

Jinx grinned. "Let's take a walk."

"To remind myself what I can't have? No. Besides, I'm not allowed to."

"I didn't say we were coming back." He barely spoke the words, but the way her eyes widened, he knew she'd heard him clear as day.

Gillian wanted to ask this man with the long reddish brown hair why he'd do that. But really, she was too busy being drawn into his eyes.

Something deep inside of her that wanted the moon was also drawn to this man.

She never trusted, but the rustling said to now.

"How long have you been here?" he asked with a sidelong glance out the single window on the door.

He was built like a warrior from gladiator times—she'd seen the show on the TV in the main room. He looked as though he could do anything.

"Does it matter?" she finally asked.

"To me, yes."

"Five years this spring." She wouldn't give him a date even if he asked outright. She needed to keep something for herself, had learned the importance of doing so in a place like this.

A scream tore through the late-afternoon air, sailed in through the window and made her cringe. "It's like that all the time," she told him. "Worse on visiting day."

"Do you get many visitors?"

"You're my first in over a year." Over three years, actually. At some point her parents had given up. There were care packages, clothes she never wore, books she never read. Nothing that could be of any value to her.

"You'll stay with my family," he told her. "They're all like you. I'm like you."

She didn't know what he meant, but the rustling did, was chomping at the bit to be with others like herself.

She didn't ask how he planned to do anything. He simply pointed to her pants. She slid them on and he knocked on the door.

"She wants to walk with me," Josh Todd said.

The orderly looked between them. "Not without a major dose of tranquilizer."

No choice, the rustling said, but Gillian shook her head and backed away. Too many injections made her feel odder than she already did. She could barely get her equilibrium during the past six months to begin with, never mind the last five years that passed in a blur of sameness.

Except for the escapes, the only time she could actually breathe, time had ceased meaning anything at all.

This wasn't going to go well at all. Josh Todd spoke to her in a low voice, but she lunged past him and threw herself at the orderly.

She hated him and this place. Hated the visitor too, who'd promised her too much and then didn't come through for her.

So what was the point of sitting here like a good girl, telling them, "Oh no, I don't need to go outside—I'll just stay here."

The next time she left, she wasn't coming back. The decision had been made but it would be on her own steam.

The orderly was coming with a dose of tranquilizers and she didn't want them. Even though the other man told her to take them, that they would help with the escape, she wouldn't submit.

Nothing inside of her ever truly would.

Chapter 3

This wasn't going well. Jinx grabbed her and she fought less in his arms. But she still fought, which brought more orderlies and more drugs and she ended up strapped to the bed, drugged to the gills and unresponsive.

And it was all his fault. Guilt, his familiar friend, rushed over him as her glazed eyes stared up at him.

You promised, they told him. Fuck you and the horse you rode in on, they added for good measure.

"We'll get out," he murmured, squeezing her hand as his heart broke for how she'd had to live. He couldn't imagine, although now he understood the dark look in Stray's eyes when he talked about his time in solitary captivity. The people who worked here didn't know how lucky they were—another few months and an episode like that would've killed them all. Might've come close today if not for his strength.

"Can I push her in the wheelchair?" he asked. "She needs sunshine. Fresh air. And she wasn't violent until you gave her the drugs."

The young female doctor was sympathetic but firm. "She's hurt a lot of people. Her anger comes out of nowhere, so this is best for her as well."

No, it wasn't, but the humans wouldn't know that. "Okay, then. I'll just sit with her."

"I'm sorry for what you saw, but she's sick. She's in the best place she can be."

That was the biggest crock of shit and for a moment, Jinx thought about shifting and watching the woman shit her pants. Instead, he walked back inside and heard the door lock behind him.

Gillian was pointing weakly to the window.

"We can't escape through it," he told her.

But she shook her head.

"She's looking for the notepad," the ghost said clearly, and Jinx couldn't ignore it. He'd tried to since he walked in, and the woman had been pleasant enough, sitting on the windowsill in the hospital johnny, her hair tied in a neat bun. She looked to be about forty, was clearer than a lot of the ghosts he'd seen, which meant she'd been around long enough to cement her place in this world.

And that was not a good thing.

"I'm Lynn, by the way," she told him.

He walked to where Lynn had pointed and found that the windowsill was hollowed out underneath. He stuck his hand inside and pulled out a small pad of paper with an orb that could only be the moon drawn over and over, until thousands of orbs blended together to show how long she'd been trapped here, waiting.

His heart ached for her. "I won't leave you here another second."

Gillian blinked, but didn't truly believe him, made evident by her whispering, "I won't go anywhere with you."

"You will. And you'll be better for it."

She rolled her head wearily to the side.

He'd rather remain here strapped to the bed if it meant her freedom. And he did remain there for hours, checking in with Jez several times and getting no response, which was typical.

When visiting hours ended, they'd have the cover of an early winter's night and hopefully Jez would take his place in the car or else Jinx was leaving him here.

He glanced around the rest of the room. There was a pile of well-worn paperback books in the corner, stacked up, obviously not thought of as dangerous.

It was clear they were loved. They were stacked carefully, all their spines showing. She'd been as careful as possible with them, and he didn't know if bringing them would make things worse or better.

Instead, he took a picture of the stack.

There was nothing else here of value. He shoved the moon drawings into his back pocket and looked up at Lynn. "What do you want?"

"Nothing."

"Have you seen anything out of the ordinary here?"

"Like me?"

"Like a monster." He bit back the word freak because somehow monster was less scary.

"Oh, that. There was one here, but it's gone. It left last night after those people came looking for it," Lynn whispered conspiratorially, confirming his intuition. "It was one of the meanest-looking things I'd ever seen."

Great. For all he knew, it had followed Marley home. And that left him with only one job here today. "Just one?"

"All I saw."

"What exactly did it look like?"

"Smelled like sulfur. It was a black blur and it ran by too fast for me to see. It growled."

He would have to get Gillian the hell out of here with a distraction. He needed Kill. The man could manipulate minds, so it was either that or a violent breakout.

Brother Wolf would prefer the latter for sure. But Rifter would have his head. And still, they were running out of time for any option to remain viable.

"There's a side door right here," Lynn murmured. "If your friend opens it from the outside, you can walk out."

"And leave you here?"

"I help," Lynn said.

"You don't want peace?"

"I'd rather give it to them." It reached out and

ran a hand over Gillian's hair and the wolf murmured something, smiled. "I'll pull the alarm. You go."

Jinx owed Lynn more, but he couldn't force her to cross over. He waited for the alarm to blare and the mass confusion that followed.

Gillian was crumpled in his arms and she remained that way until they reached the Dire mansion.

Chapter 4

After Vice left, Rogue couldn't bring himself to do much of anything. He paced the floor, realizing he might never want to lie down again ever, and especially not on that damned bed.

First order of business—burn the bed. Well, once the rest of the Dires knew he was up and functioning because they'd definitely notice a bonfire in the middle of the backyard.

Still, he turned it on its side, because he could. It felt so damned good to actually move, to stretch, to have total fucking control of himself again.

He glanced down at the healing wounds on his arms and chest, cursed the mare and rolled the stiffness from his neck. His Brother Wolf was slowing waking as well. When that wolf wanted out, Rogue wouldn't be able to control him. It was almost like being a newly shifted wolf—he would have to relearn the controls, until Brother Wolf was satiated and well run.

He stripped, began to pad toward the shower when he stopped cold.

Jinx was coming—he was close—and he was bringing trouble with him. Rogue's twin sense was coming back strong, which meant Jinx was feeling him as well. He was also pretty sure that Vice would tell Jinx that he'd woken up, but he couldn't blame the Dire for that.

Vice would've done the same for him if the roles were reversed. And it made things easier, because what was Rogue supposed to do, ring Jinx up and say, "Hey brother, I'm back and you've really fucked up big-time."

So yeah, Rogue was awake and already keeping more secrets than one wolf should ever have to. There would be a price to pay for all of this, including not going to Rifter straightaway, but for the moment, Rogue reveled in simply moving forward, in the feeling of the shower prickling his skin—he'd taken three—and watching the deep scratches from the mare slowly heal up.

What wouldn't go away were the markings on the left side of his face. Those had come out because of Seb's spell and they would be a party favor that would keep on giving, linking him to hell. He had no idea what those ramifications were, but wasn't anxious to find out. He'd sprinkled salt around his windowsills already as a precautionary measure.

After half an hour, he knew Jinx was closer to the house and he stepped out, dripping on the floor. He used his hand to squeegee the water out of his hair. No one had cut it while he was sleeping and he needed a haircut, never liked wearing it this long.

He grabbed a pair of scissors and began to chop. Maybe he should wait until he could get a professional to do so, or maybe he should just start fresh. Completely, totally new.

He hacked until his hair was an inch from his scalp, and then he grabbed the buzzers and went to work. After he'd cueballed himself, he noted that the markings were all along his skull as well. "Might as well not try to hide it."

It fit with the biker mode they had going on. Made his eyes darker.

If anything, maybe the spirits would stay away from him when they saw he'd been marked by hell.

The deadhead drove as Jinx kept checking Gillian's breathing, her pulse—which was racing—until Jez asked, "Are we just storming the mansion or are you calling ahead, wolf?"

Shit. He pulled his phone from his pocket, keeping one hand on Gillian and dialed Gwen. The new queen had been most kind to him, calling to check on him. He was sure she wasn't doing it behind Rifter's back, but Gwen definitely had a mind of her own.

"Jinx, what's wrong?" she asked without saying hello.

"I'm bringing a Dire wolf in."

"Who's hurt?" she demanded.

"No one you know. It's a full female Dire."

There was a long silence and then, "I'll open the garage for you. Come right into the clinic."

She hung up and Jinx directed Jez to park in the garage in between the Hummers and the Harleys and various other sports cars and classics. He moved quickly, with Gillian in his arms and Jez trailing behind him until he saw Gwen waiting in the hallway. She motioned for him to follow her and he did, placing Gillian gently down on the stretcher before backing away to give Gwen room to work.

But for a long moment, Gwen simply stared down at her.

"She's full Dire," she finally breathed.

"Yes. She was in a psych ward."

"So she has no idea what she is?" she asked as she turned her full attention back to Gillian. "She's pretty."

Jinx agreed, watched Gwen put two fingers on Gillian's wrist as she placed the stethoscope on Gillian's chest under her T-shirt. Jinx heard his growl, low, warning, before he could stop it.

Gwen stilled and stared at Jinx, her canines elongated.

"Jinx, you've got to back off and let Gwen check her. She's not hurting her," Jez said and when Jinx looked at the vampire, his fangs had come down too.

"Jinx is feeling . . . protective," Jez told Gwen and she stared between Jinx and Gillian. The bond was palpable, at least to Jinx and from the look on her face, she felt it too.

She looked back at the vampire, who simply smiled.

Christ. He stared at the floor, took a deep breath and tamped down that reaction because what the fuck? "Sorry," he mumbled after a long, tense moment and Gwen went back to her exam.

"Do you know if she's been drugged like this for five years running?" she asked.

"I'm assuming so, but maybe not as heavily. If they have her birthday listed correctly, she's due for her first shift in three months." Jinx went for the intercom. "Maybe Stray can look into her records."

"That's a good idea," Gwen said. "Because I have to know how bad her withdrawal's going to be."

Jinx put his finger on the button but he hadn't pressed it yet. Gwen went over to him and pressed, called up to Stray. "Come to the basement and bring your laptop. Stat."

Stray gave a sharp "Will do," and she added, "Bring Killian."

Jinx looked at her with a furrowed brow.

"Gillian might be from the Greenland pack," she offered.

"Right. They might know her." His entire body tensed at the thought of other Dires coming down here, coming near Gillian. And it had to have shown, because Gwen asked, "Are you going to be able to hold it together?"

"Of course he can," Jez said. "What? I have impeccable hearing. It's not just you wolves."

Gwen gave Jinx a lingering look and then went back to Gillian. She ran some IVs, explaining to Jinx, who'd been a medic in the Army, what each one was—he'd know what they'd do. It was nothing he wouldn't have done for any of the Dires, nothing that could hurt Gillian. Rather, this could push the drugs out of her system, but not so fast as to cause a reaction.

It dawned on him then. "You think her body's addicted to the drugs?"

"I don't know. Can wolves get addicted? Don't forget, this is all preshift," she said. "I mean, our metabolisms are really too fast for drugs to stay in long, but this kind of exposure, day in and day out . . ."

"She ran away for days at a time. And she always came back. Wouldn't she have gone through withdrawals then?"

"Maybe she was. Or maybe the wolf was urging her on. I can't be sure, Jinx. But I'll do everything to make sure she's comfortable," Gwen promised and Jinx believed her.

He heard Jez at the door talking to Killian and Stray, and he could make out the bare-bones conversation that consisted of *If you get close to her, Jinx will flay you.*

Message received, because Stray and Kill both gave him a warm greeting but stayed by his side when looking at Gillian.

"Do you recognize her?" Jinx asked.

"She's got to be from the Greenland pack but I don't recognize anything about her," Stray said tightly. "Then again, if she's not immortal, I might not ever have known her."

They both knew Stray wouldn't have known her at all, the way he'd been caged and isolated by his family in Greenland. There was no love lost for that pack from anyone in this household.

Kill walked to the end of the table and uncovered Gillian's feet. Gently, he lifted the left and checked the heel, nodded as though he'd found what he expected. "There's a marking here. A brand given at birth to everyone born to the Greenland pack, for tracking purposes."

Stray went to look at his own heel but Kill said quietly, "You weren't given one. It's a good thing, brother."

Stray's brow furrowed. "I guess it is."

Kill recovered Gillian's feet. "She looks like Arrow's family," Kill said decisively. "Are her eyes blue? Aqua?"

"Yes," Jinx confirmed.

"That's their signature. Never seen a color quite like it before. Arrow's one of the nobility—their family's been running the pack since forever. But this doesn't make sense. She'd have been too young for any of them to detect powers. No prophecy on her. Why would they let her go like that?"

"Stolen?" Jinx suggested.

"Could've been," Stray muttered. He had his laptop open and went to the corner where Gwen had a small desk set up. "Let me get on her records."

Jinx stroked the hair from Gillian's face. Gwen had given a quick sponge bath to the unconscious Dire, so now her golden skin seemed to glimmer under the lights. She'd also brushed Gillian's hair so it shone with health. But despite how healthy she looked, this would still be a rough road for her.

"I've got to go," Jinx told Gwen.

"Rifter's on his way," she started but he shook his head. This was too hard—leaving her—without seeing his king again. He wasn't ready, wasn't accepted back and none of this was right.

"Just take care of her. And keep me up-to-date."

"I will, Jinx." She turned to the vampire. "You take good care of him or I'll kill you myself."

"Impossible, but point taken," Jez said dryly.

Chapter 5

The truck was halfway down the driveway when Jinx slammed out of the moving vehicle, ignoring Jez's cursing. He was halfway across the yard in the dusk at record speed until he stood directly in front of his brother.

"You're not a fucking ghost, are you?" he breathed and Rogue shook his head, which was shaved and covered in markings on the left side of his skull and cheek. He wore a black wife beater and old jeans and he looked nothing like the wolf he'd grown up with.

Everything about Rogue had changed, and Jinx didn't know how he'd failed to notice the transformation over the past six months.

Because you didn't want to.

"I'm very much alive," Rogue said finally, his voice a rasp.

"Vice said . . . he said you'd call. But you didn't."

Rogue didn't look surprised. "No, I didn't."

"I didn't feel you," Jinx confessed.

"It took for you to be close to the house before you were on my radar," Rogue told him. "Maybe it'll never come back for you. Maybe it's not meant to."

"Right. Because I'd corrupt you and your gift." Jinx didn't mean to sound so bitter but Rogue was acting like he was a perfect goddamned stranger. Granted, he hadn't exactly rolled out the welcome wagon or raced over here when Vice filled him in, but he'd convinced himself that he was helping Rogue, keeping his secret until he was ready for his big reveal to King Rifter and the others.

But it wasn't that at all. He was scared to see Rogue, and he still wasn't exactly sure why. As he scanned his twin's face, he noted no judgment in his expression, but it had to be there. Jinx judged himself too harshly to not believe another Dire would.

"I missed you, brother," Rogue said quietly.

Jinx swallowed hard, wanted to reach out and touch the markings from hell on Rogue's face and skull, wanted to tell his twin that everything would be all right, just the way Rogue had done for him a zillion times since childhood. But his throat tightened and his head spun. He simply nodded and Rogue's brows furrowed.

He flashed back to the night he discovered Rogue and Rifter had been captured. He was supposed to be there, but he'd gotten held up at a haunting. If he'd been there . . .

"If you'd been there, you'd have been captured too. I'd never have wanted that."

That twinsense had obviously come back for

Rogue, but still not for Jinx. Or maybe Rogue was simply reading the guilt that Jinx was sure plastered his expression.

"You blame me," Jinx said.

"You're wrong."

But he wasn't—Jinx could see it in the man's eyes. A lifetime of brotherly fuckups and now it came down to this. Rogue had always been the stronger one, the one who could manage to balance heaven and hell and everything in between, while Jinx only had to deal with the ghosts who were lonely or confused.

Rogue's ability was always more dangerous and it had taken a toll on him. Jinx would never forgive himself for any of it, even though he never could've taken the wolf's place.

"Jinx, please—"

"I'm just glad you were able to let us know what to do with the Dire ghost army."

"I knew you'd figure it out." Rogue's voice was raspy and he looked pale. Jinx knew he needed to shift soon.

"Yeah, Brother Wolf is begging," Rogue agreed. He couldn't read minds but they'd always had that twin thing happening. "Ask the question you want to."

"Did you know—about purgatory? Did you know before I opened it that it would happen?"

"Yes, I did."

"You knew what I was going to do and you didn't stop me?" Jinx growled—Rogue barely blinked. "Come on you fucker—fight!"

But Rogue wouldn't, still frustratingly calm and collected, even after six months in literal hell. Jinx turned to leave, stopping when Rogue called, "Going back to your deadhead?"

"He's not my deadhead," Jinx said through gritted teeth.

Rogue snorted in response and Jinx was probably more pissed because he was going to see Jez. Because he refused to live in the mansion again and it had nothing to do with the fact that Rifter hadn't invited him. No, he would not come back here.

He and Jez formed a semi-uneasy alliance. Neither would vacate the penthouse so they both stayed there. Jinx told himself it was more helpful to the humans that way, but he'd wanted to know more about Jez and the men. Needed to keep an eye on the deadhead, all the while knowing the vamp was doing the exact same thing to him.

"What else do you know that you're not telling me?" Jinx called to him. This time, Rogue stopped, turned back until he and Jinx were back in punching distance.

"I know that some . . . things escaped." He shuddered as he spoke the word *things*.

"And you know I need your help to vanquish them."

"You should stay away from me for now. I'm too vulnerable."

"If you're vulnerable, you should be with me," Jinx argued.

"I think you're looking at it the wrong way. I'm a liability to you."

"So you're never going to hunt again."

"I didn't say that. Let me worry about me and you worry about your shit. Apparently, you're in pretty damned deep."

Rogue didn't say the "P" word, but it was for sure implied.

So this was great. Domestic issues. Oh, and purgatory. A nice mix. "Rogue . . . the others don't know what happened with purgatory."

"Yeah, I know. You, me, and Kate. And that vamp. I'll tell you what, brother—you keep my secret, I'll keep yours."

"What's your secret?" Jinx asked.

"I'm still in hell," Rogue told him before he turned and walked back into the house.

Vice had been keeping himself busy with several Weres, because even though it wasn't party night, he'd needed the stress relief. Besides, he needed to keep his mouth busy so he didn't spit out, "Rogue's awake," by accident.

Besides, there was so much fucking going on inside the house, and he was trying to convince himself that he wasn't freaked the fuck out at the thought of Liam and the twins fighting tonight. He was spinning, his being pulled in several different directions had his hormones working overtime.

Liam had trained well—he was ready. Vice wasn't sure he was, though. For the first time, he felt really damned old and he didn't like it.

He'd forced himself not to go back out to the hole by the tree, to think of anything but Eydis, but he was distracted enough that he actually made the Weres in the room as unhorny as he was. They all sat there looking at each other and Vice wondered if he should break out the Scrabble or something.

Finally, he gave a long-suffering sigh and yanked the male toward him. The younger Were kissed him, straddled him, emboldened with the sudden attention and Vice grabbed the male's hips and ground against him. Pheromones were flying around the room after several minutes of this, and with the female Were now kissing the back of his neck, he might be able to lose himself . . .

"Vice, downstairs, now," Rifter's voice floated through the intercom.

Ah shit. He had that king thing going on in his voice.

"Rogue, if you fucked me on this . . ." he muttered, sure Rifter had discovered that secret.

"Yeah, fuck me, baby," the Were moaned as she tugged at him.

"No, not fuck—ah, forget it." He slid out of the bed and the Weres pouted for a moment before they started going at it with each other. He shrugged it off—no law against them having fun.

Cyd was at the door, smirking. "Rifter sent me up to get you."

"Just make sure you get them out of here. And don't join in. You need your strength for later."

"No carbs, no sex, no fun," Cyd muttered as Vice took the stairs down three at a time. Cyd threw jeans down after him and Vice caught them but didn't put them on. Because what the hell—if he had to shift, which was usually when Rifter used his king tone, why ruin a perfectly good pair of jeans.

He met Rifter at the landing before the basement. Rifter didn't comment on the lack of clothes this time, the way he'd been doing lately because of Gwen, who wasn't always entirely comfortable with the big, naked males surrounding her. Mainly because Rifter growled every time it happened.

He followed Rifter down to the basement, Harm behind him. They all pulled up short when they entered the room to find Gwen standing over a . . .

Dire.

"She's a fucking Dire," Vice breathed. He didn't know if he should move forward or not. Killian and Stray were already in the room but they still had that wide-eyed look that Vice was sure he wore.

"Yes. And she has no idea she's a wolf. She was locked up in a psychiatric facility when she started exhibiting symptoms," Gwen said and Vice felt the anger rise in him.

"Immortal?" Rifter asked, unable to hide the shock from his voice.

"I don't know—I wasn't planning on trying to kill her," Gwen said wryly and Rifter rolled his eyes and the mood relaxed a little. "There's no other test, you know."

"She's not," Killian said. "No one from the Greenland pack but Stray and me are immortal.

But she'd live a long time if she gets through this shift."

Rifter studied her more clinically. "She's thin. Hasn't been trained well in the warrior ways, but she's got muscle. She looks like she's been running regularly."

"She has been. She escapes once a month and doesn't go back to the hospital for days. Says she's running around the woods," Stray added.

No Dires or Weres ran in the woods behind the institution—it was considered bad form and they didn't want the patients to see anything they could be labeled as more crazy for seeing. So she'd been safe running there, getting in the exercise her body needed, her mind preparing.

But Gillian had no idea what she was up against.

Gwen looked concerned, because she knew, having recently wrestled with it. The physical part would be easier on Gillian but the wolf didn't know she was a wolf.

"Who brought her here?" Rifter asked.

"Jinx," she said without missing a beat and Vice had to give her credit. "He did the right thing. He had no idea he was being called on to rescue a Dire."

Rifter didn't say anything further, moved toward the table to get a closer look. "He should've checked with me."

"I know. But he said she was in medical trouble—and I reacted." Gwen remained calm to Rifter's growly alphaness. The king was right and Gwen was just beginning to understand the rules of living with a king alpha Dire. "Jinx had to go hunting. He said he would call later."

Rifter grunted a little. He was trying to hold back his anger—more directed at Jinx than at Gwen. The rogue wolf had gotten himself kicked out of the Dire mansion weeks back and had done little to atone for his asshole behavior. Vice knew his friend was hiding something. When he figured out what, he'd be all over him.

"I think none of you should be here when she wakes up. She's quite . . . attached to Jinx." Gwen seemed hesitant to bring up that last bit of information but it wasn't news to Vice. He'd felt the tingle of the bond from the second he'd stepped into the room. He just hadn't been sure who it was directed toward.

But Rifter's gaze went sharply to Gwen and then to Gillian. "She and Jinx bonded? Because you know Dires don't bond."

"We're not vampires," Vice added. "Maybe he's been hanging around that deadhead too long."

"I don't think you can catch something like that," Stray told him.

"How do you know that? Just because it's not on your precious Internet. Put it out on Twitter and someone will know," Vice continued, sliding out of the way before Rifter was able to clock him on the back of the head.

Gwen had been waiting patiently through their dialogue. "I can't explain it. I know our bonds happened like this, but humans have love at first sight, so why can't Dires be susceptible to it?"

"Fated at first sight," Vice said. "Hell, I didn't think Jinx had it in him."

"Maybe it's lust," Killian threw in. "Because she's beautiful."

There was no arguing with that. She was built like the Dire women of old—tall and slim, her bearing regal. But there was a wideness to her shoulders, a rise to her cheekbones that foretold that she might be the fiercest fighter they had.

"This is gonna be trouble," Vice muttered as a stomp of boots that made no attempt at stealth clattered down the stairs. "And speaking of . . ."

The wolves turned, expecting Cyd or maybe Liam, but Vice knew exactly who it was.

Rogue turned the corner, wearing all black leather, head shaved looking far more badass than a man who'd recently been in a coma had a right to be.

Hell still rode in his eyes, and Vice wondered if he was the only one who could see that.

Rifter moved first, embracing Rogue. The wolf let him. The men had been imprisoned together—Rifter had saved him from the trappers, but couldn't save him from Seb.

"You look good, brother," Stray said, clapping him on the back. Rogue shook Kill's hand and thanked him for helping to save him. And then Kate came in from the garage—she'd been out at the cabin that had been in her family for generations with Cain—and she dropped the packages she held and ran for the wolf.

He caught her and the wolves heard her whispering, "So glad you're okay."

"Kate." Rogue's voice was hoarse, the only thing that belied emotion and the young witch hugged him without a second thought. "Don't get growly, Stray—it's okay."

Stray flushed but he didn't look worried. Being possessive was natural and nothing any of the Dires worried about. But Kate did move away quickly, in deference to her mate and went over and kissed Stray hard.

Vice knew Rifter was staring at him, but Vice pretended to look anywhere but, because it was damned obvious Vice wasn't surprised to see Rogue up and about. Instead, he told Rogue, "Nice skull—werechicks will dig it," and tried to back out of the room when Gwen said softly, "I think Gillian's waking up."

All the wolves stilled and waited.

The female's aqua blue eyes were stunning. Vice swallowed hard, because it had been a long time since he'd been in a female Dire's presence. Rifter moved forward, as did Stray and Killian. Vice hung back with Rogue, told him, "I kept your secret—you owe me."

"Don't bullshit me, Vice. I'm not the only one keeping secrets around this place," Rogue said, stared at him for a long moment and Vice fought the urge not to meet his gaze because suddenly it was like Rogue had these mind-bending—or at least reading—abilities and he didn't want anyone in his noggin. Especially not now.

Chapter 6

Gillian dragged herself up through the water into the light, drew a deep gasping breath and sat up, hearing the familiar rip of the restraints as she did so. Lights danced in front of her eyes and she blinked to clear them, shook her head as the now familiar rustling clogged her ears.

When everything finally settled, she took in the cinder-block walls, the soft lighting, the nonantiseptic smell.

She remembered Jinx, but she knew instinctively he was no longer here.

It was only then she realized she was surrounded by giant males. She stilled, letting her eyes wander over all of them, one by one. Warriors, yes, but none of them were *her* warrior, and she felt the nag of disappointment under the urge to fight.

She would play possum, the way she always had at the hospital. If they thought she was weak, they would let their guard down, and that's when she would escape. Here, she would have to strike, to fight.

She had no idea where these urges came from, but she did know she would fight them all.

"She ripped those restraints like they were paper," she heard one of them murmur in a language she shouldn't have understood. She glanced down at the metal cuffs that were attached to the table.

"She understands," another one said.

"Gillian, I'm Gwen. We're Jinx's family, and you're safe here." The tall blond woman didn't seem particularly afraid of her, smiled kindly.

"You're a doctor?" she asked and the blonde didn't seem to know what to say to that.

"She is," the tall, dark male said in a gruff voice.

"Really. The IV is just to get the drugs out of your system."

It took Gillian several tense moments to believe her. She ripped the needle out of her arm, even as Gwen explained about drug withdrawal and the like.

"That's never happened," she assured the tall, cool blonde. "I need a weapon."

"No, you don't. These . . . men . . . they're all part of Jinx's family too. They just . . . wanted to meet you. But they'll leave now," Gwen said and they all did as she asked.

"You have power over them," Gillian noted.

Gwen laughed a little. "Some, I guess."

Gwen had pointed to the pile of clothing and Gillian didn't argue, slipped into the comfortable

T-shirt and leggings reluctantly. As always, the clothing chafed her skin.

She thought about the big man they called Rifter, the one who told Gwen to keep her in the basement. The cinder blocks and lack of windows blocked the moon but she could sense it, and walked around the room as if she could somehow find a way outside.

She always found a way.

"I think I like this place," Gillian murmured in spite of her need to escape, the contrast maddeningly odd, more to herself than to Gwen as she moved around.

"It's nice here," Gwen agreed. "You're safe—I meant that. No one's going to drug you."

"But I can't go outside."

"For now, it's better for you to stay here. I promise you'll understand why soon enough."

"Where's the warrior?"

"Do you mean . . . Jinx?"

"Yes."

"He had to go to work. I could ask him to come back."

Gillian didn't answer that, instead asked, "Does anyone else know I'm here?"

"No one from the hospital."

"My parents?"

"We don't know who they are."

"At this point, neither do I," she murmured. Maybe she'd never really known them. There were always others taking care of her because they traveled a lot. Thinking back, there were always a lot of doctors and tests and she wondered if they'd always known she would need to go into some kind of hospital, if they were testing her early so they'd know.

But know what? That she liked to run naked through the woods? Other than that, she seemed to be able to function normally in society. She was polite, didn't eat with her hands, was well read. She'd finished all her schooling, graduating early. And she would've moved on to college if she hadn't been forced into the hospital.

How much had Jinx told them about her past? How much did he actually know? They'd barely had time to talk before she'd been sedated.

Rescued. Safe, the rustling told her. It never steered her wrong.

Her back ached. It had been hurting, as if she'd bruised it, for the past several weeks. She lifted the shirt and turned to look over her shoulder in the mirror at her naked skin, noted that Gwen was watching her too.

"I must've bumped it the last time I"—she was about to say *escaped*—"exercised."

Gwen moved closer and her tone was a little off when she said, "It looks like it's going to be just fine."

"You're the doctor." She tugged at the neck of the T-shirt. The clothing was soft, but it still chafed. And Gwen hadn't seemed bothered by her nudity, but still, she knew walking around the house with all the men wasn't appropriate.

"Are you hungry?"

"Actually, starving," she said. Gwen went out the door and pulled in a table on wheels with a big tray of covered food dishes.

"That smells great."

"Here—sit and get started. I'll be right back, okay?"

Gillian couldn't think of anything but food at that moment. At first, it was only that way after they'd sedated her and lately it was that way all the time. There was never enough food, except on the days she ran. Then, it was like her body shut down to everything but the air and the moon.

It was all delicious—lots of stew meat and potatoes and bread. She sat and ate for what seemed like hours. Finally, when her stomach stopped complaining, she looked around and noted that there didn't appear to be any cameras in this room, although they could be well hidden. She took a few more bites and couldn't shake the fact that she was alone.

They trusted her, just like they made the mistake of doing time and time again at the hospital. Gillian always took full advantage of their mistake and she'd do it here.

Really, she had to. The moon, the air, Jinx—all called to her as surely as they felt her pain of being held captive.

Her bare feet padded across the cold floor, but her blood ran hot. Her fingers nestled in the seams of the cinder-block wall, looking for any kind of weakness, a secret passage.

Nothing.

She went into the small bathroom and looked up at the vent. It was small, but it had to lead outside. She lifted the cover and smelled earth. But she'd never liked enclosed places, so she was torn.

Jinx had left her. She'd ask him why when she saw him again.

She went to the door and found it opened easily. She went to the next door and found herself inside a maze of cars and motorcycles. There was a big window about seven feet up and she climbed onto the roof of a truck and pushed it open and looked down.

You can do this.

She balanced in her bare feet on the window's ledge. Hesitated and then jumped as if it was the most normal thing in the world. Landed solidly on her two feet and broke into a dead run toward the woods, her smile wide. The wind tore through her hair, the T-shirt billowed out around her and she heard her own laughter echo in her ears.

She was free—and this was no dream.

"Your brother looks good for being a prisoner of hell. The biker look works for him," Jez said, trying to keep conversation going as Jinx brooded in the passenger's seat. "A bold choice of tattoos, though. The women are going to love them, I'm betting."

"Do you ever shut up?" Jinx growled.

"Finally. I was beginning to think I'd lost you in your broody bad-boy mood for the night, and we have work to do. Are you ever going to ask what I found back at the psych facility?" Jez asked. "I realize you were busy being all growly over your mate—"

Jinx wanted to say *she's not my mate* but the words wouldn't come out, dammit. Instead, he managed, "I talked to a ghost who mentioned a monster."

"Most of the patients saw it," Jez confirmed. "Several nurses mentioned that over the past four days, they used a lot more drugs than normal to keep everyone calm. One of them said that, and I quote, 'It was like all the freaks freaked out at once.'"

"Nice nurse," Jinx muttered.

"All the patients I spoke to—"

"You spoke to patients?"

"They won't remember me, wolf," Jez told him with a sigh. "You sure you want to talk about monsters rather than the fact that your brother woke up and you just found your mate?"

"You are not my therapist, deadhead. And we're not supposed to have mates."

"Did the Elders tell you that?"

"Centuries." Jinx slammed his hands along the dash. "We had no one forever. And now we're allowed to fall like dominoes?"

"I didn't say the PTB made sense. Ever." Jez took a corner on two wheels. Jinx hadn't realized how fast they'd been going.

The vamp was possibly more on edge than Jinx. "What's wrong, Billy Idol?"

"Fuck you, wolf." Jez yanked the car to the side of the road. "I realize you're all wrapped up in you. But I'm involved in this shit too."

"Is this about your brothers?"

"I don't like psych wards," Jez muttered.

"Why didn't you say that hours ago?"

"I didn't think I'd have that kind of reaction."

Jez didn't elaborate and Jinx figured he'd share when ready. At the moment, they were facing something bigger, because they were back outside the original scene of the crime, as it were. Beyond these iron gates that stood shakily was once the opening to purgatory.

It was shut now, but would it always be there? Could Jinx be tricked into opening it a second time? Was he somehow purgatory's bitch?

"You think the monsters would come back here?" he asked to distract himself. "I think they'd stay far away."

"Got to cross it off the list," Jez said firmly, his stiff-upper-lip composure back. The long leather coat whipped around his thighs as Jinx followed him reluctantly.

The ghosts clung to him. They were all still freaked about the recent events and too damned needy for his state of mind.

Needy ghosts were the fucking worst.

"Are you going to talk to them?"

"I'm not their therapist." But even as he spoke, they dissipated like smoke in the wind. He felt naked being ghostless. "I think I was wrong about the monsters not coming back here."

Jez circled around slowly, his fangs elongated.

"What exactly do these monsters do in purgatory?" he asked quietly.

"All they do is fight each other. Over and over."

"I'm guessing they learned a lot about stalking their prey," Jinx said. "And I've never felt more like it in my life."

"I think we should go."

"Way too late. Good thing we can't die." But it was for sure going to hurt. "What did they look like?"

"That's the odd thing—each person described them differently. It appears that the monsters morph into whatever your greatest fear is," Jez told him. "They feed off humans and wolves alike. Vamps too, I'm guessing. Equal opportunity monsters."

"You didn't think to mention this before?"

"You didn't ask."

A low growl emanated from the trees. "Jez, what's your big fear?"

"I don't really like hellhounds much," the deadhead admitted. As he spoke, a giant black beast with red eyes darted out of the woods, making a beeline for the vamp. Jez stood stock-still, muttering some kind of prayer—if vamps even prayed.

Jinx wanted to remind him that prayers didn't work so well for them the last time, since that's what opened purgatory in the first place, but he refrained, if only because his heart was in his throat.

"Jez, man, what the hell?"

There was no way to outrun this thing. Fighting

would be their best option. And what a fight it would be.

The hellhound bounded on a straight course toward Jez, who pulled a silver knife and prepared to slice at whatever he could. Jinx called out and the hellhound skidded to a stop as the vamp and wolf stood close to one another.

"What the hell?" Jinx repeated softly.

"Good puppy," Jez muttered and it advanced. Jinx took a step closer to it and it backed up.

Okay, this was definitely all kinds of weird.

"What's your big fear, wolf?" Jez asked.

Oddly enough, Jinx appeared to have none, since he was looking downwind at a hellhound, and he didn't much fear those necessarily, although it was a big motherfucker and Brother was straining at the bit, pushing for a shift.

"Not now, Brother," he hissed.

The monster hellhound stared him down. Snorted. But it was confused.

And then it bowed.

"It thinks you're its master."

"I don't want to be in charge of it," Jinx hissed.

"I'm not minding it," Jez said. "Now tell the nice hellhound that the vampire isn't a chew toy."

"Maybe. Or maybe I'll take him home with us. We wouldn't need a security system then."

The hellhound moved toward Jez and Jinx stifled a laugh. "Back off the vamp. He's with me."

The giant hound backed up.

"Yeah, down boy," Jez told it. "I bet if you followed him, he'd take you to the others."

"I'm not ready for that—what am I going to do?"

"This is like that book, *Where the Wild Things Are*. You're that five-year-old kid who wears the white suit with the horns. Kinky."

"I am not five," Jinx said coldly.

"You've created quite a wild rumpus," Jez persisted.

"I could still make you puppy chow."

"Point taken." Jez cleared his throat. "You do realize you're like their king now."

"I'm definitely not the king of goddamned purgatory," Jinx said, but the beast sent up a mournful bark that said otherwise.

"Cheer up. Things could be worse," Jez noted.

"How so?"

"You could be the king of purgatory and be inside purgatory."

"I hate it when you're logical."

Jez stilled then, murmured, "Hey Jinx, we've got company."

But Jinx already felt her presence like the soft brush of a hand on the back of his neck, a warm caress of sun. He felt her before he saw her, like there was a silken tie that stretched between them but remained unbroken. He felt tangled up. Confused. And grateful as hell.

He didn't dare turn away from the monster, had no fucking clue what to do with the bowing hellhound presence. Finally, he told it, "Go hide. Don't kill or hurt anyone. Tell the others to stand the fuck down. Wait for my call."

The hellhound did some kind of doggy nod and disappeared quickly into the brush around the cemetery.

"How very military of you," Jez drawled.

"You're from London, not the south."

"I'm versatile."

"You're fucking nuts."

"I've been hanging around wolves for too long." Jez still looked shaky as he lit a cigarette that looked suspiciously like one of Vice's special hand rolls. "This is getting weird. We might have to ask Kate if you're all evil again."

"We can just ask Rogue," Jinx said. "I'm guessing he'll say yes."

Jez sighed. "Why don't you see if you can make sure Gillian doesn't run again? Although I have a feeling she was running to you."

It was then that Jinx realized his biggest fear wasn't in the form of a monster, but rather, a mate.

Chapter 7

Instinctively, she knew where to find Jinx. In her old life, before the hospitals and the drugs, if anyone told her she'd be running through a creepy cemetery in the middle of the night alone, she'd have laughed. She probably would've been drinking at the time, in some kind of underground rave party with all the hangers-on who wanted to be called her friends because of her name and the money and perks that went along with that.

She let them, because it didn't cost her a dime, and she'd never let them inside where it mattered anyway. She'd learned from a young age that everyone wanted something from her, but that didn't mean she had to give it to them.

Here—he's here.

Her warrior was standing, tall and proud, his stance one of battle. And although she didn't see any imminent threat, she certainly felt one.

Her heartbeat pounded inside her ears, her toes dug the grass as her muscles tensed. She felt the urge to rescue him in much the same way he had her, but the rustling in her ears grew loud and she wasn't sure what to do.

He sensed her, but he didn't turn around, not right away. When he finally did, his expression was serious but his eyes . . . they glowed.

She wore what must be Gwen's clothes. As much as he wanted to see her naked, he was glad she wasn't, because they weren't alone.

Once acknowledged, she strode across the space that separated them like she owned it.

She was mesmerizing and when you were trying to tame a hellhound, it wasn't the best time to be distracted.

Maybe your fear isn't going to come in the form of a monster.

"You're angry," she murmured when she got close.

"No. Worried."

"Don't be."

She was so goddamned pretty. His instinct was to fall to his damned knees and take her down with him, Jez and hellhounds be damned. Even Brother Wolf egged him on and it took him a long moment to gain control. "Gillian," was all he could say before he brought his mouth down on hers.

So much for control. Jez would have to deal.

Her hands wrapped around his neck as he pulled her close. Her body molded to his perfectly, a fit he'd never thought possible.

I'm the worst possible wolf for her.

And that didn't stop him from playing his tongue along hers, his canines elongating just enough to scrape her lip, a sign that Brother Wolf wanted to claim her too. His cock hardened and she moved her hips to rock against him. He ran his hands along her sides, cupped a breast before realizing that if he didn't stop soon, he wouldn't be able to.

When he pulled back, she put her hands on either side of his face and stared at him. "You're worried."

"About you, yes. Because you shouldn't be out here alone."

"I've always been alone. But now, I'm with you."

Ah Christ. "Gillian—"

"You feel it too, when we're together. It happened back at the hospital. That's never happened to me."

She was so much like the Dire women of old. Strong. Self-assured. Fate at first sight didn't happen often, but they'd locked and loaded onto each other in the hospital room and nothing was going to change that.

He wasn't worthy of this. She was nobility. Royalty. "It's never happened to me either."

"I couldn't help leaving to find you."

"I'm glad you did," he admitted.

"The doctor—Gwen—said you were working."

She was absorbing the Dire culture so quickly—

being around him would make everything happen faster for her. She'd scented him here, and she knew instinctively that he was hunting.

"She's right."

"You're hunting ghosts." Her eyes flashed for a second and he swore he saw them change. Prayed it was a trick of light.

"Yes. I'll tell you more, but we should get out of here."

"I was worried about you. You were fighting, I think. I didn't see anything but I feel . . ." She trailed off, shivered.

"Those are the ghosts."

"And the monster?"

"What do you know about that?"

"They talked about it. At the hospital. I never saw it but a lot of them did." She slid her hand into his like it was the most natural thing in the world as they walked, with Jez several steps ahead of them. "I don't want to go back there."

"To the hospital? You won't."

"No, to the house with Gwen."

"Did something happen?" he heard himself demand with a growl to his tone so fierce Jez stopped walking for a second and turned to look at him with warning.

Yeah, Brother Wolf, back it down.

If Gillian noticed, she took it in stride. "No, they all seem nice. I just want to stay with you."

"You met all of them?"

"Lots of males. They were big, like you. But

none of them were you," she said quietly. "I wanted to go outside, but Gwen told me I couldn't. So I left."

"And they followed you," Jinx said, noting Rifter's truck. Vice would've been the first one on her tail, but he was no doubt helping Liam get ready.

Liam. Cyd. Cain. Jinx felt the guilt of not being there ball in his stomach. As if sensing this, Gillian squeezed his hand a little tighter.

"That's Rifter. He's my . . . boss. Both he and Gwen are." Technically, it was the truth.

Rifter came toward them and Jinx willed himself not to growl as he got close. But the possessive feelings couldn't be ignored or tamed.

Gwen must've mentioned it to the king, because Rifter stayed at a respectable distance as he spoke. "Gillian, you scared the hell out of us."

"I can't believe a girl gave you the slip," Jez said and Rifter growled at him. Jez crossed his arms and looked unimpressed.

"You've got to go back to the house," Jinx told her.

"No, I don't. I won't."

She might only be out of prison because of him, but she wasn't giving up any other freedoms easily, if at all. Hell, he was lucky she wanted to stick close to him, because her Houdini act was hard to top.

"It's dangerous, Gillian," Rifter said. "You don't understand yet—"

"I'm staying with Jinx." Her words were firm and for a long moment, the king pondered in silence. Finally, he nodded his consent.

He hadn't asked Jinx to come back and stay at the mansion, which was a relief.

"Fine. But Jinx, you need to report in and make preparations. Come use the yard, the woods at night. Much safer," Rifter said.

Jinx nodded and Gillian smiled at him. "Will you get in the truck with Jez? I'll be right there."

Jez motioned to her and she nodded, slipped her hand from his. He immediately missed the contact.

"Thank you for bringing her to Gwen, instead of asking Gwen to come to you," Rifter said. "We both know she would've done it."

Jinx nodded, didn't know what else to say.

"You know Rogue is awake."

"I saw him when I left the mansion, yes."

Rifter opened his mouth as if to say something else, but stopped. Jinx broke in with, "Liam's going to fight any time now."

"Yes."

And you should be with him and your twins was the unspoken phrase. More guilt.

"I'll make sure her shift is smooth. I'll try to have her at the mansion when it happens," Jinx told his king, because he owed the man, his brother in arms, that, if not more. Rifter nodded and dismissed him. Jinx ran his hand along the deep scars on the side of his neck that Rifter had given him recently and knew that nothing between them would ever be the same.

Chapter 8

It was close to three in the morning, Vice's favorite time of night and it was rapidly becoming Liam's as well. That afternoon, Liam had captured a young Were who'd been working with the outlaw wolves. In doing so, he gained valuable intel on his biggest enemies, Tals and Walker, the wolves in charge of the outlaw werepack currently trying to oust Liam as rightful king. Now, with only the sliver of a moon for company, Liam was tense—Cyd, not much better.

Cain, his omega, was remarkably calm, which Liam took to mean they were on the right path, hopefully both literally and figuratively. Their truck cut through the night quietly, purposefully as Cain drove them and Cyd remained in the backseat, armed and dangerous.

The twins had permission from Jinx to fight. Cyd had proven his control a couple of months earlier when he took down a rogue Were who threatened Jinx and the entire werepack with his actions, and again during Seb's most recent attempt to take over the town. But tonight's fight would be different, enough to push a Were who'd suffered from moon craze over the edge.

Cain was worried about his twin, Liam knew, and Liam wasn't sure if he was as worried about himself. But they'd made their decision about tonight—none of them were immortal and all three had to be prepared to suffer life-threatening injuries during a kill like this.

Was anyone really prepared? Liam wondered now. His father hadn't been—Liam could still hear the man's screams echoing in his ears, his death anything but peaceful.

"What are you doing with Max?" Cain asked him as they neared their destination, ripping him from his heartbreaking reverie and throwing him into another one of almost equal pain.

"I can't answer that now. How the hell can you ask me that at a time like this?" Liam ran his hands through his hair and he heard Cyd's muffled curse from the backseat. No doubt that alpha was as pissed as he was for Cain's question, but the omega was undeterred, and undaunted.

"You have to. You need to be decisive in every damned thing you do," Cain said, his voice strong and sure.

The pain of having Max, his mate—his human mate—cheat on him with an outlaw wolf was something that could rip Liam's heart out if he thought about it too much, which was why he'd been avoiding anything to do with the subject of her unborn son.

"You let that pup out of your sight, he's going to come back and kill you," Cain told him.

"You're a soothsayer now?" Liam demanded.

"You know I'm telling the truth, right?"

Liam thought about Max and the last time he'd seen her, holding her swollen belly and staring out the window. "He could kill me either way when he finds out what I did to his father and mother."

"I guess you've made the decision on what you're doing with the human. But the baby, keep him close." Cain spoke quietly but every word was a boom to Liam's ears.

"And what? Lock it up?" Liam asked.

"You could raise it as yours," Cain agreed.

"You're kidding, right?"

"Nature, nurture." Cain paused. "You don't know what kind of half wolf you'll be turning away. Sometimes, it pays to keep your enemies close."

"The Dires took us in when our own Weres didn't want us," Cyd said. "I don't think they made the wrong choice."

"The Dires can't die," Liam pointed out and the twins left him in silence for the rest of the trip, with Cain's favorite Floyd, *The Dark Side of the Moon*, playing.

Liam let him have that. Stared out the window at the dark road ahead and thought about his night to come—and the long stretch of road that lay after it.

He was charged with getting all the Weres to follow him, without question. He wouldn't tell the majority of the Weres about what their mission was until their loyalty was completely secured.

Even then, it was a risk.

Half the Manhattan pack was behind him. Another quarter was undecided and the rest were decidedly rebelling with Tals and Walker leading them after Liam had killed Teague, who'd been the real leader of the outlaws.

Which was why those wolves needed to die.

"I'm ready," Liam said, not bothering to ask Cyd or Cain if they were. They had to be, if for no other reason than the man they'd decided to call their king was, and the two fell into step next to him.

Flanked by Cyd and Cain, he prepared for his first official act as king. His first unofficial one had been killing Teague weeks ago, after which he'd announced his intentions to take over for his father—and to kill every single outlaw unless they renounced their new leaders and came back under his pack's protection.

Liam had already made a statement to the outlaw werepack by killing Teague in front of Max. And while he hadn't made up his mind about her child, if he didn't kill Max—as was his right since she was his mate and she'd betrayed him—he would lose a great deal of the ground he'd gained establishing himself as the successor to the crown as king of the alphas.

Too young . . . not strong enough . . . not ready. Liam

saw red when he heard those words. And he was willing to go balls to the wall to prove himself.

He and Cain and Cyd planned their ambush with only a few hours notice, staked out Tals and Walker, who met only once a week under heavy guard since Teague was killed.

The first group of wolves they encountered was twenty feet from the small house, the guards for the outlaw pack. Boys he'd grown up with. His throat tightened at their betrayal but he forced himself to remain calm. He would give them a single chance at life. They deserved only that, or maybe not even, but he would toughen with each kill, Vice promised him.

Come to think of it, Vice hadn't looked happy about that.

Now, Liam stood in front of the small pack of young wolves who he knew wouldn't back down easily. It was necessary to pull them back from outlaw-ville, or take them out completely.

"Where's your Dire backup?" one Were sneered at him. Able, a wolf three years younger and several inches shorter, with a big mouth and an even bigger attitude.

Liam told him, "I've got my own pack. I'm the new king. Abide by my law or die by my hands."

The smallest one paled, but the others couldn't let down their show of bravado. Liam watched the five Weres come toward him as the smallest lagged behind, knew this would be a violent, frightening show for all, especially if he let himself go the way Vice had taught him.

"I guess your decision's made," Liam said, and then he struck, faster than he'd ever thought possible, with a decisive energy that seemed to stun the Weres. Two went down with broken necks before Cyd jumped in, and then Liam took out Able as Cyd and Cain each made their own kills.

"Your name," Liam demanded of the small Were.

"Pat," he answered.

"Don't move—you're my witness. Move and die, understand?" Liam asked and Pat nodded as Cyd and Cain moved past him to infiltrate the house and get rid of the guards.

As king, Liam needed to allow his pack to keep him safe, to do some of the dirtier work. And so he hung back, knowing Cyd and Cain wanted to prove themselves to him as much as to themselves, watched his Weres infiltrate and kill the guards.

Seconds later, Cyd and Cain were dragging a surprised Tals and Walker out, the young twins' strength and fighting skills far surpassing what it should be at their age, thanks to their training from the Dires.

While Tals and Walker looked cocky when the twins let them go in front of Liam, he knew they didn't have the fire, the need to prove themselves. There was so much pent-up anger inside Liam, he could take them on one by one and it wouldn't be enough.

He'd planned a brutal assault. There wasn't a chance of a fair fight. This was a message—and if it turned into a bloodbath, so be it. "You'll die tonight—and it will be a lesson to other Weres to not disobey their king."

Tals snorted. "We don't recognize you as our king, little boy."

"You were just dragged out here like a sack of beans, so I'd watch who you're calling little." Liam cocked his head and stared down the two men, knew his eyes had turned lupine.

Knew there was no turning back as a newfound strength roared through his body like a freight train—heavy, well greased and unstoppable forward motion. The rage was a focused one, a steadily mounting sense of what he needed to do to avenge his father's death and take back his role.

He would take Tals, because Tals killed his father. "Walker's yours, Cyd," he told the alpha Were, and Cyd didn't hesitate.

Cain stood guard and kept an eye on Pat as Liam circled Tals.

"Just because you took down Teague doesn't mean I'm as weak."

"Prove it," Liam urged, and when Tals lunged, Liam faked left and took him down with a hard elbow to the back. Then he threw his body on the prone wolf and all hell broke loose.

Tals fought. He was excellent—Liam had sparred with him before. But this time, Liam took no prisoners. As his hands tightened to fists, he grabbed Tals and began slamming his face until his human form was a bloody, bleeding pulp with no doubt every bone broken and then he hit him some more.

We tortured your father until he begged to die.

Liam knew—he'd heard all of it, allowed himself to crawl away only when his father's screams stopped.

Jinx assured him that Linus had passed, crossed over successfully. At least he knew his father was in that place of peace he deserved.

Tals was headed where he deserved, too. Liam was sure of it. He'd taken Liam's family, no doubt encouraged and laughed when Teague had taken his mate.

Liam had the wolf by the neck and squeezed until Tals bucked frantically under him. "You didn't give my father the chance to fight. I'm returning the favor."

"Liam . . . we were friends," Tals managed through his mangled mouth.

Technically, that was true—Liam had been closest with the man currently bleeding underneath him. "We were never friends," he spat back as his canines elongated and he ripped the man's throat out, felt the life slip away from Tals even as the alpha leader inside of him stood up and finally reared his head.

You were meant for this, his father's voice echoed in his head. He'd heard it a million times growing up, but it was hard to believe it when you really didn't feel it.

There was no mistaking it now. Taking this action had not only been right, but just.

He didn't stop there, ripped the wolf limb from limb. Before he tore Tals's head off, he turned to see Cain holding the mounting spike at the ready, an old Were tradition.

In his haze, Liam could see the light Cain was bathed in, a thin shadow that glowed like a protective skin.

Tradition said only the true pack alpha could see the omega's glow. Cyd and the Dires swore it was there and Liam had been ashamed to admit he couldn't see it.

But now that he could, he was even more determined that he was doing the right thing. Blood and sweat mixed with tears of rage and revenge, ran in rivulets down his face and neck. He tasted the metallic tang and his wolf wanted out.

Vice told him that Weres had no control, not like the Dires, but that Liam could learn some measures of control. He didn't want the out-of-control wolf to take him over. No, he wanted to be in control, to take the wheel, to be present for every brutal punch he threw.

He wanted to never forget.

Liam twisted Tals's head with a roar, ripped it from the man's body. As the blood covered him, his eyes turned, his chest coated and he and Cyd both looked like primitive gladiators. There was enough gore on the field for a horror movie.

Now, Cain held two spikes steady and Liam and Cyd mounted their enemies' heads, prepared to wrap and drag the pieces of the bodies behind them on tarps to the meeting with the outlaws that Liam had called before this fight.

"This is what we'll do to any and all who betray

our kind," Liam growled at Pat now. "Pass it along. It's the only reason I'm letting you live."

The Were who'd witnessed the brutal battle scampered off and Liam had no doubt the tales he'd tell. Liam's legend was just beginning. The bodies in the middle of the outlaws' clubhouse to be discovered soon would tell the rest of the story.

He fully expected there would be noncompliant wolves—he would do this, killing one by one until he reigned with an iron fist. This wasn't the time for forgiveness—it was a time for war.

Liam and his new pack would win it, battle by battle, not caring if he was soaked in the blood of his enemies. This was a message to any other Were who was thinking of rebelling, and it was also a risk, but one Liam needed to take.

"Fine job, king," Cain told him. "Fine damned job."

The packs would talk about this forever. Vice knew that as surely as he did his vices.

His canines elongated with the violence, the smell of shed blood. The scene in front of him had been so fucking brutal that he was both hard as hell and sick to his stomach, his emotions swinging on a violent pendulum of their own.

It had taken every ounce of self-control he had, which wasn't much, to not join in the fray. Brother Wolf was mainly responsible for holding him back this time, because his wolf trained with Liam's.

There are some things a pup has to do alone, Brother Wolf said, and besides, Liam wasn't alone. He had an alpha and his omega and he had to come into his own at some point.

Doesn't mean you're not needed—now, more than ever, Brother Wolf said and Vice sighed as his wolf saw right through him. As much as Vice had fought the pairing at first, spending time with the wolf pup who would be king was good for him. Spending any amount of time with someone balanced was always a plus, and although those effects were only in the short term, Vice still liked how it felt.

But his emotional pendulum swung the other way more quickly than he thought and sorrow washed over him as he watched his charge—and Jinx's—covered with blood, eyes still lupine and fierce, howling with all the frenzied power and lust that came with victory.

Cyd looked . . . stronger. The kill he'd made had brought out more of his inner alpha. Vice wondered how long he'd stay with Liam's pack before breaking off into his own. The omega was gaining power too, and it should've been the signal of good things to come.

But Vice was so fucking sad. The loss of a certain kind of innocence that these young Weres would never get back.

Vice never had it, but to watch the young ones doing what the Dires had trained them for made him so proud and sick at the same time.

"Hey." Liam stood in front of him now, uncertain for only a moment before Vice grabbed the back of the young wolf's neck and pulled him in for a backslapping embrace, a warrior's congratulations. A charge's comfort, as Liam buried his head against Vice's shoulder for a little longer than he should have, as if trying to gain back what he'd just lost.

There was no going back now. There couldn't be. And humans would be the better for it.

Vice pulled Liam's head back up, looked the young king in the eye and made sure he knew it too.

Chapter 9

Instead of going straight to the penthouse, Jez pulled into the parking lot of Mo's Diner.

"I thought we decided home was the best option," Jinx said, wondered when and how he'd begun to think of the place as home in such a short period of time.

"She's got to eat, right?" Jez asked and Gillian's stomach rumbled. She blushed and laughed a little and Jinx felt himself grow lighter every time he heard the sound.

Fucking pansy ass. "You know who owns this, right?"

Jez smiled. "Of course."

Jinx kept Gillian close when they went inside. Most Weres wouldn't be able to sense what she was—they just didn't have that kind of nose when a Dire was preshift, and Dires were good at that kind of camouflage for good reason. But still, that didn't always stop stupid things from coming out of wolves' mouths.

"Grab a seat in the back," the owner called. He was a big Were, head of this family-run business. The Were family considered themselves their own pack, owing loyalty to no one. And yet, Jinx heard they pledged theirs to Liam, if push came to shove.

A smart move to align themselves with the once and future king.

Obviously, Jez had been here before, as none of the Weres looked at him oddly. In fact, the waitress asked if Jez wanted his usual.

Jinx raised a brow when Jez nodded.

"I don't think I want to know what a deadhead's usual is," he murmured without thinking.

"You like the Grateful Dead?" Gillian asked and Jez gave her a smile.

"I followed them one summer."

Jinx rubbed a hand along the back of his neck as he watched his mate and his vampire roommate bonding over "Sugar Magnolia." He supposed things could be worse.

They all ate heartily once the food came. Jinx ordered another round of fries for Gillian and a burger and shake for himself—they would be his third—and she didn't seem to think the way they ate was odd at all.

"I see someone I need to do some business with." Jez excused himself and made his way to a table across the room where two werechicks sat. They'd been staring at Jez from the moment he'd walked in and Jinx made a mental note to ask his roomie what the hell that was all about.

The extra food came and Gillian put ketchup

carefully on the side of her plate. Took a sip of his shake when Jinx offered to share.

"Thanks. This food is so much better than the hospital." As she spoke the word, her expression tightened a little.

"It's okay, Gillian. I'll make sure you stay out of that place."

"Why are you doing this? Hiding me? Helping me?" she asked.

"Does it matter? You're free."

She nibbled a fry dipped in ketchup, then said, "In my experience, there's a price you pay for everything."

"I think you've paid enough, Gillian."

She smiled. "I like the way you say my name. You don't have an accent, but every time you say my name, you do."

Because he slipped into the cadence of the old language whenever he was around her, couldn't help it. He felt like he was in the old country; expected he could look out and see the bloom of the Reinrose, the delicate purple Revebejelle that circled around the center of town hall where all the celebrations took place. He could see Gillian dancing in a loose white dress, her hair glinting like diamonds in the sun.

You are losing your ever-loving mind. And after living with both Vice and a vamp, he didn't have all that far to go.

Jinx seemed far away for the moment. She took the opportunity to study him carefully. He was like no man she'd ever met before—a mix of modern motorcycle badass and somehow old-fashioned in his manners, the way he opened her doors for her, pulled out her chair. That wasn't some act, like her father and his friends. No, this was ingrained in him, like it was second nature.

His eyes were green like the fields she ran in during the springtime—she slept on the pads of warm grass during the day, hidden away from the prying eyes of the others in the park, and at night, she ran, smelling the musk of the flowers. His eyes warmed her. His hair felt as silky as it looked and she wanted to run her hands through it again. To kiss him again, although granted the cemetery was possibly the least romantic place for a first kiss.

She grinned at that thought and it faded when she saw his expression had gone serious again. "Whatever happens, Jinx, just don't send me back."

"I won't."

She pushed her plate away. "My parents won't give up easily."

"What do they do when you run away?"

"I always come back within a couple of days." She left her clothes folded, a sign like DO NOT DISTURB AND I'LL COME BACK PEACEFULLY. "For all I know, the hospital doesn't even tell them I leave and come back."

But this time was different. They would know this man took her and while he didn't appear to be scared of anything, he'd never been up against her family.

Then again, neither had she and as the dust settled and the enormity of what she'd done began to hit her, she realized she would be on the receiving end of their ruthlessness for the first time.

Gillian Margaret Blackwell. She could still hear her mother middle-naming her after all these years and she winced.

"What's wrong?"

"Nothing. Just . . . memories."

"None of them good, by the looks of it."

No, there hadn't been good ones for a long time. Maybe, with Jinx, there would be.

Liam stared at his hands. He'd woken up four times already in the past two hours, convinced he could see the blood on them still. He knew it couldn't be so—they'd been washed several times already, but the smell . . . the howls . . . rang in his ears.

The spoils of war.

"Ten more surrendered tonight," Cyd had told him just before he came in here to get some quiet. The rooms they used were at the end of the Dire tunnel, where it was safest for them and yet gave them enough independence to begin functioning as a pack of their own.

In time, Liam would move back to Manhattan with the twins and the majority of his pack.

Max was being held in the room next to Harm and she had everything she could want, except freedom.

Liam felt the yoke around his neck as surely as she did.

It was hard to stay away from her. Cyd offered to find him other comforts but Liam refused.

Didn't want to ever fall in love again but he didn't want meaningless shit either.

Cyd took the comfort instead. As an alpha, all his desires were strengthening exponentially. After their kills, they'd never be the same.

As it's meant to be.

He heard the two weregirls' cries of pleasure throughout the night. Cyd obviously satisfied them completely and then some, as they'd had come out to breakfast smiling.

Cain was quieter about his needs, as he needed to be as the omega, but he fed his appetites as well. And when they gathered again, the strength of that trio would cement them all a great place in Were history.

Would it be enough? His father had done it for twenty-one years, since Liam's birth, with not a single companion, no true mate. He said it was much easier without the entanglement and for the first time, Liam understood what he'd meant.

His father could've stopped him from mating with Max, but instead let him make his own mistakes. Linus saw nothing wrong, saw mistakes as something to learn from.

Liam saw a hell of a lot wrong with it.

So what, you'll keep the boy and protect him from everything?

The pup was innocent and a hybrid. It would

deserve none of the scrutiny and rejection it would get. But could Liam show the whelp love? Because without that . . .

"Liam? The California alpha's on the line for you," Cain said. "He wants to congratulate you on a job well done."

A job well done most likely meant Liam had his support. The thrill of that helped to erase some of the heaviness in his heart at what good pack law really meant.

Chapter 10

Jinx's wolf did not like closed spaces, but he offered Gillian the option of the elevator. She seemed to accept his claustrophobia in stride and walked up with him.

"I don't much like small spaces either," she told him as they started up the stairs together. Jez took the elevator, mainly so he could make sure all was right in the penthouse.

Jinx was sure they would've sensed trouble, but Jez was more careful than most, a trait Jinx appreciated.

"I really like the other house. Why don't you live there anymore?"

"It was time for me to get out on my own." They rounded the landing to the halfway point of the upstairs.

They finished the walk in silence. Jez met them at the door with a nod to Jinx as Gillian stepped inside.

"I like this place too," she told Jinx. There were

lots of windows in the main part of the room. Most vampires would hate that, but Jez wasn't most vampires.

"I'm going to head to the roof," Jez told them.

"Do you sleep there?" Gillian asked.

"I don't sleep much at night, no."

"I'd like to sleep outside, I think."

"I'm never going to have any privacy again, am I?" Jez grumbled, but he didn't look all that put out as they went out onto the rooftop terrace under the stars.

It was so calm—too calm for monsters to be roaming the night. Then again, most humans thought wolves were monsters too. He settled with Gillian in one of the double loungers while Jez took one on the other side of the roof for maximum privacy.

She snuggled in against him. "Do you see them now? The ghosts?"

"Yes. They're everywhere."

"I could only see the one in my room. I liked her," she said wistfully.

There'd been a time he'd liked ghosts too—thought maybe they were misunderstood. He'd spent what seemed like a lifetime trying to hold to this theory. Since it was his ability, shouldn't he be kind to the things?

Rogue never had that issue. He'd wanted the spirits to go back to where they came from, no niceties at all. And by the time Jinx was convinced he was right, Rogue was far ahead of him in the *sending them back into their box* thing.

But Jinx had learned. "You shouldn't ever get that close to a ghost. Don't let them talk to you. Ignore them, because most of the time, they lie."

That was true about half the time, but for the inexperienced, the ignoring thing was generally the best rule of thumb.

"You make them all sound scary."

"You don't know what's underneath what you're seeing or hearing."

"It sounds like a hard job. I used to want to work at Carvel when I was younger, but mainly so I could have ice cream all day long," she admitted. "What about you? Did you always want to hunt ghosts?"

He couldn't tell her yet that, as a Dire, you didn't really have a choice as to what you wanted to be. You just were—and he was a warrior alpha wolf born into a great warrior family big on tradition and worried as hell that the twins would ruin the line with their witchy ways. "It's what I'm good at."

There was a long, comfortable silence and then Gillian turned her head against his chest and went to sleep. It was a calm, peaceful sleep, with deep, easy breaths and the hint of a smile on her face. He covered her against the coolness of the night, since she hadn't officially turned yet. Her metabolism was faster, she was warm, but he wouldn't take any chances.

Shifting—especially the first shifts—on any Dire were very hard. In his day, on average maybe half survived the transition.

Brother Wolf whined in his ear and he didn't blame him. Jinx didn't want to think about the possibility of losing Gillian either.

As Gillian slept under the stars, he and Jez moved back over to the small table in the middle, bringing beer and chips and salsa with them. Their talk turned back to the other matter at hand while they had the opportunity. Decided that reopening purgatory was the worst idea ever, but neither had a clue about how to send the purgatory monsters to hell.

"Hell might not even accept them," Jez pointed out.

"How can you be rejected from hell?" Jinx asked.

"I was." Jez sniffed.

"You sure there's no one innocent in purgatory?"

"There's another place for the innocent who haven't moved along yet. They're not all walking the earth."

"And you've seen this place?"

"I've had a rather extensive tour of all the areas except purgatory. And I can assure you that none of these monsters were in hell." Jez sucked back the beer and then grabbed for the chips. Odd deadhead, this one was.

"In order for you to travel through hell, you can't be innocent."

"That I'm not innocent is news?"

He'd never asked exactly what the vamp had done, but he supposed, by the very nature of vampires, that killing was up there on their list of sins. "I'm going to have to get Rogue's help on this."

"I'm thinking it couldn't hurt."

The hellhounds listened to him for now and in turn, corralled the monsters. He couldn't help but wonder how long it would take before the monsters actually ruled him. This kind of power was something you couldn't wield for very long without losing a hell of a lot of yourself.

But he couldn't deny that he'd allowed himself to think about how he could use the monsters for good.

"When are you going to tell your girlfriend that you run purgatory?" Jez asked.

"I will fucking stake you."

"That's a myth. And it was a simple question. You need to get laid."

Jinx grabbed the phone and dialed Stray.

"I say get laid—you call a male wolf. Odd," Jez moved and Jinx gave him the universal shut up signal in the form of the middle finger.

"Yeah, it's me. When you go to the hospital, can you find the books that were in Gillian's room? Yeah, there were some classics, a few romance." He rattled off some titles. If Stray couldn't find them, Jinx would replace them with new copies, because everyone deserved to have something that made them feel good when they were in a strange place.

Hell, even Jez had done that for him, had orchestrated moving Jinx's old comforter and pillows from the Dire house to here, with Vice's help.

Brother Wolf greatly appreciated the comforts of home. It had only been a few weeks, but when they'd faced battles together, warriors tended to bond faster. He wasn't sure what would've happened to him had he not approached Jez in the first place, and he didn't want to think about it.

Chapter 11

Jinx carried a sleeping Gillian in from the roof around dawn, put her in his bedroom and resisted the urge to crawl in next to her. They had enough issues to deal with already and truth be told, the king of purgatory thing was going to be a nice wedge in their relationship.

On his way to the shower, he grumbled something at Jez while the vampire ate his Cocoa Pebbles, wondering if the deadhead needed any sleep. Superfuckingvampire, he was.

He contemplated the day ahead as he let the hot water sluice over his back. Brother was pissed about the no-running thing. Rogue was pissed. Rifter was pissed. Vice would be pissed soon enough.

Maybe the hellhound could be housebroken. The building obviously didn't have a problem with pets.

Brother Wolf growled. "I wasn't talking about you."

And maybe you're punch-drunk on lack of sleep.

He'd barely gotten out of the shower when Jez opened the door.

"I think we're close enough that I don't feel the need to shower together," Jinx told him.

"Stray's on the phone—said it's an emergency. Asshole," he added and Jinx dried himself as he walked into the living room to grab the phone.

Jez had put it on speaker. "Stray, what's wrong?"

"Your girlfriend's famous," Stray said. Jez was already turning on the TV where a special news bulletin was splashed across the screen.

There was a picture of Gillian—and a drawing of a guy who he guessed was supposed to be him.

"Looks nothing like me," he scoffed.

"You're lucky I managed to destroy the video footage. Took all night—neither you or Jez was really slick. And Kate was the sketch artist—she helped make sure the sketch is just off enough."

"I'm not supposed to show up on celluloid," Jez mused.

"No one says celluloid anymore," Jinx said as Stray continued, "You were all over it in black and white."

Jez frowned but merely said, "They're offering an obscene reward."

"Her parents are the Blackwells. As in Blackwell Industries," Stray told them and Jinx couldn't tear his eyes away as the press conference with Gillian's parents began.

They didn't look anything like her, which of

course made sense. In a way, he'd been hoping they were Dires, even Weres, but no way. He'd be able to tell.

"I've got a call in to Marley—she knows a couple of the camera guys at the conference. Parents are human," Stray confirmed.

Mrs. Blackwell looked suitably teary, her husband, stoic and firm. They pleaded for their daughter's safe return and offered five million dollars.

And now there was a bounty on Gillian's head the size of fucking Earth.

It made sense that Gillian would've used the name Black. Using her real name would've attracted the media as well as making her a target for, well, kidnappers. Like him. "We're screwed."

This new world of wolves and humans living so close—mixing—was inherently dangerous. She wouldn't be the first accidentally adopted wolf. But the fact that she'd been locked away and forgotten, and now they were trying so desperately to get her back, struck him as more than a little strange.

". . . She's a danger to others. She tried to kill several members of the hospital staff," one of the doctors was saying now as the camera lights flashed and members of the press called out questions.

"That's a lie," Jinx said.

"Is it?" Jez asked.

"Wouldn't the orderly have shared that with me?" Jinx demanded.

"None of this makes sense," Jez agreed. "But this is going to get everyone's attention—and Gillian is hard to miss."

"Please call law enforcement to help bring Gillian in. Do not attempt to grab her yourself," the New York City police chief was saying. "We are working with law enforcement in the areas around the hospital where Gillian disappeared. Yes, I'll take a question."

"Sir, does it appear that Gillian Blackwell left of her own accord?"

"According to reports, she was carried out by the man you see in the police sketch. We believe he has taken her against her will."

"Sir, have there been any calls for ransom?"

"Not as of yet," he confirmed.

Jez shook his head and Jinx stared at the floor.

"Does the Greenland pack have TV or Internet?" Jez asked finally, without a trace of irony.

"That's a good fucking question," Stray muttered across the line.

"We've got to get to the bottom of this—now," Jinx said.

"Kill's got a lead," Stray assured him.

Jinx had forgotten how damned hard the memories of the Greenland pack were for the brothers—and it wasn't like they could saunter in and say, "Hi, we're the other Dires and we've got one of yours."

"I'm sorry you and Killian have to deal with this, Stray," Jinx told him.

"It's all good. For your mate."

All Jinx could say was "Thanks."

"Obviously lay low," Stray added.

"She's got to run."

"Fill her in when she wakes," Stray said. "You can't ease her into this."

And then what? Jinx wanted to ask, but he couldn't. Because the "then what" would entail hiding her. Sending her away, possibly back to a pack they all hated.

Gillian had been watching TV in the bedroom. She sat up, hugging the covers to her body, her eyes glued to the screen of the channel that prepared to run the news on a continuous loop. She didn't acknowledge him at first, until he said, "I didn't know you were, ah . . . you know . . ."

"An heiress?" she answered without tearing her eyes from the news conference.

"Rich as shit."

"That too." He'd wrapped a towel around his waist, as all his clean clothes were actually in this room, washed by whatever vampire cleaning fairies Jez employed. He never saw any of them, but everything was always pretty damned impeccable and there was always a ton of food, including a lot of meat, so he had no complaints.

Now, he grabbed a pair of jeans and dropped the towel to yank them on. She was glued to the TV screen, so not the biggest confidence booster.

He took the remote from her and turned it off.

She grabbed it back from him and turned it on. "I have to know what they're saying about me."

"Why?"

"Because." She shoved the covers aside, frustrated, and he tried not to stare at her long lean legs. "You don't understand. My family is so fucked up."

"Yeah, I definitely wouldn't understand fucked-up families," he muttered.

She was staring at him because she'd heard him. Goddamned wolf hearing. "All I'm saying is—"

"Am I?" she interrupted.

"Are you what?" Jinx braced himself as she asked the next part of the question.

"Dangerous. They kept telling me how sick I was. But they never tried to find me when I left. And I don't remember trying to hurt anyone, but I had blackouts."

"What kind of blackouts? From the drugs?"

"Maybe. I lost time. Days—weeks, one time. But the doctors always told me that things were fine." She gave her parents on the TV a hard look. "I shouldn't have believed any of them."

Jinx was studying her. She wondered if this was the point where everything that had been so wonderful and easy between them would break down, that he would reconsider hiding her.

Five million dollars was nothing to sneeze at, and ghost hunting couldn't pay that much, if at all.

Granted, she had no idea how he afforded this place, but maybe Jez paid for it.

Another doctor was on-screen now, discussing Gillian's diagnosis without saying the exact word schizophrenia, because that would violate all kinds of HIPPA policies. Instead, he talked generally about what happens to a mental patient who stopped taking meds suddenly.

He had no clue the daily meds did nothing for her. She didn't even bother spitting them out anymore because she was convinced they were sugar pills. And she certainly wasn't suffering from any kind of withdrawal symptoms as far as she could tell.

She would, however, kill for a nice, stiff drink. And a rare hamburger. She wanted to go to a bar and dance on tables and kiss Jinx all night, end up in his bed.

She'd settle for not being put back into the hospital at this point. Moved nervously under the covers until Jinx finally spoke.

"You said last night that your family could be difficult. Didn't you think it might be important to tell me who they were?"

"No," she said coolly. "I liked that you didn't know."

"I could've been lying."

"But you weren't. I would've known. I lived my entire life growing up around people using me for that damned last name." She fisted her hands on her bare thighs as she watched her mother daintily wipe her eyes, her father's comforting arms around her. "This is the most they've touched each other ever, and I'm counting their wedding night."

"Wow."

"They've slept in separate bedrooms as long as I can remember."

"Maybe they have, like, conjugal visits?"

"In separate wings. My father's lovers sleep over."

"Ouch."

"I'm adopted," she said suddenly. "They didn't want to tell me, but I hired a detective to find the lawyer they got me from. At least my father's money did me some good."

"You're their only kid."

"Yes. And no, I don't want any of their money. They can keep all of it." There was a time in her life she couldn't have imagined saying that, never mind meaning it. But she had and she did.

She was angry—at Jinx, herself, her parents. All of it.

"I don't understand why they're even doing this. It's got to be for show."

"Maybe they're sorry?" Jinx asked.

"They haven't even come to see me in years. People don't change that much." Granted, even before that, her parents had never really taken a huge interest in her. Like most of her friends, she'd been raised by staff, rarely seeing her parents except for important functions where she'd been shown off to the society she was supposed to become a part of.

Poor little rich girl.

"Look, Gillian . . . if you decide to go home, I don't want you to think you're not free to do that," Jinx told her.

"There's no point. There's nothing to go back to—my parents don't even want me inside their house. And I'm not going to live in a psych ward for the rest of my life. So no offense, but you're not helping this at all."

But what was she going to do? Hide out here forever?

It seemed, at least for the foreseeable future, that was the best thing for her to do. "I'm sorry, Jinx. I'm being a bitch."

He didn't seem worried or offended. Concerned a bit, yes. But he didn't seem to mind her, moods and all. It was an enlightening and completely new feeling. "I'll bring you in some breakfast. Best you stay inside for the time being, okay?"

She nodded and he closed the door halfway. She could see the big TV was on in the living room, of course, on the news station. She was causing a lot of trouble for both men now.

Apparently, they'd somehow signed up for it.

She looked around Jinx's bedroom. It was furnished in clean, modern lines like the rest of the penthouse. Very few personal touches, she mused as she looked around.

It was then she noticed the books on the shelf.

The books . . . the titles she'd kept in her room at the hospital. They were here, neatly lined up on the bookshelves. Not the same books, mind you. No, these were brand-new, no creases on the spine.

He hadn't been able to get hers back in time, because they'd probably thrown them out once they realized she wasn't coming back. But he'd gotten her every single one and left them here. It was the only explanation.

When he came back in with a tray filled with bacon and eggs and toast, among other things, she was up rifling through the books, smelling the pages. "How did you . . . ?"

"I have a good memory," he said. "It seemed like you really liked them."

She put one to her chest. "They were all I had."

"I didn't want to bring back bad memories."

"They're not. You didn't. Thank you." She reached out and hugged him, not wanting to tell him that, at this moment, that was all she had of them.

Chapter 12

Cain dreamed of Angus almost nightly. Sometimes they were sex dreams, but most often it was his wolf stumbling on the battered, broken FBI agent, too late to do anything but mourn him. When he woke, his stomach knotted and he wondered what the thin line was between dreaming and prophesying.

Yeah, he much preferred the sex dreams. Because in those, no one was bloody or broken . . . well, maybe Angus was a little bloody from Cain's teeth, but he enjoyed it.

Did Angus need him? He hadn't changed his number but the man hadn't called him at all.

You're turning into a female.

"You were tossing around so much you shook the damned floor," Cyd complained now. "I don't want to be inside those dreams anymore."

The twin thing assured that, more often than not, Cyd would feel whatever Cain did when he was in distress. And since Cyd knew all about the

Angus situation, he knew who his twin was having those feelings about.

There was far more judgment that Cain felt that way about a human than the fact that it was another man. "I'd think you were too busy with your own floor shaking to worry about mine," Cain said dryly and his twin laughed as he headed into the shower. Cyd's back was covered in scratches, which would match the screaming werechicks who'd ended up in Cyd's bed last night.

"Hey, I offered you one," Cyd reminded him.

"Yeah, yeah." Cain lay back on the pillows, covering his eyes with his hand. It was dark out, but too damned light in the room since Cyd turned on all of the lights to wake Cain up. His cock was half hard, because this particular dream had them finishing what they'd started the night he'd saved Angus's life.

He'd pressed Angus up against the sink—the fed was holding on and they were both staring into the mirror, his cock inside Angus's hot, tight—

"Better get moving—you're babysitting today," Cyd called out from the shower, breaking the mood for the umpteenth time. Cain sighed and tossed the covers off.

"Don't let Rogue hear you call it that," he said darkly. The Dires had been staying with Rogue around the clock. According to Liam, who'd heard it from Vice, every time Rogue tried to sleep, he'd wake up screaming.

Cain could only imagine the literal hell he'd been through.

Speaking of dreams, he wondered if Rifter was wandering around in his mind too. He hadn't exactly caught sight of the shaggy gray Dire but, then again, he really wasn't paying attention to anyone but Angus.

Angus. Gone for just a short time but it felt like months. You'd think Cain would have better judgment or at least survival skills after all he'd been through.

He guessed love really did make you goddamned stupid.

Rogue had stayed up all night and all the next day, because fuck sleep. He'd had enough to last him a lifetime. Stray and Killian hung out with him, and then Vice came back and they smoked some hand rolls, because at that moment, Vice seemed more fucked-up than he was.

He'd heard the wolves talking in low tones about Liam's big fight. The twins' involvement. And then there were the visits to his room—the just-checking-on-you glances, the let-me-know-if-you-need-anything looks.

He was drowning.

It was after midnight by the time everyone cleared the fuck out for their runs and Rogue was alone. Semi-alone, since a much-subdued Cain trailed into the attic and he enlisted the young Were to help him burn the bed.

He wasn't surprised by Cain's quiet. Young Weres usually had enough energy to bounce off the walls no matter how hard they ran, but last night had been a battle. And even though they'd won, Rogue knew they'd lost something as well.

As they watched the giant bonfire roar in the middle of the yard, Cain said, "The female Dire escaped. She's with Jinx now."

"She didn't look like much could hold her. If she could do that before a shift . . . well hell, from what I remember, the females were actually stronger than the males. Granted, I think it's like that in every culture, although the males aren't likely to admit that."

Cain gave a soft snort but his eyes didn't lose their sadness.

"You miss Jinx."

"Don't you?" Cain asked.

"I miss a lot of things," Rogue admitted, ran a hand over his shaved head. It would take some getting used to for sure, but he liked the feeling of freedom. "Thanks for babysitting me."

"That's not what this is."

But Rogue held out a hand to stop him. "Don't bother. It's okay. But I want to shift and run."

Rifter had told Rogue to wait at least a couple more days before trying to shift. Cain didn't seem all that worried about disobeying that order. Rogue supposed that, after the last couple of months, what he wanted to do was mild in comparison and as natural as breathing.

But hell, if he was going to shift, doing so with an omega around seemed like a good idea.

"Think you're ready?"

"Brother Wolf's singing. But he's nervous."

Cain put his hands on the bare skin of Rogue's back, over the glyph. Rogue felt the warmth sink in until he was heated from head to toe.

The pup had gotten stronger since turning twenty-one. He was coming into his destiny.

Inside Rogue's head, Brother began to howl. Without warning, Rogue shifted and although it seemed to take a little longer than normal, everything else appeared to have fallen into place. Brother shook his fur and howled. Cain walked around his big wolf as if checking to see if it was all systems go before stripping and shifting himself.

Brother watched the young Were's pain, the way the scars on his back pulled during the transformation. Those scars had been put there purposely by a cruel packmaster, so Cain would always feel the pain of them during his shifts.

Cain always said it was a reminder of how lucky he was now that he'd escaped. The pup had a good attitude. And now, the wolf in front of him motioned with his head as if to say, you first. Rogue took him up on it and burst like a shot through the woods, his wolf humming as he picked up speed. The forest blurred as he ran, the scenting almost overwhelming, but welcomed. He was worried he wouldn't be able to tolerate handing over the reins to Brother after what he'd been through, but Brother had suffered as much as he had. They both deserved this. Needed this. And with Cain on his six, they ran until they hit the lake.

It was still a little icy, because the nights remained cold, but his wolf walked in and splashed around in the freezing, clean water. Cain waited and watched, and Rogue swore he spotted some amusement in the lupine eyes.

Cain needed this as much as he did. And after several more minutes in the lake, he got out and shook. Prepared for another run when he scented humans. Cain obviously had too, and they moved toward a thicket of brush where they could camouflage and make sure there was no danger approaching.

Rogue's hackles rose, but both wolves remained still as night as the humans passed them with weapons readied as if searching for someone. Or something.

Hunters.

Hunters were like Switzerland. They were equal opportunity, believing live and let live. They policed humans and shifters alike. They lived above human and shifter law, hated by trappers and rogue wolves, tolerated by most Weres and other shifters. Most humans didn't know who or what hunters were, as they were also still in the dark about the existence of the supernatural world.

They hadn't been seen in this area for a long while. Weres stayed clear of them for the most part, although some packs sent their wolves inside the organization to make sure the hunters were on the up-and-up. For the most part, any Weres that worked with hunters were seen as disloyal. Weres made their own laws and they didn't want—or need—humans policing them.

So far, hunters had proven to be evenhanded, on the up-and-up, but Rogue knew that most organizations started out like that. Absolute power corrupted absolutely and all that crap. He'd seen history repeat itself on a loop like *Groundhog Day* for centuries.

He watched in silence as the group, who all bore the traditional hunter bow-and-arrow tattoos on the backs of both hands, met in a tight group. They were discussing Gillian, which was unsurprising, considering the five-million-dollar bounty was the news of the day, but as Rogue listened, it appeared they were simply patrolling the area, not looking for trouble—or Gillian.

"Listen, if they're giving away that money, better that we find Gillian Blackwell and not the trappers or the Weres. At least we'll bring her in safely," one of the men was saying.

"I don't disagree that we're the best ones for the job, but I won't pull us off our posts to hunt for her. If we come across her, we save her, deliver her to her parents before any harm comes to her," another man said. "Beyond that, we've got a job to do."

There were four humans in all, three men and one woman, not a Were among them. And they seemed serious and capable and Rogue wondered what would happen if he and Cain stepped out in front of them. That would tell the tale for sure.

But neither wolf did, their own sense of self-preservation more ingrained than that.

It was only after the hunters passed and he and Cain ran for several more hours did Rogue realize he hadn't seen a single spirit. Not a real one, anyway, but it had gotten to the point where he'd begun to realize that his flashbacks of his time spent in hell might not be flashbacks after all.

Maybe, for the first time in his life, the spirits were as scared of him as he was of himself.

Chapter 13

The roof was the second-best place for this discussion. Jinx would've much preferred the woods, but everyone was on high alert looking for Gillian and her five-million-dollar self. So Jez would go out hunting around, making sure the monsters from purgatory weren't out and about, and Jinx wondered if Rogue would be too.

When Rogue saw the monsters for himself, Jinx knew he'd hear from his twin. For now, he led Gillian to the rooftop terrace where he'd laid out Chinese food and beers and for the better part of an hour, they ate and laughed a little. She'd spent the day parked in front of the TV, getting angry with each sentence her parents spoke, but she hadn't mentioned it yet.

Instead, she curled her feet up on the chair, her bare feet under her, beer balanced on her thigh. "That was great. Thanks."

"Welcome." He drained his own beer. It would take him at least a case to feel any kind of drunk, and tonight, he'd welcome that. He thought about Rifter—he could've gone to his king, asked what it was like to have to tell a woman who thought she was human that she wasn't. Could've asked Gwen's advice too. Hell, Gwen might be the best person to give this talk.

But Jinx's wolf didn't want anyone near Gillian. Brother was . . . attached. And ready to attack anyone who got in his way.

"How're you feeling?" he asked finally. "I know you're restless."

Indeed, when she wasn't staring at the TV screen, she'd been pacing so much he was sure she wore the floor down.

"I've got a lot of energy lately," she admitted. "I wish I could go for a walk."

He nodded in understanding, but they both knew it wasn't possible, not with the amount of scrutiny her picture was receiving at this moment. Even if she cut her hair and dyed it, covered her eyes with contacts, he had an odd feeling she'd still be discovered.

And she'd told him she didn't relish the thought of walking around in a disguise for the rest of her life. If it came down to it, however, she would do it before she ever went back to her parents or the hospital.

"I have a few things I need to know about you," he started, breaking her from her reverie. She stared at him with something akin to disappointment in her eyes, but not surprise. She had to have known he'd need to know about all of it sooner or later. And maybe because he'd saved her or maybe for other reasons he didn't yet know, she said,

"You want to know more about why I was in that institution to start with."

"Only if you want to talk about it."

She shrugged, and he knew she'd rather talk about anything else. But learning her symptoms was an important lead-in. "I was always a little hard for them to handle. My mother always looked at me like I was some alien who'd landed on her doorstep. When I started to refuse to wear the fussy dresses, she shipped me off to a boarding school. I didn't mind that so much. But when I came back for summer vacations, that was the worst. The year I turned seventeen, I was doing the same things as others in my so-called social circle—running around, drinking, smoking. Making out with boys . . . did you just growl?"

He touched his canines with his tongue, keeping his mouth closed because they'd extended. *Down Brother . . . she's talking past.*

But Brother didn't differentiate. "Just clearing my throat. So yeah, basically what teenage girls do."

"Right," she said, casting a doubting look at him. "I mean, I had my parents' money behind me, so my idea of partying was probably more extensive. I felt indelible, like I couldn't get hurt or in trouble. My behavior was wild—and it was escalating. Staying out all night, taking lots of dangerous risks. I had the means to get out of any kind of trouble."

But whatever happened made her face grow dark with the memory. He wanted to wipe that pain away, stop her from thinking about it, but this was important shit. He had to know it.

She sighed, grabbed a second beer but held it instead of drinking it. "I'd had a lot of shots that night. I was spinning. I was high as well, but the weird thing was, I don't think the drugs were actually making me feel the way I did."

"How's that?"

"Indestructible. I got behind the wheel of a car and I ended up crashing into a telephone pole. I was so lucky because I could've killed someone. As it was, I broke my legs and spent time in the hospital recovering. My parents told me they were placing me under psychiatric care because of the drugs and drinking, and I agreed. I felt so guilty. I was dangerous. They'd been warning me to get myself under control for months and months and I just kept ignoring them. I thought the hospital could fix me, but things got worse. I knew that I'd never be released. No one could figure out what was wrong with me. I didn't respond to meds. I couldn't just behave, no matter how much I wanted to. After a while, they placed me in a long-term facility and I figured I'd be there forever."

"Plenty of kids are wild, Gilly, but not all of them get sent to psych wards."

"I was clawing at the walls. One night, I woke up howling. I jumped through windows. I would get bursts of anger and adrenaline and throw tables at the staff. I was uncontrollable at times," she told him in a burst of angry confession. "None of that's normal."

It was. His heart broke for just how damned normal it was, but she continued. "I feel like I'm two people. Gillian—the girl who just wants to find a boyfriend and have fun and this other person who likes to run naked and lately, it's like they're blending and it's getting harder and harder to separate them and I hear this voice—it tells me things. It calms me. The doctors said I'm the right age for schizophrenia to manifest."

He put his hand over hers, his palm searing heat onto her skin. "I can promise you that you're not schizophrenic. That you don't have any mental illness."

"How do you know that?"

"Because you can't. Genetically. Physically. You do not get mentally ill or get any other diseases."

Maybe Gillian had been right the first time—Jinx did belong back in that mental ward. She could go back with him and they could grow old together there. Because that was all she wanted—to be together with him.

At least he appeared to want the same thing.

"What I'm going to tell you—well, you might laugh. Think I'm joking. And then you'll probably get scared. But a part of you, the part you told me about, will understand."

"Okay, tell me."

"There's no good way to do this," he muttered. "Gilly, you're feeling this way—the urge to be naked, to run under the moon—because you're a wolf."

She blinked. Once. Twice. Held back a laugh as she waited for his.

None came, from either of them. "So all of this is happening to me because I'm a wolf?"

Still, no laughter. The man was serious. Dead serious when he said, "Yes. Part of you knows instinctively. And part of you has been taught it's too crazy to believe. But still you do." Jinx handed her the book with her moon drawings that he must've grabbed before they left the hospital.

She took it from him but refused to look inside. It represented so many years of pain. "I'm not a very good artist."

"It's the way you interpret her. Raw. Primal. Basic, like your needs."

Jinx's voice whispered to something she'd already known as it skittered along her back and tingled like a caress. She wanted to mount him on the warm grass, take him inside of her so deeply until she . . .

Howled.

She blinked as Jinx's eyes shifted. They looked like the ones she saw in her dreams. "You're not . . . human."

"Neither are you, sweetheart," he murmured before directing her to look in the small mirror he'd brought outside with them without her noticing.

She gasped. Had this ever happened in the hospital? In front of her parents? "Wolf."

"All wolf. Dire wolf. This is just the form that allows you to pass in this world unnoticed. Although you're too beautiful to be ignored."

Everything that had happened to her since Jinx found her led to this moment.

Mentally ill versus wolf. She figured she hadn't drawn the short end of the stick.

And if he's lying?

He's not, the rustling said.

"You're hearing rustling. That's your wolf talking to you. And your back—I'll bet if I looked, I'd see bruises there, but you don't remember falling or hurting yourself."

She took a step back. "Maybe I am going through some kind of drug withdrawal."

"I have a glyph of my wolf on my back."

He pulled his shirt up and waited, standing patiently as she circled him. A wolf stared at her from Jinx's back. It was the color of Jinx's hair, a handsome, ferocious creature. It had Jinx's eyes, only with an otherworldly light shining through them. This was more than a tattoo. This looked . . . alive.

She thought back to the large pattern of bruising she'd seen on her body yesterday and tried to picture a similar creature on her skin.

"It will have your hair color. Sister Wolf will be as pretty as you are," Jinx told her without turning around. He was talking low, as if speaking to some wild animal he was trying to tame.

Except she got the feeling that Jinx would never try to tame anything about her. "In the hospital— I had dreams about the wolves. I told the doctor that when I was a little girl, I used to dream about turning into a wolf and running away. She told me that was my unconscious ego—that I was too little to protect myself, so in my dreams I turned myself into something that no one could hurt."

"Sometimes, a wolf is just a wolf," Jinx told her.

She reached out and touched the glyph. It seemed to move under her fingers, like the way heat off a sidewalk steamed and made everything look hazy and fluid. "I'm not dreaming."

"No." This time, he did turn to face her. "There's a lot more for you to know."

"I'm not ready to hear it." She moved forward, touched his chest, pulled him close to her by the belt loops on his jeans. She was all revved up. Needy. And Jinx's erection pressing her belly told her he had the same needs.

At that moment, she realized how badly her body ached with need. She reached out to touch Jinx, palms flat against his chest for a long moment before she surprised herself by viciously ripping off his shirt.

"Holy Odin," Jinx murmured. "Gillian . . ."

"You can't stop me."

"I don't want to."

She cocked her head, not quite believing that. She sensed apprehension, but not about sex. "What is it?"

He moved away from her, sat heavily on the double lounger. "If you knew what I've done. When you know . . . you'll be ashamed to be with me. When you know what I can do—"

"You got me out of jail. You saved me. That's all I need to know."

"I wish it were that simple."

"For tonight, it will be." They were the last words she spoke before pushing him on his back and straddling him. He looked surprised, especially when she took his wrists and raised them above his head. "I feel like I need to tie you. Bind you."

When her hand moved to curl around his throat, something changed in his eyes.

"No binding," was all he said.

"Not this time," she agreed and his face flushed. She noted he left his hands above his head though, and she liked that. Instead of stripping herself under the cool night air, she first moved so she could unzip his jeans. She got them all the way off so he was totally naked under her.

I can't wait to see his wolf, the rustling said.

She'd had some experience with boys, but never with a man. Not like this. She let his long, thick cock rub against her wet sex. Took her shirt off, played with her nipples, never taking her eyes from his face.

"I want to touch you," he told her, his voice a growl. She leaned forward, teasing him with her breasts near his face. He reached up and caught a nipple in his mouth, suckled as she groaned in pleasure at the contact. His cock seemed to swell under her and all she knew was that she needed him inside of her. Foreplay didn't matter—she didn't have the time, the patience for foreplay.

She wondered if this was what it was like to be a guy and decided she liked it. Jinx didn't mind it at all—he was thrusting into her with abandon and her body was taking it and wanting more.

When he came inside of her, he let out what sounded like a cross between a growl and a howl. The sound actually made her come again, her climax milking him to completion.

No condoms necessary. No diseases.

Because you're a wolf.

When she looked down, she saw that his eyes— *his eyes* had changed. They looked like the wolf's eyes on his back and for really the first time, she believed.

He couldn't help the partial shift any more than he could've stopped his climax. Nor did he want to. She knew and now, he just had to wear her out in a way she'd never been before. He knew how to please a wolf warrior female and he would prove it.

She tried to push back as her eyes never left his, but he refused to let her. Put his hands on her biceps and pulled her back toward him. His cock was still encased in her sex and he was hard.

She hadn't had nearly enough orgasms.

"Don't be scared," he told her.

"I'm not."

"You're lying. You can't do that when I'm still inside of you." He slid his grip to her hips to make sure it stayed that way.

"I'm scared."

"You're free, Gillian, in a way you never thought you could be. Everything you've been feeling, everything you thought wasn't normal was normal for you. For a Dire wolf. That's why I pulled you out of the hospital; and if I'd known you were in there before this, I never would've let you linger there."

She believed him, because she'd stopped fighting his grip. There were tears in her eyes. "Those years—they were wasted."

"We'll make up for them."

"You're not going to leave me?"

"Why would you think that?" he asked, a tug in his gut when he thought about how bad for her he actually was.

"Because in the past, everyone has," she told him and he sat up and kissed her so fiercely, a promise, a pledge and everything else in between. Her tears wet both their cheeks as she kissed him back. They remained like that for a long while, kissing, the air cooling their too-hot skin. She was content, but didn't remain that way for long.

When she pulled back, he noted that her pupils were shrinking. Her wolf eyes wouldn't show themselves until her shift, and if anyone else saw her right now, they'd accuse her of being high.

"I feel edgy," she told him.

"I can take care of that. I'm built to take care of it. Sex is a need for us—much more than it is for humans. If it's not satisfied, there are consequences. You'll never have to deal with those again."

Before she could protest, he'd flipped her onto her back and her legs and arms instinctively wrapped around him. He'd begun to rock into her again and she couldn't stop the jolt of pleasure that ran through her. He bent and suckled a nipple, bit it lightly but enough to make her gasp.

It was then she noted his canines were elongated.

A part of her was truly terrified but a larger part was definitely thrilled. She remained still, watching him brush those sharp teeth across her nipple lightly. Her sex was so wet and his cock seemed to get bigger as it remained inside of her, pulsing against her clit.

He wasn't human. Jinx was taking her—claiming her, she supposed—and she could do nothing but remain open to his advances.

You started it.

But apparently, he'd be the one who would finish it. His body weighed hers down, and even though he slid out of her quickly, he managed to pin her hips to the lounge as he brought his head between her legs. She looked down and watched his wolf's eyes as he scraped his teeth against her soft, hot flesh and then used his tongue to flick the tight bundle of nerves once, twice, until she gripped the sides of the chair so hard she thought she actually heard them crack.

His eyes never left hers. She wanted to look away, should be embarrassed by such a blatant show of sexuality. Legs spread, his head bobbing between them and all she could do was cry out because she needed to come. And when she did, he didn't stop licking her, not even when she begged. And oh, how she begged, with her hands tight in his hair, her actions the complete opposite of her words.

Whatever beast was inside of her wanted these releases, needed them, despite how the line between the pleasure and the pain blurred.

When he'd had his fill of tasting her—that's what he told her, that he loved tasting her and chuckled when she shivered—he turned her onto her stomach, pulled her to her knees. Her body was limp and she was beyond fighting. For the first time in a long time, that nervous, restless energy seemed to have dissipated. She was near satiated—the rustling in her ears calmed, her muscles loose, her body humming.

"You want more?" he asked her.

"More," she managed. "Please."

He didn't ask a second time. On her knees, he took her from behind. She could barely remain upright, but he held her up with an arm around her waist as he thrust into her.

She met him, thrust for thrust, arching her back, pushing her ass back to take him deeper into her core. She didn't recognize herself. Didn't want to. The searing, all-consuming pleasure threatened to slay her and she would let it overtake every bit of common sense and reason, if only to continue feeling this good.

She looked over her shoulder. Jinx's eyes were still otherworldly, his cheeks flushed from exertion but the look on his face was sheer pleasure.

Because of you, the rustling told her and, for the first time, she felt a pride within her that felt right.

Chapter 14

The nightmare woke him up again. Rogue considered giving up sleeping for good, because this getting himself back on a regular wolf schedule of up all night, sleep the day away wasn't working for him. Then again, he pictured hell in most of his waking moments too and decided he'd never be able to get away from it. Not in the near future, anyway.

He made PTSD look like a walk in the park with the shit he saw.

Gwen had encouraged him to try to get his patterns back to normal as soon as possible, but she didn't argue when she discovered he couldn't. Instead, he would come down to the clinic and help to organize her things. Like Jinx and the others, Rogue had also served in the military alongside his twin, becoming a Ranger and a medic in his company.

And since Jinx was out of the house, Rogue figured he could at least be useful and take up that role.

Gwen was doing a lot of research into wolf metabolisms and the like, learning which medicines Weres and Dires could tolerate. In truth, it looked like she was readying for a war, and considering what was happening with Liam, she might be right.

Several hours later, he had all the new boxes opened up, meds labeled and the second room set up with stretchers and curtains.

"You must've worked for hours," she said, brushing the sleep from her eyes with her fingers. Her hair was loose, feet bare and she was so pretty. His queen. The woman who, along with Kate, had saved him from a fate far worse than death. He'd be forever in her debt, would lay down his life for either of them.

In fact, just being in either's presence seemed to calm him, and neither Rifter nor Stray objected.

"It's good for me to keep busy."

"How bad is it?" she asked.

"I should go back out hunting. I need to. But it's hard getting back in the saddle."

Also hard, because he knew what he'd find. But the odd part about no spirits bothering him still confirmed what he knew—the spirits were more scared of him than anything. Instead of seeking comfort from him, they ran from him. He hadn't been lying when he told Jinx he was still in here— hell was a part of him—how could he make it let him go?

"I was there, Rogue. I saw."

"What do you mean, you saw?"

"I saw everything." She whispered it and he wondered if her nightmares of the place were as bad as his. "I know what you went through. I can't imagine how you're feeling right now. But you've got to keep moving forward."

"Suppose I never shake the images? Suppose it never goes away?" He asked it more to himself than to her.

"You've literally been to hell and back, Rogue. I can't imagine that ever leaves you. But you've got to do something with what you've learned. It's what you do."

It was. Since childhood, he manipulated spirits into going where they needed to, heaven, hell— but he'd never dealt with anyone who was in that place in between. "I don't know where to start."

"How about with your twin?" she suggested softly. "I'm worried about both of you. I think you need each other."

"I was kind of an asshole to him the other night," he admitted it. "But he started it."

She smiled a little and he continued, "Fine, I'll go talk to him."

"Good."

"What else's on your mind?" he asked. "I might not read minds or dreamwalk, but you've been avoiding asking me something."

"I have." She looked down at her hands. "Did you mean what you said? About me being both healer and destroyer."

"Yes."

"Well, I know about the destroyer part, unfortunately. But the healer—is that just because of the doctor thing or—"

"Don't you know the answer to that?"

"I was born of a Dire with abilities and a human. I have no idea of the answer."

"Does it matter?"

She looked at him with complete honesty in her eyes. "I guess it can't be helped if it's here. I just see all of you with abilities and . . . it seems like they take so much out of you."

"It's okay to be scared, Gwen. I'm surprised you're not spinning with everything that's happened to you in the short span of time. But you're taking to all of it—you're dealing. Whether or not you've got it, you'll handle it. We may not like it, but we handle it. And that's the most important thing." He turned and headed away from the room. "Now I'm going to take my own goddamned advice."

He didn't have to turn around to know that she was smiling.

They stayed under the stars for a long time, until Jinx mentioned having to go to work, which Gillian supposed meant ghost hunting. She didn't bother asking if she could go with him. Today, of all days, that would be a death wish. They reluctantly dressed and went inside. Jinx returned some calls and she paced around a little, exhausted but still wired from the sex . . . and the news that she was a wolf.

Jinx suggested a long bath and she did that,

soaking under bubbles in the Jacuzzi-sized tub for a long time, her sore muscles enjoying the warmth. When she got out, she stared over her shoulder at the bruising on her back, trying to picture how it could actually form a glyph like Jinx's.

She heard Jez and Jinx arguing about Jinx going hunting alone, with Jinx saying something about how *those dogs will listen to me more than they will you*, and finally Jez agreed that staying home to protect her was more important.

"It's the most important thing to me," Jinx had said and that made the vampire relent.

Now, Jinx was gone but Jez was there, sitting on the couch, drinking a beer. She grabbed a soda from the fridge, because Diet Coke in the morning was the best thing.

"Rough night?" he asked.

"A little," she admitted. "Are you a wolf too?"

"Hell no." Jez looked so offended that she nearly laughed, took a drink of soda as he said, "I'm vampire."

She choked on her soda. When she finally stopped coughing, she told him, "No admitting things like that when I'm drinking, all right?"

"Wolves are all so odd. Worse than humans," Jez observed, offered her the box of fresh-baked doughnuts he must've snagged on his way home from . . . vampire-ing.

"Do you have to hide during the day—from the light?"

"No," Jez sniffed. "Not my kind of vampire. I'm sufficiently indestructible, but I much prefer to sleep during the day. I guess old habits die hard."

"I'm a wolf, sitting next to a vampire. I'm a wolf who hangs around with vampires."

Jez watched her steadily. "You're not going to have some kind of breakdown, are you? I signed on to watch out for you while Jinx had business to attend to, but he didn't mention anything about crying."

"I'm not crying," she protested. "Mildly freaking out, maybe."

"Want to watch a movie? *Dracula? The Wolfman?*" he asked and she looked at him, astonished. "That was my attempt at humor."

She snickered in spite of herself. Wiped her eyes with the back of her hand. "It might've worked."

"It'll get easier, Gillian. You're surrounded by good wolves."

"What about other vampires?"

"Tired of me already?" he smirked. "How about some Chinese food? I know a place with great sesame noodles."

He was looking through a pile of papers on the table in front of him and triumphantly pulled out a menu like he'd found the prize in the cereal box.

"You're worried about Jinx being out there alone," she said quietly and before he could say anything, there was a knock on the door. Jez moved toward it silently, looked out the peephole and then opened it to reveal a handsome, tall man with a shaved head and glyphs running down the side of his head and neck.

Wolf, the rustling said.

"Jinx's twin," she heard herself murmur, but he'd heard her anyway. Nodded in her direction.

"I came to talk to Jinx."

"Good timing, since he's out hunting by himself," Jez told him, named a cemetery in the area.

"I'll go to him. He won't be alone tonight," Rogue said. "Are you okay, Gillian?"

"I will be once I know Jinx is all right," she said honestly and his expression softened. He even smiled a little and she had a feeling that didn't happen often.

Chapter 15

Jinx thought about reaching out to Vice the entire way to the cemetery, but he knew the wolf would insist on joining him, and Jinx couldn't forgive himself if anything happened to Vice. But he'd do anything not to come out here alone.

It had taken him several rides around the cemetery grounds to actually force himself to park outside the iron gates. Another long twenty minutes of waiting in his truck, listening to music as loud as possible to try to get himself in the right headspace. Ghost hunting was definitely a way to ruin his afterglow, and he'd wanted to stay next to Gillian tonight. Laying all the wolf stuff on her and then sleeping with her and running would make her vulnerable. Maybe even angry.

As he moved forward and took a few steps inside the gates, a truck rumbled up next to his that looked like it could ride through fire, and he turned to see Rogue climbing out of it.

Jinx, of course, immediately thought of hellfire and waved for the wolf to turn around and get the hell out, to not walk through the iron gates. But Rogue ignored him.

"Jez told me where you were," Rogue called.

"Of course he did."

"He didn't want you out here alone. I told him we had to do this alone. Get our rhythm back."

"I thought you weren't talking to me."

"Yeah, I thought that too," Rogue admitted. Jinx didn't push him, just grateful to have his twin back by his side. "You didn't sense me coming."

"No."

Rogue cursed under his breath, but his ire didn't seem to be directed at Jinx. "I felt you a little. But we're being blocked from each other."

By what's out here, Jinx thought, but Rogue would see it soon enough. Together, they walked through the cemetery.

"Yours here?" Rogue asked and Jinx nodded, ignoring them.

"They're subdued. Can you really not see anything?"

"No. Not yet," Rogue confessed. "I went out the other night. Got as far as finding some hunters before I turned around and went back."

"They're really still not . . . coming around you?" Jinx asked, perplexed. The Dire house was a ghost- and spirit-free zone, the mare being an exception. But once Rogue hit the outside air, the spirits usually rushed him.

"No."

"What does that mean, Rogue? Are there none? Or are they scared of you?"

"I'm not sure which option I like better." Rogue rolled his neck like it was stiff, brought a hand back to massage it.

Jinx glanced at his brother, the one he'd been closest to for centuries and he wondered if anything had really changed inside of him. It didn't appear that way, but . . . "If you want to go back. Want to keep not seeing things . . ."

"Of course that's what I want, but I won't go back. It's my lot," Rogue said. He'd tied a black bandana over his head, reminding Jinx of their Army days. For eight years, they'd worked side by side, kicking ass and saving humans. There were no trappers to worry about, nothing but pure, unadulterated battle, as they'd been trained for.

But the ghosts and the spirits on the battlefields, they'd been a bitch.

"Maybe we should've stayed in the military," he said now.

"I've thought about that. But we already knew Seb. What would be different?"

Seb. Jinx hadn't said his name since he'd disappeared, and now it seemed to echo across the field. "Where do you think he is?"

"I don't give a shit, but I hope he's in hell."

"I think he's been there for years," Jinx said, although the hatred for Seb burned brighter than Rogue's, which was difficult to do.

"Good." Rogue stuffed his hands in the pockets

of his leather jacket. They walked for another thirty feet, were too far into the cemetery for comfort when the ground started to shake.

"Salt circle?" Jinx asked and Rogue nodded. They hadn't used one since they were kids, but Jinx figured it would make his brother feel better. He used the rock salt in a wide arc around them. It trapped them, but if need be, they could sleep safely on the ground until morning light.

The ghosts began to depart, running, yelling. If Rogue heard anything, he didn't say, and Jinx listened for the sounds of the dogs he'd heard the other night. The hellhounds' howl came first, and then Jinx heard them running, the earth shaking beneath his feet. And then, Rogue put his hands over his ears and closed his eyes as a shudder went through him, and Jinx figured he'd heard that.

The hellhounds ran, circling around the salt, whining unhappily that they couldn't get closer to Jinx. Finally, they sat and waited expectantly and in that silence, Rogue took his hands away, opened his eyes.

"Aren't you . . . worried?" Rogue asked.

"They kind of, ah, listen to me."

Rogue's neck practically snapped as he turned to stare at Jinx. To his credit, all he said was, "Good to know."

And that's when it all started. Out of the woods behind the cemetery came thick black clouds like fast-moving smoke over the graves. They rushed toward the wolves, stopping behind the hellhounds.

"Keep them back," Jinx told the dogs, who turned and growled.

Rogue's voice sounded strangled when he said, "I think I liked it better when I didn't see anything."

"I hear you." Jinx stared at the shapeless clouds of smoke, blobs of grayish black, ready to form and take over whomever or whatever they wanted to.

"They're fears," Rogue confirmed what Jez had spoken of the other night.

"And they're waiting for us to give them orders."

"Order them to go away," Rogue said through clenched teeth.

"That's one thing they won't listen to." He'd lose control of them all together. "How bad can it be, having them protect all of us?"

"Bad, Jinx. Really, really bad."

But in the interim, it might be all they had. "Is this all of them?" Jinx asked and the hounds howled. "I guess that's a yes."

"These things thrive on using people's intentions of evil—they're not going to hold out much longer without doing something." Rogue rubbed the side of his head. "They're trying to talk to me, but I can't understand what they're saying."

"Hey, I'm their king."

"Seriously? This is not the time for formality. Maybe we need a banishing ritual."

The spirits groaned and tried to rush forward at Rogue.

"He's kidding." Jinx put his hands out, but the salt was what stopped them. "We've got a job for you. Soon."

That seemed to make them happy.

"What are you thinking?" Rogue asked.

But Jinx had no idea. He simply sat on the ground and lay back to look at the stars, pretending none of it existed. Rogue did the same and as the hellhounds panted and the fears circled them in a tight knot, the twins lay there, protected. Hunted. Haunted.

At first, they just remained silent. Finally, Jinx rolled to his side so he could concentrate on his brother and refused to acknowledge the other shit around him. "Can you see any other spirits?"

"No—just the hellhounds and the fears," Rogue said. "You can still see the ghosts?"

"Yep. If any were left here. These things seem to be the fastest party ender in the free world."

"What else are you carrying around, Jinx? Any other secrets I should know?" Rogue was being sincere.

"I killed our father. And although I had nothing to do with him dying the first time, I wasn't sorry to see him go," Jinx confessed.

"I know you tried to shield me from the worst of the abuse," Rogue told him.

"It never worked."

"Doesn't matter."

"Yeah, trying is the story of my life," Jinx muttered.

"Trying and failing are part of life, Jinx—you know that as well as I do. Dad always had it out for you because you were born last."

Because he'd been born at all, Jinx knew. Six minutes younger than Rogue. He'd been told it enough times by both parents for it to echo inside his mind at the worst possible times. He'd heard the words hissed at him when things went wrong in the house, in the village, when he was being beaten for not performing the warrior ways the way his father thought they should be performed.

But he could handle it. When he heard Rogue being beaten, however, that had made him physically ill.

It's not as if Rogue couldn't hold his own—he was stoic in the face of pain, maybe more so than Jinx himself. But the twin thing—Jinx seemed to feel Rogue's pain and fear more explicitly than his own. The old saying "When you get cut, I bleed" was true for them.

The entire time Rogue lay on the bed under the mare's spell, Jinx had been in hell, a part of him cut off from the world, deadened and yet he felt the sharpened pain of the mare's claws, the clutch of the markings from hell as they crawled up Rogue's face and head.

He'd told no one—hadn't even hinted it to Vice. He wouldn't have been surprised to wake up in the morning to find matching markings on his face. But since Rogue had them, they were both connected to hell forever.

Not that they hadn't been before. Anyone who could see ghosts and spirits had connections to heaven, hell . . . and now purgatory.

As Jez told him, this was always meant to be. "What did you see in hell?"

"I'm not talking about it."

"I can ask Gwen."

"Don't bring her back into that place." Rogue's markings were back to normal. "It was everything you can think of and more."

"So why were these creatures in purgatory, rather than hell? Are they not bad enough?"

"No, they're worse. They'd corrupt hell."

"Hell's got to take them. Where else could they go? Hell's going to have to buck up and grow a goddamned pair."

"Can't we vanquish them?"

"Vanquish fear? Good luck with that."

Jinx thought about purgatory opening, how he'd dropped to his knees when he'd seen the freaks—the monsters, as humans liked calling them—circling the air above him. If he'd concentrated more at the time, he might've noticed them watching him intently.

"Hey, at least we can't be possessed for long. Well, except for Vice, but he likes it," Rogue said absently.

"I'm glad you're awake, brother."

Rogue looked at him and smiled. "I wasn't so sure I was, but now I am."

Chapter 16

In the dead of night, after she'd had twenty-four hours to try to process what Jinx told her, Gillian found herself inside a truck with blackout window tints on the way to the Dire mansion. She sat in the back, Jez driving and Jinx in the passenger's seat.

She was nervous about going back there—maybe more so since she wasn't sure if Jinx was going to try to leave her there again for her own good.

After a night in his bed—the roof—his arms—she wasn't ready to give him up. Heard herself say, "Are you leaving me at the house?"

"Do you want me to?" he asked, the surprise evident in his tone, which was guarded.

"No."

"Good, because I'm not. But we can run in the woods there—we should be safe," he told her.

"Really?" She heard the eagerness in her own voice. "We'll be safe?"

"We'll have guards."

The thought of being able to run—really run—

without being thought of as crazy—made her smile. She leaned back and let the Grateful Dead music Jez played envelope her as they pulled up a long, winding driveway and into the garage she'd escaped through. The house was sprawling, the land surrounding it more so and she rubbed her hands together in anticipation of seeing all of Jinx's family again.

"I've got stuff to do, so I'll meet you back here in a couple of hours. Call if you need me sooner," Jez said. Jinx looked as though he wanted to say something but held his tongue, nodding instead.

"Keep out of trouble, vamp."

"You know me, wolf."

"That's why I said it, dipshit," Jinx muttered as he led her from the garage to the house.

Once inside, they bypassed the basement room where she'd been held originally in favor of the first floor, the kitchen, specifically. She was greeted by Gwen.

"I'm sorry. I hope I didn't get you in trouble when I left," she told the young doctor—wolf. Looked at her to see if she could tell anything and noted she had the same long-limbed figure that she did.

"I'm just glad you're okay." Gwen's smile was warm and genuine. Jinx had told her that Gwen was also a new wolf—and mated to the alpha king, Rifter. She remembered that dark-haired male as well, and when he introduced himself to her again, she wondered if she was supposed to bow and settled for a handshake instead.

In short order, she saw Rogue and was reintroduced to Vice with the silver eyes, tattoos and piercings and Stray and Killian, the brothers with the dark hair and the close relation with her.

"Tell me everything you know about me," she couldn't help but ask after they shook her hand solemnly. They couldn't deny her that and to her relief, they didn't.

"I guess we're getting right down to brass tacks," Stray said with a nod, motioned for her to sit down.

"You've got the markings of the Greenland pack. Your family's surname is Arrow," Killian started. "You're from my and Stray's extended pack."

"So you two are like family."

Stray flinched and she wondered if she'd offended him, said something wrong. Kill continued, "Yes, like family. All Dires are connected. And while Weres often mate with humans, a Dire can't. Couldn't, before recently. Dires are insular. I can't believe they would've given you up."

"I can believe it, because they were horrible to both of you. Jinx told me your history." He'd actually filled her in on it before they got in the truck, giving her only the sketchiest details, but she knew that Stray and Killian had been innocent. That their pack—her pack—had tortured them for little more than having abilities.

Stray was watching her carefully. "I guess we don't know for sure, but it's the only thing that made sense."

"Can you contact them?" she asked, and the mood at the table went somber again.

"We could. I don't know if we're going to," Rifter said. "We can try to get the information more covertly. But as of now, they don't know that we realize they exist. We'd like to keep it that way until it suits our purpose otherwise."

"Your pack doesn't get along with them . . . because of what they did to Stray and Killian?"

"That's a large part of it." Rifter didn't elaborate. "But just because we don't contact them doesn't mean you can't. Just not yet. We need a little time to figure things out."

"Take all the time you need. I don't want to go back to them."

"Gillian, the Blackwells have plastered the world with your photo. The Greenland pack has the isolation you need. You might not have a choice."

"I don't want isolation," she told Rifter. He growled at her, but she didn't have the sense yet as a new wolf to care. She was still heady from the taste of freedom.

And then she realized that everyone had stilled but the growling she'd attributed only to Rifter continued, but Rifter wasn't making the sound.

It was Jinx. His eyes had turned to the wolf, his chair pushed back and the growl was low and menacing . . . and directed at Rifter.

"Stand down, wolf."

When Jinx didn't, Gillian stood and moved nearly in front of him. "Leave him alone. He's worried about me."

And every eye turned to her. Vice's eyebrows raised but no one said a word. Gwen put her hand on Rifter's arm and Gillian wondered how badly she'd just stepped out of line. But she'd never been much for social etiquette and figured pack etiquette wasn't for her either.

"I think we should leave Jinx and Gillian alone," Vice suggested. "Or else there's going to be a brawl."

"I think you should stay out of it." An order masked in suggestion, but there was no mistaking Rifter's tone.

"Jinx, you gotta stop challenging him. You know what he's going through—mated alpha equals fucking nuts," Vice continued, even as he backed away from Rifter and Gwen pushed the wolf behind her.

But Jinx couldn't, not if his life depended on it. Rifter was challenging him by calling out his mate—and this was much worse than when he'd had to make Rifter kick him out of the house. "You don't make decisions for her," he told his king now.

"I make decisions for the pack. You all gave me that title, that respect—"

"I withdrew my respect, remember?"

"Ah, Jinx," Vice groaned as Jinx heard himself actually snarl as he pushed Gillian behind him, keeping a hand on her arm. Like he was prepared to fight to the death for her—which he was—and then drag her out of here, caveman style.

He guessed the old ways were still very much ingrained in him after all. And as Rifter moved closer, Gillian was struggling against Jinx's grasp. Like she was trying to help him.

She broke free because he was afraid of hurting

her if he held her wrist too tightly and she jumped in front of him, onto the table, stared down at Rifter. And she growled.

The entire room went silent.

"Wolves, we have bigger problems. Something other is surrounding the house." Vice's eyes glowed silver, his voice a growl at the outside threat. All of them were suddenly caught between wanting to shift and waiting to assess what was happening.

"Nothing can see this house but us," Stray said.

"Greenland pack?" Killian offered, standing close to his brother as he spoke.

"They've come here for me?" Gillian asked.

Jinx's Brother Wolf listened to the growls that seemed to shake the walls with his heart in his throat. Because he'd heard those sounds before and they were most definitely not wolves. "Don't go out there," he said. But he had no clue if they'd follow him inside if they thought it necessary.

Like Gillian, they were attempting to protect him.

"Do you know who's there, Jinx?" Rifter asked, his rage barely concealed, and yeah, Jinx couldn't blame him.

Jinx glanced at Rogue, who was standing in the corner, pale as anything. The markings on his skull looked brighter and Jinx said, "Ghosts," and headed toward the living room. Only Rogue knew it was a partial lie. There were always ghosts. What waited for him outside was far worse.

Everyone followed, including Gillian, who said, "Jinx, no," and grabbed him. He shook her off as gently as he could and jumped out the window, shifting as he went. He hoped these monsters could recognize the wolf form, because otherwise, he might just end up puppy chow.

Jez was there, trying to calm the dogs down. Since they'd been told not to eat him, they hadn't, but they weren't paying him much attention either. His fangs were out and he didn't look happy.

"I followed them here," Jez told him.

The incessant growling quelled when Brother walked around them. Jinx shifted so he could talk to them, telling them in a low voice that, "I'm fine. Leave this place and do no harm to it or any wolves within."

The hellhounds bowed their heads. Some whined. Obviously, they didn't like being told not to kill things, since that was part of their job description. He didn't see the black smoke, so he added, "Keep the smoke away from this house. From everyone—now."

Reluctantly, they went, but one of them turned to look at Jinx with a gaze he found chilling.

He's thinking of rebelling, Brother told him. And Jinx wished he knew of a way to kill a hellhound, even if it was just to make a point to the others. Instead, he returned the stare until the creature turned its massive head forward and began to gallop away, the others following.

"Gillian's coming," Jez told him. "She's getting good at escaping."

"Don't go far, Jez. I'm going to let her run a bit."

"Do you think that's wise?"

"Nothing I've done tonight can be considered

wise at all. I'm fucked. But she shouldn't suffer because I don't know which way to turn," he said honestly. Jez looked pained but he disappeared into the trees as Gillian came up on him. "How did you get away this time?"

"They were busy looking out the window you jumped from. I went into another room and went out the door." She looked pleased with herself and he couldn't help but smile. Obviously, she hadn't seen the hellhounds but she looked around now, rubbing her arms against the evil, like the last time.

"It smells funny out here," she said.

It was the sulfur. The hounds carried it with them. "Everything's clear now."

She looked like she wanted to say something else about that, but asked instead, "What was all that about back at the house with Rifter?"

"You already know enough to make your head spin." He looked around for the hounds, covered a few footprints as he walked along. Hopefully, once they saw him safe, they'd back off.

"I'm not spinning. I'm confused. Rifter looked like he was going to hurt you."

"He was." And Jinx would've hurt him right back and things would've escalated, gotten uglier than they already were. He knew Rogue would try to smooth things over, but ultimately he'd be forced to choose—admit what he knew or else leave the Dire house.

"Jinx, you know all my secrets," she persisted.

"Can't we just enjoy being out here?" Because as long as they were alone—guarded by the hellhounds, they might as well take advantage of it. "You've been begging to go outside and now we're here."

"And here I thought I was the expert in avoidance," she murmured, although she began to strip.

He stopped her. "As much as I want to see you naked . . ."

"It's safer if I'm clothed, right?"

"You're more camouflaged this way." He indicated the head-to-toe black she wore.

"I've spent days in the woods naked and avoiding people. You'll just have to trust me on this."

He had no choice, unless he wanted to try to forcibly keep her clothes on. And once he saw her bare breasts, he was decidedly on team naked. Camouflage was overrated. He had hellhounds.

He stood there for a long moment to admire her. She was stunning—he wanted to take her, claim her, but the mating rule of three times rang in his head. Three times and he'd be laying claim to her for life. He'd have to explain that and he was tired of explaining. Just wanted action and plenty of it.

"Go run," he told her.

"Are you going to try to catch me?" she called over her shoulder, laughing.

"I'll do better than that," he murmured, stripping and shifting, Brother Wolf passing her in a blur.

Chapter 17

The thrill of being in her element made her tingle. The cool air hit her skin, and she went up on the balls of her feet for a long second, then propelled forward with a small grunt as she ran along the small, twisted footpath before veering off it into the woods.

She'd never gotten lost before, never really thought about why but obviously being wolf gave her some kind of internal GPS system that kept her on track.

The air washed over her skin, her face stretched in a smile and she might've been laughing out loud with the joy of it all. Her feet stung a little from the rough branches and brambles she ran over, but it didn't matter. That would heal.

She heard Jinx behind her, felt his breath on her back . . . and that's when she realized it was Jinx's wolf following her and she knew it before she turned around. Did so slowly and saw the extra-large, gorgeous wolf waiting patiently, head cocked as if to say, "Problem?"

She swallowed, girding herself before stepping forward and reaching out to touch him, sinking her hands in the fur around his neck, pressing her cheek to the top of his head. A soft whimper greeted her. The wolf was so warm with wise eyes and huge paws. Strong, sleek.

"This is what I'll be," she whispered and the wolf nodded, because he understood. "Can I run with you?"

He opened his mouth, threw back his head and he howled, a sound that sent shivers down her spine, made her hot and wet with need. And then, with what she swore was a smile, he ran, leaving her to catch up.

She held pace with him, her thigh muscles burning, her body screaming as she wove through the trees, ducking so the low branches wouldn't touch her.

She didn't know how long they ran, but when Jinx stopped by a lake, he bent down to drink. She waded in past him, went in waist deep and then dove under, coming up to stare at the sliver of moon that hung in the sky.

There was no beating the real thing, she thought as she floated on her back.

She heard the splash, assumed the wolf was joining her. But Jinx's face popped up in front of her and she realized she'd missed the shift. She'd ask him to do it later, but for now, she wanted something more.

"You okay?" he asked.

"Very. Thank you," she told him, grabbed for him, surprised at her own strength. "I want to kiss you."

His mouth parted. "Go ahead. I won't bite. Much."

"I might," she told him before she did so, bit his lower lip in a light nip that made him growl with a pleasure that zinged through her entire body.

She was alive, more now than she had been when running. This was what she'd been waiting for. Under the water, her legs wrapped around his waist, urging him inside of her.

Instead he pulled her back, turned her so she faced away from him and used his fingers between her legs, stroking her to completion. The combination of the heat between her thighs and the cold of the water made for an intense orgasm that came on more suddenly than she'd expected, caused her cry to echo through the woods.

She leaned back against him, her body as liquid as the lake around her. He floated with her in this serene setting, so at odds with what had happened back at the house.

"If we could stay like this . . . forget everything else," she murmured.

Jinx wished the same damned thing, because here, in this water, with her hands on his shoulders, her body close, there was peace.

But they had so much to conquer still. He figured Rifter and the others were holding meetings back at the house trying to figure out the Gillian and Jinx situations. And soon enough, he'd have to answer to everyone.

For right now, he could just keep Gillian close and pretend nothing else mattered.

Rogue saw Jinx's blood on the broken glass that was once a picture window. The growling they'd heard outside had retreated momentarily, but he knew what made the sounds weren't gone. Not by a long shot.

They all watched out the window until Gwen mentioned Gillian and then they all moved away to find her.

She'd gone out the door, though. Rogue had listened for her, knowing she and Jinx were impossibly close. Just the way she'd stood up to Rifter told him that.

He wanted to tell them they shouldn't go out there, but the questions that would invite were more than he was willing to say.

Trouble, trouble, all around . . .

"We need to talk."

"Not now, Vice." Rogue refused to look at the wolf, but knew Vice wasn't letting this go. At least Vice was able to restrain himself from not doing this when Jinx was there or in front of anyone else, but no way was this discussion going to remain between the two of them.

Rifter was lurking—he believed Rogue knew what was going on with Jinx. And Rogue was torn between his brotherly loyalties and loyalty to his king.

Maybe outing what was happening with Jinx was the only way to get him help.

And maybe it would make him angrier, and the situation more impossible.

Because if Jinx got angry, the monsters who suddenly saw him as the once and future king would go after the Dires and anyone else who got in Jinx's way. It was a delicate balancing act and Jinx had taken only a few steps on the tightrope, not nearly enough to know if it would hold his weight for any considerable length of time.

"Now." Vice's big hand on Rogue's shoulder turned him around and Rogue bared his teeth as a growl escaped his throat, louder than intended. The tattoos on his skull and face throbbed as though activated by his anger and that scared him in its unexpectedness. The nightmares he could deal with. Unintentional fallout from being marked by hell was in the *oh shit* box.

"What do you want from me, Vice?"

"What the fuck is wrong with your brother? What the fuck is wrong with you?" Vice demanded, not giving a shit if hell itself was on his heels. Rogue should've expected this—Vice had no filter, no worries about consequences when he was in the moment. It was the wolf's nature and Rogue should've considered getting the hell out of Dodge the second he looked out the window and saw a hellhound looking back at him.

It cocked its head and looked confused. Sniffed the air and Rogue suddenly understood. They were protecting Jinx since he freed them from purgatory. And by extension, Rogue, since he was part of Jinx.

"Be nice to me or they'll eat you," he told Vice.

"You're serious?" Vice asked, his hands in his pockets, his tone non-threatening.

"They're Jinx's protection," he said.

"Jinx needs protection from us?" Vice looked astonished.

"No. It's a long story, Vice. And none of you should follow Jinx out there."

"Obviously, I'm going to need the story," Vice said and then pointed to Rifter, who was listening by the door. Rogue had been so focused on the hellhounds that he hadn't heard the other wolf come up behind him.

"I can't, Rifter."

"It's not disloyalty to Jinx—it's necessity, to help him," Rifter told him.

"Don't do this to me. Don't make me choose."

"There is no choice in this. There is only goddamned obey." Rifter's voice rose to shake-the-house levels. Vice trembled as his wolf struggled to stay contained. Rogue's glyphs pulsed with pain and he heard Gwen and Kate talking, didn't want either of them to feel Rifter's wrath because of him.

But Rifter was circling him and Rogue felt cornered. Something in him was ready to snap, to go over the edge uncontrollably and what if he couldn't pull himself back?

Jinx had always been able to do that for him. Would if called on again. But bringing his twin here in the first place was a mistake, even if it wasn't his.

The growling was louder and more inhuman than any wolf he'd ever heard. It sent shivers down the base of his spine, called to him in a way it shouldn't have.

His wolf wanted to join them and that was wrong on so many levels.

"What the fuck, Rogue?" Vice asked. He was circling the room staring out the window and seeing nothing, but sensing the evil surrounding them.

Vice stopped asking nicely and shook Rogue by the shoulders, which enraged the hellhounds. It was as if they were ready to jump through the windows, and Vice, who wasn't scared of anything or anybody, didn't stop pressing Rogue.

Just as suddenly, they were gone. Rogue heard them running, the beats of their paws inside his head, their massive jaws gnashing. He could only imagine what would have drawn them away from their threats outside the Dire house.

Only one thing. "Jinx is in trouble," he told them, before he shifted and went out the already broken window, following Jinx's trail of glass and blood.

Chapter 18

Letting the air dry them, Jinx and Gillian walked together through the dark woods, arms around each other. The bruising pattern on her back was looking more glyph-like and she said it was tender to the touch, so he made sure his arm didn't press on it.

Halfway back to the house, his scenting diverted him. He smelled wereblood, tasted the violence like a bitter wine and he motioned to Gillian to follow him.

Quietly, they wove through a makeshift path that wasn't here a week earlier. Trappers came here and did things like this all the time—typically, the twins found them and took care of it, re-camouflaging everything and restoring it to its original state. But they'd been caught up with Liam's war lately.

At the end of the path, he stopped, scanned the area and saw the bodies, hurriedly buried beneath some old leaves. He raced over to them, Gillian on his heels.

Dead Weres. Two of them, younger than Cyd and Cain were when they came to Jinx. They'd been through their first shift, but they hadn't been shifted during the attack. They hadn't even been given the chance, probably drugged to make the shift impossible, and wrapped in silver chains to stop it from happening, judging by the burns around their necks and wrists.

He bent to look more closely at the other injuries, saw electrical burns and deep cuts made from a hunting knife. And the way they were tied made it easy for Jinx to assume they'd been raped. Tortured. Held for who knew how long. For what? For being what they were born to be. He knelt next to the bodies, touched their foreheads. They were no doubt coming to find Liam, as they had directions to the meeting place and a note from their packmaster who'd sent them along as a show of faith for the new king.

Brother's impeccable hearing told him that whoever dumped these bodies was close enough to have heard Jinx and Gillian. They were lying in wait, and Jinx's hackles—and the violence held tight within him—rose.

The near miss with Rifter, the feelings Gillian brought out in him, the troubles with Rogue and purgatory, all of it conspired to make Jinx goddamned angrier than he'd been in centuries. The feeling grew quickly until it rattled everything inside of him.

More than anything, Gillian brought out his most primal side, the warrior who would fight for what was his. And he was more sure that Gillian was meant to be his than anything he'd ever known.

"Jinx, what happened to them?" Gillian was looking for a pulse on their necks until he stopped her with a shake of his head. "Were they . . . ?"

"Wolves. Weres, not Dires. They were tortured."

"Why?"

"Because they're wolves." He wanted to sugar-coat it for her, but he couldn't. Wouldn't be fair to her anyway. She had to know what kind of world she was coming out in. There was no changing it—she had to know things to keep her safe.

"What kind of people do this?"

"Weretrappers. They're angry at all of wolfkind because we killed their leaders and threatened their entire organization." The Dires had expected blowback, but seeing innocent Weres bear the brunt of it turned Jinx's stomach.

She looked around like she felt the trappers were still near them. "They're still close, aren't they?"

"They heard us, yes." Their voices were low, their heads close. "We're going to need to try to get back to the mansion."

"We should stop them. Fight them."

"You're not ready for that. I'll go after them after you're safe," he promised.

Shots rang over their heads. He shoved Gillian in front of him and he ran, because he would shield her with his body. And as much as he wanted to stop, rake his claws over the men who'd hurt the young Weres, they couldn't stop—he couldn't afford to have Gillian taken. But they were closing in on all sides and he pushed Gillian to climb the big oak, handed her a gun and told her to shoot anyone who came close who wasn't a wolf.

She did so as he shifted. Turned, prepared to run into the trappers, confuse them by turning the chase onto them. He could handle bullets—the wounds would heal. At this point, Gillian's might not.

He waited until he saw them in the clearing, maybe fifteen feet away, and he began to run. As he did, the earth beneath his feet shook. The air chilled and as the trappers descended, so did the dogs of hell. Shots rang out, and something caught him in the neck. It took Brother Wolf mere seconds to realize it was drugs, not bullets, and he cursed and tried to force himself to shift as the hellhounds passed him.

He tried to tell them to stand down but the tranquilizer was strong, had him wobbling, unable to shift. Hellhound didn't understand wolf. All they understood was that they were supposed to keep Jinx safe. And that's exactly what they did.

Through his position prone on the ground, he could see the way the hellhounds poised to rip the unsuspecting trappers to pieces. Three men who never stood a chance.

He was finally able to convince Brother that he should shift. It hurt like hell but he did it, managed, "No," and the hellhounds whimpered but stopped. "Make . . . them . . . run."

They did. The trappers had no idea that hounds of hell were at their heels but they knew something was after them and they ran for their lives.

Jinx lay on his back, staring up at the dark sky as his brother came up on him. "Gilly . . ."

"I'm here." She moved closer, still holding the gun. "They're gone."

"I know." He rolled over onto his side as Gillian told Rogue, "Help him, please."

"Can't take him back into the mansion," he heard Rogue say and then someone—Jez—picked him up. He was vaguely aware of a rocking car ride, muttered something about deadheads being terrible drivers.

"Asshole wolf," Jez told him, carried him up the stairs instead of taking the elevator without Jinx having to ask. So yeah, he owed the vamp.

"Gilly?"

"She's with Rogue in the elevator—checking the apartment."

"I think I can walk," he mumbled but Jez didn't listen, carrying him the entire way to his bedroom, where he laid Jinx on the bed and began to get supplies together.

"Gwen told me to run saline to get the drugs from your system," he explained.

"You know how to do this?"

"I know how to find a vein," Jez deadpanned and Jinx groaned and closed his eyes.

Cain, Cyd and Liam had been preparing for a night of patrols and meetings when they heard the ruckus. They'd run through the underground hallway that connected to the main mansion and burst into the living room in time to see the Dires headed out the window. Kate was following them and Cyd helped her out the window, picked her up and carried her to where everyone had gathered.

Cain passed him by when he smelled wereblood. Liam was right behind him. And now, minutes later, he was trying to process what he'd just seen.

Bigger than Dires. Blacker than night, foul smelling with glowing yellow eyes that looked more than other. Unworldly. And they were chasing the trappers through the woods.

It was obvious they could've caught them, ripped them to pieces. The question was, why didn't they?

"What was that?" Gwen asked. She was shaken—they all were—but none of them could put a handle on exactly what they'd seen.

Vice was tracking whatever it was and nearly tripped over the bodies. "That's why Jinx was running. He was trying to save Gillian."

Cain came up behind him and knelt by the bodies. They were too far gone for anything, but he still passed a palm over both young wolves eyes to close them so they were no longer staring vacantly in death. "Things are getting more violent."

They were. Nothing was as downright evil as when the weretrappers had both the Shimmin brothers in charge but since their deaths, the trappers had gone Wild West on all wolves. *If we're going down, we're taking as many wolves as we can with us* seemed to be their motto.

Liam would be upset by this.

Stray and Killian were out there, both of them looking unhappy, and Killian more than a little disoriented as he sniffed the air. Cain's wolf was pissed and confused, maybe more so by the fact that he hadn't been allowed to help Jinx recently, and since that's what he'd cut his teeth doing, he was lost out here. But only for a moment, because he'd gotten through his moon craze and was going to be the omega for Liam. He had other responsibilities, and he'd help Jinx whether the Dire wanted him to or not.

He approached Kate, who was staring off into space, hand on her chin. "You all right?"

"Not really. Rogue left with Jinx."

"Do you think that's a good thing?"

"It's the best thing for now. Do you know what was in the woods?"

"I know of only one thing that makes tracks like this, but I've only seen pictures of it in books. Depictions, actually." He stared down at the massive footprints again and back up at Kate. "These were made by hellhounds."

Kate's mouth opened and then closed. Finally, she said, "Do the others know?"

"I want to make sure before I open this up to them."

"Rifter overheard Rogue saying they came to protect Jinx."

"Why does he need protection from the Dires?" Cain asked, completely confused. He could feel the empathy coming off Kate in waves. She knew more than she was saying, probably because of her connection to Rogue when he'd been in the coma. There was a bond between them and he was grateful that at least someone knew what the hell was going on.

Finally, he said, "Jinx isn't bad."

"No, he's not," she said quickly. Sincerely. "But he's in some real trouble."

Cain would lay down his life for Cyd and for Jinx. For any of the Dires and their mates. Kate put a hand on his shoulder, told him, "Rogue will help him, Cain. He won't let anything happen to them. Let's concentrate on what we can help with now."

"I can track the trappers," he said as Vice joined them. He knew the Dire wouldn't say no. Those men needed to be brought to justice. And wolf justice meant an eye for an eye. "When you're done, bring the dead to Liam." He pointed to the young Weres. "He's their packmaster, even though they'd never met him. But they served him. And they fought."

Cain nodded. Called to Cyd with a long howl and waited until his twin bounded through the woods, already shifted.

"We're tracking," Cain told him and Cyd took off, Cain at his heels without waiting for further instructions.

Cain noted the hellhound prints as his paws passed through them—it looked like there had been at least six of them, maybe more. He smelled the sulfur in the air and something else that reeked of rotten eggs and dead things. It was easy for them to follow that scent, as it overpowered that of the trappers, but the underlay was there.

He ran side by side with his twin for miles. The trappers wouldn't have been able to keep the running up for miles and miles, and they'd find it impossible to evade the hellhounds. They were trapped in this ring of woods and Cain's wolf bared his teeth as he thought of the young Weres who'd been sacrificed.

Even through all their injuries, Cain could smell the fight—and the fear—they'd carried. They hadn't gone down easy.

Finally, the trail was getting colder for the hellhounds, stronger for the trappers. It was as if they'd gotten bored of simply cornering the men or they'd gotten distracted and Cain was glad. Hadn't wanted to come face-to-face with those creatures.

As the scent of human trapper became overpowering, the wolves passed quietly. Cyd paused, Cain at his side, and for a long moment, they waited in silence. The hellhound scent was gone suddenly and a rustle in the trees told them the trappers were near. They didn't know how many tranquilizers they had, so it would have to be an ambush. There wasn't time to call for help. Neither wolf had any desire to, either.

Instead, Cyd circled to the back of the large tree where the trappers were hiding and in a graceful leap, jumped up to the branch, scaring the three men who'd been perched precariously. Cain lunged for all three as they fell as if they were bowling pins, taking them down by slamming their legs out from under them. Cyd leaped onto them and without thinking, they acted like the wolves they were, avenging the Weres' deaths. Acting in Liam's stead. Doing what warriors would. There was no pleasure in the task—it was purely necessary justice and the trappers' throats were torn out in rapid succession, with no excess torture. Far more care than the trappers had given the Weres, but that was the Weres' tradition and the twins honored it.

And when the trappers lay dead, excoriated so there was no doubt they'd been killed by wolves, it was only then Cain and Cyd stepped back. They howled together, the sound echoing in the quiet night, bouncing through the woods and possibly the town beyond, and tonight, neither wolf cared.

No mercy can be shown, Cain thought and his twin answered him with a growl of approval. The time for mercy was over. The time for revenge was here.

Liam made calls all night, with Vice at his side.

"Keep going."

The list was long and so far, the response had been good. News of Liam's kills of Tals and Walker had continued to spread and the respect in other alphas' voices had been evident.

Good thing they couldn't tell how freaked he was.

Now, he traced the smooth surface of his android phone with his thumb, staring at his reflection in the back screen. He had others to contact, to make inroads with and still, he couldn't get the idea of calling a meeting with the head of the hunters out of his mind. He dialed the phone and left a brief, firm message that he wanted a meeting with the head hunter ASAP. Now he'd wait to see how much respect he actually commanded.

He'd been doing his best to still push Max and the baby from his mind as he worked the command center of his pack from inside the Dire house. But what he would do—whether or not he'd follow the tradition demanded of him—was on the mind of all the packs who'd stood behind him thus far.

He couldn't forgive or forget. The love he'd felt for her had morphed into a kind of hatred that still signified his feelings.

That's what you get for hanging with a human.

The baby was late. And even though he dreaded asking about it, he forced himself to pay Gwen a visit in the downstairs clinic she was setting up.

"I figured you'd come to see me soon," she said as she unwrapped a bottle of medicine and wrote on the label.

"Sorry—I didn't mean to avoid you."

"You did. That's okay." She paused and then told him, "She's not showing any signs of labor yet. And I won't induce because I don't know what that does to a wolf pup."

He nodded. "Why's she late?"

"It's either stress having the opposite effect on her body or she was just off as to when she was impregnated," Gwen told him. She moved forward and took his hand in hers.

"I'm sorry, Liam. I know how hard this must be. But the baby's coming soon. You need to make a decision so we can make arrangements. A few packs have come forward with offers of foster care. They don't want a half Were in human hands. That would cause too many problems."

Liam agreed. What he didn't know yet was whether or not he was keeping Max's child. Vice's words echoed in his mind.

We don't blame the child for the parents' mistakes.

Vice was too damned wise for his own good. But it still didn't help him with his decision regarding Max. And it didn't make him feel any more confident about keeping this pup.

Chapter 19

Gillian paced nervously as Jinx slept. Since she'd known him, albeit, not for that long, he rarely, if ever slept and woke on a dime. Seeing him out like this . . .

"He'll be okay, Gillian. They shot him up with some powerful drugs." Rogue was next to her, hadn't left his brother's side since they'd gotten back here either.

"And if they hadn't been stopped?"

Rogue's brow furrowed. "They would've taken him in. Experimented on him. Tried to, anyway. We wouldn't have let him stay for long."

"That's what these people—these weretrappers—do?"

"Yes."

She stroked a hand across Jinx's brow and he stirred for a second, whispered her name. She put her palm into his and squeezed. "You were captured by these trappers."

"He told you?"

"No, you did." There was something in his eyes when he spoke of them. "I'm sorry."

He didn't respond, and she continued, "What were those things? They smelled like . . . they were around Jinx when I escaped from the mansion and found him by the cemetery."

"They're hellhounds." He paused. "You couldn't see them?"

She shook her head no, then swallowed. Hard. "Am I supposed to?"

"No. That takes a different kind of ability."

"You see ghosts too?"

"Spirits."

She didn't ask about the distinction. "I'm guessing the hellhounds can take down wolves."

"I'm thinking yes."

"But they didn't. Why?"

"I think Jinx should be the one to tell you that. Let's just concentrate on him for now, okay?"

"Is this how you all live, all the time?" she asked. "Or is it worse now because of me?"

"You don't want me to answer that. No matter how I do . . ." He trailed off and she supposed he was right. Then again, they all lived with something. Rogue was as worried as she was—he couldn't hide the anger and fear and she decided she loved him for that alone. The fact that he was related to the wolf she'd fallen in love with made it that much easier.

"I might want you to answer that for me when all of this is through," she told him truthfully. "For now . . . Jinx."

He gave her a small smile and nodded. "For now, Jinx."

He smelled the hellhounds, heard their paws stamping and swore the ground was moving underneath him. He struggled to get up, to move away from them but they drew closer. Followed him. Worshipped him. Wanted him to run with them and all he wanted was to escape.

They're never going to let you go.

Jinx's eyes opened with a start and he nearly sprang from the bed. Caught himself before he toppled over, because he was all twisted in the blankets and there were no hellhounds here, just wolves and a vamp and he was safe. For now.

He blinked a few times and saw Rogue's form standing facing the window in the dark. Heard Gillian's restless footsteps outside the partially opened door. Scented Jez, who was hopefully ordering Chinese food, because he heard his own stomach growl.

A good sign.

"Hello, Sleeping Beauty," Rogue said without turning around.

"You okay?" he asked, his voice still groggy.

"I don't know if I'm okay. Might not ever be again," Rogue said honestly.

"You shouldn't have come with me the other night."

"It's what I'm supposed to do, Jinx. Cut the guilt shit."

"Then you shouldn't have come back here with me tonight."

"Didn't exactly have a choice. It's not like Rift doesn't know where I am."

"What did you tell them?"

"Enough, to Vice. Rifter overheard some of it, about how the hellhounds protect you." He leaned back, the bottle of Johnny Walker Green balanced on his thigh, half full. He took two more long drinks, nearly draining the bottle before he said, "What the hell are we going to do about this, brother?"

Jinx stared out the window. "What am I going to tell Gillian?"

"The truth."

"I don't even know what that is anymore." He groaned in frustration. "How the hell are we going to get rid of them?"

"I think I know a way," Rogue said.

"Well, come on—I'm listening."

Rogue crossed his arms and said, "We can't open purgatory again—can't risk it. But we can banish the monsters to hell."

"They won't just go," Jinx pointed out.

"No, but they might follow. If you get the prayer done at the right time, I can lead them into hell."

Jinx stared at Rogue, waiting for the joke. None came. He opened his mouth, then closed it, because what the hell was he supposed to say? Besides "No way in hell."

"Nice pun."

"You know what I mean. Even if that would work, you're not doing it."

"Maybe you're just jealous that I could be, like, a king there."

"I would kill you if I could," Jinx muttered.

"We can't keep trusting hellhounds," Rogue said. "I know it will pain you to give up your king status."

"Screw you."

"That's better. I hate being treated like glass."

"I'll beat the shit out of you if it makes you stop talking about going into hell."

"I'm there, Jinx. Location isn't much more than a state of mind."

"I'll sacrifice myself before I let that happen."

"That would be stupid. You have a mate."

"I'm not having this discussion now."

"Something's got to happen soon. Very soon," Rogue warned him, and Jinx planned on ignoring his twin and his stupid, stupid suggestion for as long as possible.

After what seemed like forever, Rogue called to her and Gillian left Jez eating moo shu pork.

"Is he all right?"

"He's up. He wants to see you." Rogue slid past her and she hesitated for a brief moment. "Don't be scared of him. He'd die if you felt like that."

"I could never be scared of him. Of any of you," she whispered.

"Except me, right, darlin'? Because I'm the big bad scary vampire," Jez called through the pancake he was eating delicately with chopsticks.

"Yes, Jez. I'm terrified," she said, went into the

bedroom as Rogue chuckled. She closed the door behind her and went toward Jinx, not sure if he was going to be angry or not for the way she'd gotten in between him and Rifter.

He wasn't. He leaned back against his pillows as though drained, patted the bed next to him for her to join him. She did and he started with, "I'm sorry. Rifter and I are going through a difficult time. I didn't mean to put you in the middle."

"You didn't. I did."

"Yeah, I guess that's true."

She sat on edge of the bed, legs dangling. He reached out to run a hand along her thigh. "What did you think of Stray and Killian?"

"I like them. It makes me feel better that not everyone from my pack is an asshole."

"You could still meet them, if you wanted to. Sometimes people need to see where they came from with their own eyes."

"I don't want that. And obviously, I have nothing to offer them."

"You're a Dire," he told her, like that meant everything, and maybe it should, but she couldn't accept it yet.

"They didn't want me."

"That hasn't been proven, but no matter what, we do. I do."

She wanted to trust that. "Why would my own pack disown me?" It felt so right to say that word and for the first time in forever, no one corrected her. "Why abandon me? They must've felt something was off."

"Dires don't let their own go."

"They let Stray and Kill."

He sighed. "Different circumstances. You were left as an infant. They wouldn't have known if you had an ability yet. There are no prophecies about you."

"How about an unwanted pregnancy?"

"Not the same thing in the wolf world. Mistakes happen, children aren't punished for that," he told her. "But the thing is, a Dire's not able to give birth till she's shifted. So none of it makes sense unless you were taken."

"Like stolen or kidnapped?"

"Maybe. And it's not like those Dires could go to the police. Tracking you would've proved too risky."

She wasn't buying it. Something fierce and primal inside of her told her she'd track her missing child to hell and back. "I hear . . . rustling in my ears."

"Normal. That's your wolf, letting you know your time's close."

She'd missed everything because her body had spent its lifetime trying to prepare her and doctors spent the same amount of time telling her she was schizo. Her parents had tried, but they'd grown weary of her supposed psychosis and delusions, the outbursts of violence that came out of nowhere that she could never explain.

"I have a terrible temper."

Jinx's grin was . . . well, wolfish. "Join the club. It's supposed to be. You're going to be all right. I'll make sure of it."

She wanted to believe him, and so this time, she did. "What's really going on with you and Rifter?" she asked. "Or is that a sore subject?"

"It's a shitty subject." He couldn't tell her that he'd disobeyed Rifter purposely to get thrown out of the house. Or maybe he could—should. Why get closer to her when ultimately, she wasn't going to want anything to do with him? Not that he could blame her.

"Hey, lots of thinking going on in there. I don't like seeing you sad."

"I have stuff to tell you."

"About Rifter?"

"That. The hellhounds. I'm sure you've got questions. And you've been patient. Dealing with the wolf shit you've learned about and you've been sticking up for me. And you shouldn't."

"Because it gets you in trouble?"

"Because I don't deserve it." He scrubbed his face with his hands. "I don't even know where to begin."

She moved to sit next to him. "Start with the ghosts. Your ability. Rogue said that you see ghosts and he sees spirits. I think I know the difference, but it seems like a burden, which is why I guess you don't call it a gift."

"Doesn't sound like it should be so terrible, I know. It's just . . . ghosts, spirits, they don't shut up. Ever. And they aren't just going to talk about mundane shit most of the time. They like to tell you about how they died, over and over. They share every brutal detail, like they're compelled to do so. And when you hear those gruesome stories day in and day out—and it doesn't matter if you ignore them because they'll still talk and a part of you will still hear, whether you want to or not—and you can't be a wolf twenty-four/seven. You can do the salt thing outside the room but they're still outside. Spells are dangerous because they can be used against you or backfire and I've seen enough proof of that to last a lifetime, which in my case, is centuries."

"So they're there, even when you're ... when we're ..." She motioned between the two of them.

"Most have the decency to stay away when I'm fucking. Either that or they know that an interruption will ensure I'll be too pissed to help them afterward or that I can pretty much ignore anything when I'm coming. But afterward ..."

"They bother you right away?"

"I guess they feel like I'm relaxed enough and hopefully in a damned good mood." Jinx shook his head. "But it's death, all day, every day, morning till night for as long as I've lived."

"Centuries," she murmured and he nodded.

"Sometimes I feel like I'm crazy. Sometimes I wonder if, in the end, it will drive me crazy." He gazed at her. "I told you I understood how you felt all those years. That wasn't some kind of empathetic lie."

It was probably also the most honest he'd been with a woman—or anyone—including himself. Because he never talked about it, tried even harder not to think about it. Just wanted to get through the day and find relief as Brother Wolf at night.

"Gwen said you gave Rifter dreamcatchers. Does that help you at all?" she asked.

"Ghosts are nothing like dreams."

"I'm sorry. That was stupid. I'm just trying to help but you've obviously dealt with it for a lot longer than I have."

"I like it that you try to help me. I'm just not very good at accepting it, and that's a Dire trait."

She laughed a little. "I guess I can see that in myself."

"Admitting it's the first step."

She hated to break up the few moments of levity, but she pushed him, her voice gentle. "Why are the hellhounds protecting you?"

"Because I freed them from purgatory, along with the monsters that people at the psych hospital saw. I'm responsible for that, and until I figure out how to handle it, everyone I care about is in terrible danger. Look, I can live with the ghosts. Got no choice. But this other shit that escaped— the freaks, monsters, whatever you want to call them—they're fears personified. And while fear's a part of everyday life in healthy doses, these are stripped free of any limits. They're pure, unadulterated fear that can wreak havoc on the world. Turn man against man. And Rogue is talking about leading them into hell."

"What does that mean, exactly?"

"Means he'll be locked in there with them. You don't drop things off in hell and skip back out."

He hung his head. "Right now, it's the only solution I see. I have to choose between my brother or the human race."

She didn't know what to say. Realized there was nothing she could say and, instead, pulled his head down to her shoulder, cradled him against her, wanting desperately to make it better.

He allowed it, the touch, the slight rocking, the murmur that they'd figure it out together because there was nothing else to do.

"I can't imagine living the way you've lived without help. Protection. You're so strong, Jinx. But now I'm here and I'm stronger. You have to let me help."

"How? You can't bodyguard me against ghosts."

"What if I could? What if I can protect you and Rogue when you hunt? What if word got out that nothing could or should bother you two when I'm around?"

"That's too good to be true."

"But what if it's not?"

"Even if you could, I'd never let you. Do you realize how exhausting that would be?"

"Yes, I do." She touched a hand to his cheek.

He blinked and looked at her. "Thank you, Gillian. But I don't deserve—"

"You deserve everything good. I'm a lucky wolf to have found you."

Jinx wanted to believe her, and a part of him did. But that didn't change anything. "I can't be what you want me to be. What you need me to be. I don't regret anything we've done, Gillian, and my family is still yours. We'll help you. But I can't—we can't—be together. Not in the way we've been."

She stared at him, her expression sad. "What's wrong, Jinx? I know you've been trying to shield me from things while you're helping me with my problems. But can't you let me help you for a change?"

He hadn't wanted to tell her like this—or at all. But things were slipping further out of his control. The magic he'd once held over these monsters seemed to be fading and the slippery slope was turning his soul into something he may not recognize soon—not for much longer if he kept trying to keep these things from killing. "No, I can't. And trust me, you shouldn't want to."

"But I do."

"Gillian, please. I want you to walk away without hating me."

"I could never."

"I almost believe that." He hung his head, stared at the carpet. He curled his toes, wishing it was fresh grass instead.

It was too tempting to shift, to let Brother Wolf take the wheel on a more permanent basis. Brother couldn't help the ghosts so they didn't bother him. In wolf form, Jinx could run away from his responsibility, let the monsters run wild over the humans.

But they would hurt wolves too, and other shifters and vampires alike. They would pervert the world and that would always be his god-damned legacy. Because he was easily tricked, like his father said.

And so he told her about his family. About how he and Rogue trained as hard as any alpha Dire in the warrior ways. They had little choice in the matter, as it was done for survival. And their father, a proud beta, should've been even prouder of his alpha sons.

"My father used to say that my mother was cursed before we were born and that's why we came out being able to see the things we see." Jinx paused. "He was right."

"What do you mean?"

Jinx pressed his lips together, like he was trying to hold back the secret he'd held for a lifetime. From his twin, from everyone. But it was always in the back of his mind, and while the idea of never having a mate always concerned the others, for Jinx it appeared to be a blessing in disguise. It began to surface uneasily for him when Gwen appeared, but how often did lightning strike twice? "My mother was told by an old gypsy woman at the market that she was having twins. She tried to shrug it off, but the woman told her that the second one out would cause all the ruin. That we were both cursed with abilities that could ruin us. That we'd both know evil—that we'd court it. That it was in our blood."

The twin curse had been passed down for generations. Some said it came from a human superstition, others said it was a bad Dire omen. When

twins were born, there was no birth celebration—
no, the village was as somber as they were during
a funeral dirge. And no matter why that superstition existed, Jinx and Rogue had always been regarded with suspicion. Which meant they always
had to work harder, be stronger, better, faster than
the other Dires they grew up with.

Being saddled with a twin was bad enough, but
then for both of them to have abilities? He was surprised his father hadn't actually followed through
with his threat to kill them once he'd found that
out.

The only ones who knew about their abilities
were their parents. The twins preferred it that
way. Jinx couldn't have imagined the hell it
would've brought down on their heads had anyone in the village found out they could see ghosts
and spirits. That in itself would be proof enough
that the curse of the twins was true.

Their father thought so.

At first, he'd tried beating it out of the young
wolves. Daily. And all of that healed up, because
it was made preshift. Once they shifted, any scars
made by another Dire would've remained. But to
this day, Jinx's back ached where he'd been hit
over and over with a belt, the buckle slamming his
vertebrae. They were made to sleep outside to
toughen them up. Those nights were the worst,
because it was open market for the spirit world.

"She never stuck up for us," he remembered
Rogue saying when they'd sifted through the rub-
ble of their village, post Extinction, and found

their mother's body. He hadn't sounded upset, but there was sadness in his tone. They'd been lucky to have each other. Jinx couldn't have imagined going through it alone.

Whether or not the other Dires knew about their torture, Jinx didn't know. He'd certainly never spoken of it, preferring to shove it to the back of his mind and be grateful he didn't have to go back to it. The Dire massacre had actually been something of a relief to him, something he never voiced aloud. He had no idea if Rogue felt the same way.

"She couldn't. Father would've killed her," Jinx told Gillian. "He almost did a few times."

"Then he was an abusive asshole, not a warrior," she said.

That was the truth.

Gillian was watching him carefully before she continued, "So you were an outcast, just like me."

"Ah, Gilly—"

"There's no Dire world left like the one you describe. No one to stop me from being with you because of things beyond your control."

"If you stay, you'll get hurt. I can't protect you."

"But you already have. Several times plus, by my count. You've been hiding too much from me," she told him. "I can't blame you for that, but my life's an open book."

"Because you're on the news," he pointed out.

"Because you broke me out of a mental institution to tell me I'm a wolf."

"Well, if you're going to get technical about it," he muttered.

"Jinx, please. I'd like to help."

"You can't. Trust me—if you could, I'd be eternally fucking grateful, but you can't. You shouldn't even be here."

"If it's that dangerous, maybe you shouldn't either."

"I have control of it."

"Of what? The ghosts?"

He turned to her then and she actually took a step back when she looked into his eyes. "The monsters. For now, I have total control of them. But there's going to come a time when the roles are reversed, and I don't want you anywhere close to me when that happens."

Chapter 20

After Cain and Cyd came back bloody and took the bodies of the Weres to Liam, Vice and the rest of the Dires went back inside the mansion. Killian boarded up the window so nothing could accidentally find its way inside and then they sat in the living room, all of them uncharacteristically quiet.

Or maybe stunned was a better word. Even Harm, who looked like an arrogant shit on the best of days, managed to look worried. Whether it was for them or for Jinx, Vice didn't know. He also didn't know if it mattered.

Finally, Killian said, "Why the hell did the Arrows give Gillian away?"

"Only one reason makes sense," Stray said quietly.

"She has an ability," Gwen murmured, finishing Stray's thought. "How would they have known? The Blackwells have had her since she was an infant. Her baby picture's been splashed all over the news. At most, she was a month, but I'd say closer to two weeks."

Stray answered, "She probably walked long before she was supposed to. Had to be a month old but presented closer to a year."

"And thought to be an abomination, just like me and Stray," Killian added. "I don't understand why the Elders would allow that pack to exist in such ignorance."

"Because they knew you guys and Gillian and Odin knows who else is going to be born from their bloodlines," Vice said.

"So Gillian was given to a human family instead of the Elders, who could've passed her to us?" Stray asked angrily and Vice closed his eyes and tried to picture the Eydis he'd known going along with something like Jinx's scenario.

"The Elders are more fucked-up than I am, and that's saying something," he finally muttered.

Cyd and Cain brought Liam the young Weres who'd been killed, apprised him of the situation. He'd remained inside after the panic started, and even though it killed him, he knew it was important for the king to remain alive and well. It was far too critical a time for another loss.

He placed a call to their original pack, thanking their leader and informing them that justice had been done swiftly.

"I'll send you other wolves, Liam. And I'm grateful for your honoring Weres you'd never met."

"They fought bravely," Liam told them. "And I'm grateful for your solidarity."

A few more brief words and he hung up.

There would be more days of this—months, years, even. And even though Cyd and Cain were weary of the outlaws and trappers, they were still primed for the fight. Now, they lay together on the couch, unwilling to split apart just yet.

The blood bond of the fight was strong—none wanted to break it. But a knock on the sunroom door sent them all into action, Liam pushing his way there first to find a weregirl waiting.

"What's your business here?" he demanded of the dark-haired, pretty Were dressed in black leather pants and a white tank top with a pink bra underneath.

He practically heard Cyd panting behind him but something inside of Liam was claiming possession of her, even as his mind said he was done with that kind of shit for a long time. Still, he opened the door and waited for her answer, his body seriously demanding he do more than just talk to her.

He told his dick to shut up and waited for her answer as he waved away the other wolves.

"You called for the head of the hunters," she said, and he had, not more than four hours ago through a weremessenger.

"You're a Were."

She shook her head like he was the stupidest wolf alive. "You're *really* the next king?"

"I am the king," he told her in a growl that

shook the room and she had the good sense to take a step back and bow her head.

She was a beta—he sensed that now, even though she'd come off as very alpha on first approach.

"I'm Violet," she told him, her chin raised in a show of pride or defiance or maybe both. "I want to join your pack."

"And leave the hunters?"

"I'm not their leader."

"Then I didn't invite you here."

"I don't wait for invitations," she told him. She was slim with cool green eyes that drew him in from this distance. Full Were.

There were tribal tattoos circling both slim biceps. Other tattoos down her arms, words and symbols in black that Liam should want to take his time reading.

Instead, he wanted her out. "You can go. I'm not taking visitors."

"You need me on your team."

"Why's that?"

"I can fight."

"I have plenty of fighters."

"Not ones who are as good as I am—no females. I'm your surprise."

He snorted. "Take it up with Cyd—he's my alpha."

"I'm taking it up with you. I'll fight my way in."

She turned on her heel to leave. Before she could get far, he grabbed her arm and she was trying her best to look calm—halfway succeeding.

He had to give her credit since his reputation for bloodletting was growing to legendary status every hour that passed.

"Tell your hunter leader that he made a mistake by not coming here to pay me some goddamned respect. Tell him I might have to teach you some while I'm at it."

"Maybe I'd enjoy that," she bit out with a snarl, her canines lengthening a little and fuck it all, he was hard.

"Maybe you should be careful what you wish for."

He let her go with that and she bounded off into the night, her white top glowing in the moonlight, the damned pink bra teasing him. He wanted to shift, run her down and yank it off with his teeth and dammit, it was happening.

Where was all the control Vice taught him? He couldn't tell if Vice would be proud or pissed but he didn't care either way now that the wolf was in control.

She still ran in front of him, unshifted, looking over her shoulder. She had to know she had no hope of winning this race and finally, her shirt flew in the air, like she knew she had to save her clothing so as not to walk home naked.

She whirled around and held him off as she tugged off her heavy boots and her jeans. And then she simply stood there in her pink bra and matching lace pink thong, a large tattoo of a dragonfly fluttering delicately across her taut middle. Whirled around and kicked him in the face with a hard roundhouse kick that sent him backward and brought his wolf out hard.

He forced it back, the way Vice taught him, but that came at a price. His anger would be uncontrollable if this Were continued to assert dominance by fighting.

For a few moments, she did—when he caught her, she bit and kicked and scratched, her own wolf half out. Finally, she stopped struggling when he howled at the sky and threw her to the ground. Instead of trying to get up, she lay there, watching him. Waiting.

He jumped onto her, pinning her.

And she bared her throat to him.

"I don't care that you're a woman. Do you get that?" He'd never be taken in by soft hair or a pretty face or general anatomy again.

"Good. Think of me as your beta and we'll be just fine."

He took her down, poised his open mouth over her throat, his canines elongated, ready to rip open her life force.

Her pulse raced but she remained still, throat bared, submissive.

She was fucking lying.

He pushed off her. "Don't ever come back here again."

She didn't say another word and he fought not to limp all the way back to the sunroom, giving himself credit for never turning back no matter how badly he wanted to.

He stripped in front of the bathroom mirror to

survey the scratches from the beta. She hadn't exactly held her own with him, fight-wise, but he hadn't expected her to. Still, she hadn't backed down and that, he hadn't expected.

"What the hell? A girl beat you down?" Cyd asked.

"Can I have some privacy?"

"You want that, close the bathroom door."

Liam glanced at Cyd. "I know you both researched her while I was gone, so what do we know about her?"

Cyd smiled. "I knew you'd ask. But maybe we don't have to have this meeting in the bathroom."

Liam complied, trailing the alpha into the living room where Cain waited with a file.

"Violet used to bounty hunt for her old pack out in Wisconsin," Cain started as Liam flipped through the papers. "There's no details here about why she left—or whether or not she was kicked out, but after that, she started working with the hunters against the weretrappers. She passed for a while, and by the time they discovered she was wolf, she was too valuable to be let go."

"So why come to us?"

"Why the hell not?" Cyd demanded.

"We need a beta," Cain added.

"Forget it," Liam said firmly and neither twin argued. "Find out why she left Wisconsin." Because he would never let himself be burned by a woman again.

Chapter 21

It was three days until Jinx felt that all the drugs were out of his system. And he waited an extra few, just in case. By then, both his wolf and Gillian were climbing the walls. There was only so much the roof, fresh air and orgasms could do. And she didn't understand why they weren't having sex again—but he wasn't about to talk mating with her. Not when she already had more than enough to deal with going on inside her head.

A Dire wolf due for her first shift couldn't be controlled—he could only hope for containment. Between the Dires and the goddamned hellhounds, he had coverage, but relying on hellhounds to keep monsters out of the way was the most perverse game he'd ever played. And yet, he was trapped inside of it with no way out for the foreseeable future and a potential mate running loose in the woods.

The one thing they had going for them was that they weren't likely to run into anyone looking for Gillian Blackwell in the woods, running naked.

He had to let her run. Tell her that on her birthday, he would take her farther up, maybe even Canada to let her run, but he wouldn't make a promise he couldn't keep.

But tonight's promise already made her cheeks flush with excitement. She was practically vibrating on the ride over to the mansion. He parked in the garage and they went through the house and the tunnels, and she barely looked at anything. She was focused on the outside and nothing would deter her.

It was quiet inside the house—he assumed the Dires were out running. Cain and Cyd had left him check-in messages a few times but he hadn't returned the calls. Instead, he'd texted them.

Rogue and Jez, he knew, were out in the cemetery, looking for any obvious issues with the monsters. Everything with the trappers had been quiet. And Cyd had personally vetted the woods for him tonight. Maybe he and Cain were out there, prepared to watch out for Jinx. He hadn't asked them but he wouldn't put it past them.

Once in the sunroom, Gillian stripped, faster than he did and she took off. For a second he watched, mesmerized by her speed—and her beautiful bare ass—and then he snapped to, stripped, shifted and let Brother Wolf catch up with her. Or try to. He didn't know if it was the drugs doing it or what but, dammit all, he was having trouble catching her.

And the worst part was, he didn't think she was going at her top speed. She kept looking over her shoulder, slowing to let him catch up and then eluding his grasp.

He was so caught up in the game that he didn't realize how far they'd gone. He couldn't howl and expect her to stop, so he had to shift instead, which cost him. Thankfully, she slowed a bit and he waved his hands, called quietly, "Gilly, you can't go any farther—time to turn back."

If she heard him, she ignored it, speeding up. If anyone tried to catch her on film and clock her time, they'd know for sure she wasn't human. The speed with which she moved was incredible. Jinx would have to shift back to keep up and fully protect her from whatever dangers lurked in these woods, ones she seemed oblivious to.

Brother had no problem with the quick shifts and finally, with effort, he caught her, running in front of her and waiting, forcing her to stop. She did so. Smiled. She wasn't even out of breath.

She'd let him catch her. He shifted and grabbed her by the waist as she giggled.

"You told me I could run. That I needed to." She put her hands in the air. "That was amazing!"

He couldn't be angry. "We just have to be careful."

"I'm sorry—I just couldn't stop. We can go back now." She managed to look a little chastened but her smile broke through. "When can we do it again? When will I be able to shift, like you?"

He'd told her everything but that. "On your birthday."

"My birthday?" she echoed, her voice suddenly

hollow. "Why didn't you tell me it would happen so soon?"

"Your birthday is in three weeks," he said, but she shook her head and his gut tightened.

"My parents shortened the last name and changed the birthday to keep anyone from connecting the famous Blackwell daughter to the crazy thing they locked up. My twenty-first birthday's tomorrow, Jinx."

Tomorrow, as in five fucking minutes from now. They were exposed, out in the open and too far from the Dire house for his comfort. "We've got to go back. Come on."

He kept his tone light and guided her through the woods, joking, "You can't tell my brothers that you beat me running. Or Jez—the deadhead would never let me live it down."

She laughed a little, then said, "Wouldn't running be faster?"

"It might bring the shift out."

"So it doesn't happen exactly at midnight?"

"Not always. And it's past midnight."

"Okay, that's good. Maybe we'll make it."

"Gilly, no matter when it happens, I'll make sure you're just fine."

She was so vulnerable. He couldn't call out for fear of calling attention to them, just waited for the familiar signs of the shift and tried to keep her calm.

They were five miles from the Dire mansion when she said suddenly, "I feel . . . weird," and yeah, there was that. She clutched her chest and then her throat, stared up at him.

"Let's keep going," he suggested, but a snarl came out of her mouth and as he moved to hold her hand again Brother warned him to back the fuck off. "Okay, we can stay here. But Gilly, this is important as hell—whatever you do—when you shift, you can't run anywhere but toward the house. You can stay wolf inside the house. You can tear the place apart, but we can't stay out here."

"I thought . . . you said . . . safe?" she asked, more growls escaping. She trembled too.

"You're okay," he soothed her. She was so goddamned beautiful, so gloriously naked. Would she always take his breath away like this?

"Make love to me, Jinx. Please. Now."

So dangerous. All he could do when he was around her was do goddamned dangerous things, and this was no exception. And since he was already good and naked, it made the decision that much easier. Because Brother was tired of thinking all the time, of making the right choice, of watching out for the humans instead of enjoying his own primal nature. Watching Gillian had reminded him of that.

Maybe he understood Rifter's position more than he thought. Maybe the king was also hanging on to his structure by a thread.

This isn't mating sex, he justified. It was their second time.

And she's readying to shift.

"Fuck it. Time to live on the edge," he muttered as he yanked her close, ignored the snark and kissed her until she was putty in his arms. Pliable.

Maybe Sister Wolf would hold out until they'd gotten their fill.

He kissed her breathless, until he was barely thinking. Until everything base and primal inside of him took over, laid her on the mossy floor of the woods.

It was hot. Dirty. The way it should be for them. And Gillian was locking her legs around his waist, driving him inside of her almost immediately.

"Yes, Jinx." She arched up into him as he thrust deeply, over and over. Wanted all of her—wanted to own her.

A part of him already did.

He wasn't sure how long they made love in the woods like that—it seemed too short but it was probably closer to an hour, more like a promise than a mating—the second time typically was.

"Don't let go of me," she begged him and he buried his face against her neck, bit down along her collarbone and she groaned. "Do that again."

He laughed, did so. And then she bit his shoulder, hard enough to cause his orgasm. It pushed her along and she climaxed with a loud cry—his name on the wind and he bit back his own howl as he tried to preserve any privacy they might have left.

Maybe they were meant to escape all of this unscathed. Maybe, for once, it would be easy because it felt so right.

She was stroking his hair. He was still inside of her, still hard. Wanting nothing more than to take her again. But that would have to wait.

"Gillian," he started, but something flashed behind her eyes and they glowed a little more.

"It's happening," she whispered. He rolled off of her before she threw him off. In seconds, she was on all fours, her fingers digging into the dirt, shaking her head against the rustling that he knew from experience was deafening by now.

"Go with it. Sister Wolf knows what to do."

"Suppose I don't make it."

"You will. You have to. I need you," he told her.

It was a feeling Gillian knew she'd never be able to describe thoroughly enough. There was pain—she heard bones popping but she was so absorbed, it was as if she was having an out-of-body experience. The rustling in her ears was as loud as it was calming and she breathed and gave in, because there was nothing else she could do.

She was done fighting her body's natural instincts. She'd done that for twenty-one long years and finally, she was allowed to shed her skin. Still tingling from the orgasm and Jinx's touch, she felt confident. She closed her eyes and felt herself transform.

She wasn't sure how long it took, but when she blinked, she knew she was looking at the world from an entirely different angle. She threw back her head and Sister Wolf howled, a loud, mournful sound even though her heart was light.

She looked down at her paws—the soft fur that covered her was the same color as her hair. Her eyes would have the same glow Jinx's did. And the rustling was gone, replaced by a low, growling voice that told her, *Sister Wolf is here to protect you.*

And me, you, Gillian told the wolf in return.

When she looked at Jinx, he'd shifted as well. Brother and Sister Wolf nosed one another. And then, they ran, her wolf reminding her of the promise she'd made to Jinx to run toward the Dire mansion.

She did so. The power she released as she ran was incredible, a rush beyond her wildest imagination. Her paws were strong on the earth, her balance, perfect. She jumped and sidestepped, swiveled and cut as she navigated the dark woods path, her eyesight better than ever.

Her life would never, ever be the same. And if Jinx hadn't come to find her, to save her, who knew where she'd be.

But now, she was happy. And she simply kept running, because that was all that was expected of her.

Gillian was happy. Sister Wolf was gorgeous. Graceful. Jinx would have a hard time talking her out of staying a wolf for days at a time, but taking the first three shifts quickly was important.

They'd already run for hours before her shift and she showed no signs of wanting to stop. She was powerful—he'd been right about her warrior ways. They were a part of her bloodline, bred into her, a birthright she'd come into.

She was trying to run in a direct line toward the mansion, but Sister got easily distracted by scents, different trails and he had to rally her to stay on track. They still were several miles away when shots rang through the air. He saw something whiz by his head and hit the tree behind him. Tranquilizer darts.

Trappers.

And they were after Gillian, for no other reason than she was a wolf. He knew he should be grateful for the small miracle of them not being able to recognize her as Gillian Blackwell, but that didn't make the danger any less real. He supposed they were here and out for blood to avenge their friends.

When the darts went right above her head, it must've frightened her enough that she shifted. Naked, crouched on the ground of the woods, her face shone fearful in the moonlight as she looked to Jinx silently.

He didn't shift, went to her and crouched down, hoping she'd understand. She did, pulled herself flat onto his back with her hands in the thick scruff around his neck and she hung on for dear life as he ran them out of the darkness and toward the Dire house, where they'd be safe again. As they ran toward the house, Vice's white wolf ran past him, followed by Stray and Killian.

Jinx didn't stop until they were safely inside the screened-in porch that would forever be protected by Seb's magic. Jinx eased Gillian off of him and shifted. Gathered her into his arms and walked her through the hallway until he got to one of the guest bedrooms in the twins' apartment area. He wrapped her in a blanket because she was shivering, checking her first to make sure she hadn't been hit.

Her eyes hadn't changed back all the way yet.

"I froze," she whispered, lowered her face as though terribly ashamed.

"You're new at this, Gilly. Not used to shifting, never mind having people shoot at you."

"I'll do better next time," she promised.

"I don't mind being your hero."

She hugged him, her body relaxing a bit. She was still shaking, though. Most Dires weren't the object of target practice during their first shift and it was most definitely affecting her. He was about to called for Gwen—or just carry Gillian to her when Harm came around the corner with a medical bag. Jinx studied him for a long moment before nodding that it was okay for him to come forward. When he touched Gillian's arm, though, Jinx growled and Gillian said, "He can't help it."

"I know. I'm Harm."

"I haven't met you before."

"They keep me in the attic," he deadpanned. "I'm Gwen's dad."

"Oh," she said and Jinx added, "We don't force him to stay in the attic anymore—he just likes it there."

Harm rolled his eyes but continued checking on Gillian. It was, of course, something Jinx could've done himself, but since all he wanted to do was bed her, it was best to have someone else make sure she was all right.

"Any problems coming out of the shift?" he asked.

"It just . . . happened. I got scared when the shooting started."

"That's natural," Harm told her. "But you have to let Sister Wolf take over next time that happens. Because, for you, you're safer in wolf form these days."

"Right. So no one will be able to know who I really am," she agreed. "Okay, that makes sense. I'll know what to expect next time."

"It gets easier. And you seem to like what you are," he said as he checked her blood pressure.

"Don't you?" she asked and Jinx waited to see what Harm said. It took a good minute of silence before the Dire male who should've been king said, "For a long time, I didn't. But since I've been back among these particular wolves, I'm beginning to."

Vice's white wolf had blood marring his otherwise pristine coat. Stray and Killian weren't hit but they'd bested this group of weretrappers, catching all four of them.

Inside one of the men's backpacks, they'd found disturbing pictures of other Weres the weretrappers had captured and tortured recently, all over upstate New York. These groups were working without a leader and they were thugs, just taking down as many Weres as they could.

Hunters had been taking these kinds of were-trappers down as well, but Vice wondered if the hunters would be able to tell if these trappers died because they'd tried to hurt wolves, or if wolves killed them for sport.

The thing was, Weres hadn't killed humans for sport in centuries. They'd learned it was the only way to survive in this world filled with more humans than wolves. And if the hunters didn't know that . . .

"You all right?" Killian asked.

Vice had been hit in the biceps. Burned like a bitch but, of course, he'd live. "They were trappers," he said.

"After Gillian or all of us?" Stray asked and Vice shrugged and asked, "Does it say Kreskin on my forehead?"

"You can be such an asshole," Stray muttered and Killian smiled.

Chapter 22

That night, Vice ran with Cain and Rogue. Rogue had asked for Cain specifically, and it made Cain proud that his omega skills were helping the Dire. Liam also liked knowing that a Were in his pack was in high demand.

It was better this way. Liam needed an alpha with him at all times and Cyd was good playing the role as bodyguard for him. He excelled at fighting.

Cain was still trying to shake off the violence of the other night, even though he had to admit that a part of it had excited him. His wolf needed the violence, the fighting, to survive. But as an omega, Cain was built to crave peace. To have all of that coexist in one body was at times frustrating and exciting and scary as fuck.

"Come on, Cain, let's roll," Vice said, and speaking of coexisting and scary as fuck . . .

"Have you heard from Jinx?" he asked as they stripped down in the woods. He'd texted and called, gotten a brief *things are fine* text in return.

"He's in hiding with Gillian," Vice said. Cain noticed the tightness in Rogue's expression when Jinx was mentioned and he made a mental note to keep his mouth shut on the subject around the wolf from this point on.

The shift went from pain to pleasure in minutes. Cain ran between the two Dires, slowing as they scented humans around the same area he and Rogue had seen the hunters gathering.

Quietly, Cain padded forward, camouflaged in the heavy brush. He peered out and what he saw made his groin tighten.

He was back. Holy mother of the moon, *Angus* was back and he looked . . . like a goddamned warrior.

The scars were still there, marring his chest and back and neck and they didn't distract from his beauty. Cain hadn't lied when he'd told the man that, the last time they'd seen one another.

The conversation had gone downhill after that, but Cain knew he'd come back.

He'd just never thought the ex-fed would come back as a hunter.

Angus had always been damned handsome and strong to begin with. He'd always had an edge, but it was more pronounced now, especially the way his eyes glinted as he spoke with the other men in his group.

Cain took him all in, especially the silver knife and the tattoos on the backs of the man's hands.

Hunter.

He drew a stuttered breath, found himself at a

total loss for words as he watched Angus shoot the bow and arrow and hit the target exactly in the center. His muscles bulged and the look on his face meant business.

A woman came out of the trees and hugged him. And then another guy came out too—human— and clapped Angus on the back.

And Angus smiled at the guy.

Son of a bitch. Cain knew that smile. And he wasn't about to compete with anyone.

"And that's why you don't fall for humans," Vice told him.

He hadn't heard the Dire approach, which was part of the problem, hadn't realized he'd even shifted, dammit. He was off his game and couldn't afford to be. Not now, with the impending move to Manhattan. He was Liam's great white omega hope, and he wasn't supposed to be out anywhere alone.

But he wasn't, technically. He was with Angus and his new boyfriend.

It had been less than a month. And Angus seemed to have gotten over Cain just fine.

It's not like you had a relationship.

But they'd had something and Cain valued loyalty. Had thought Angus did too. But Cain had obviously been wrong about many things. He could barely bite back a growl when the other human male put a hand on Angus's shoulder. He could bite that hand off easily and he gave serious thought to doing so.

"They could just be friends, you know? Wolves

are extremely jealous and possessive," Vice continued, giving Cain a lesson in weredom that Cain already knew. He didn't bother denying anything to Vice.

"Is this going to be a problem?"

"Hunters hunt weretrappers and other bad things, especially Weres gone bad. We're not bad things, hence, the hunters shouldn't cause us trouble," Vice said. "Sounds good in theory, right?"

"Too good to be true," Cain muttered.

Angus knew the Were was close. He could feel the tingle on the back of his neck and wondered if being bitten by a Were hadn't done something to him after all.

But Cain hadn't been the one to technically bite him. Not enough to scar him, anyway. And he'd always been able to sense the young Were. He'd done this purposely, come to the same spot twice to make sure Cain saw him.

Maybe you really do have a death wish.

Or maybe he missed the young wolf more than he cared to admit. But he had a new life now, and he had to make sure his loyalties remained true.

"You with us, Angus?" Joe asked, turned down the music.

"Just reminiscing about the last time I came to town," he said honestly. The people in this truck all knew that hadn't gone well at all. But from there, things had looked up.

He'd heard rumors about this group, usually in derisive terms from his brief encounters with the weretrappers. The hunters worked against the weretrappers, *like the hunters actually had some kind of in with wolves,* Al had said sarcastically.

But it wasn't really like that at all. In fact, Angus had learned that many hunters did get killed by wolves, even though they were actually helping the breed. Their main goal was to take down the bad supernatural influences and keep the good.

Angus knew that finding that line in the sand wouldn't be easy at all.

"Do you have an *in* to the Were world?" was one of the first questions the hunters asked, and Angus said no, because he wasn't using Cain like that. Hell, the way they'd left things, he wasn't sure there was any connection between them left.

In reality, he was still mad as hell at the Were.

Chapter 23

Gillian had her second shift two nights later, with the other Dires and some Weres making a circle in the woods to keep her protected. She ran and ran like the wind and Jinx hung back and watched her.

She was safe and happy. And he was dreaming of hellhounds while Rogue dreamed of hell.

"After we run, I'd like to come hunting with you," she said when she came back and shifted in front of him.

"Ghost hunting?"

"Isn't that what you do?" she asked.

"It's safer for you back at the apartment."

"I think you're safer with me," she asserted. "You're always saving people. When are you going to let someone save you?"

"It doesn't work like that."

"Why can't it, Jinx?" Gillian asked softly. "What if that's what I'm built for?"

"You're fast and strong—a warrior, yes," he started.

"Faster and stronger than you," she pointed out.

"That hasn't been put to a real test." Shit, he was so going to lose this bet and she wouldn't let it go.

"Then let's put it to the test." She crossed her arms, challenging him.

"I can't do that."

"You will. Let's start with a race," she suggested. "Last I recall, you could barely keep up with me."

"I didn't want to crowd you," he said defensively but she'd already taken off, flying across the field. She stopped on a dime, turned and told him, "I'll give you a head start."

"You'll give . . ." He laughed a little. "You'll give me a head start?"

"That's what I said, slowpoke." She motioned for him to run past her and he muttered, "Oh, honey, you are so going down."

He took off at a speed that would make him a blur to her as he ran by. Suitably impressed with himself, he raced toward the woods as a blast of air whooshed past him. . . .

There was *no* way.

But it was her. He ran faster, but she was already so far ahead of him he could barely see her disappearing figure. He fought the urge to yell at her not to get too far ahead but that would mean admitting defeat and he was not doing that. Forget it.

Something whizzed by him again, this time going the other way and he stopped and heard Gillian's laughter behind him.

"Have you always been this fast?" he asked and she shrugged.

"I've learned to push it down because the boys never liked to be beaten."

"I wouldn't say I was beaten," he huffed and Brother Wolf was equally offended and wanted the challenge reissued, wolf to wolf.

But hell, that could prove to be equally embarrassing.

"You were so schooled!" she called over her shoulder, fell to the ground, tickled over this fact.

He walked over to her. "Okay, fine, you might have the speed. Maybe. But the strength . . . never."

She rolled onto her stomach and looked up at him innocently. "Wanna arm wrestle?"

"You're serious?"

"Totally."

"You can't arm wrestle on the ground," he pointed out.

"Then we'll wrestle wrestle."

"Forget it. I don't wrestle chicks."

"You're really worried you're going to lose."

Before he could say anything, she'd goddamned flipped him. And that was no mean feat, because he'd flipped hundreds of wolves, including Dires who were bigger than he was without breaking a sweat.

"How the hell did you do that?"

She shrugged, like it had been the easiest thing in the world for her. It *had* been. It came naturally to her. And now it made sense why no one had ever been able to find her during the times she'd left the hospital to run in the woods, because you'd think a beautiful naked woman running wild would've gotten spotted at some point over the past six years.

But she never had, because she could practically outrun wind.

"Why didn't you mention this?"

"When we first met, it didn't seem relevant. And after you told me about the wolf thing, I assumed that all Dires were fast and strong—everything fell into place for me. I never thought my boyfriend would be a slowpoke."

He was offended and stuttering at slowpoke, but he was more worried about the boyfriend part. This was the perfect time for the *I'm no good for you; it's not you, it's me* speech but the words wouldn't come out of his mouth.

"Can we run some more?" she asked.

"No," he said, a little too loudly, then added, "Too dangerous to go much farther."

She nibbled her bottom lip a little and nodded. "Wrestle more, then. Maybe I can show you some moves."

"Maybe you can show me . . ." He couldn't finish his sentence and she smirked at him.

"Your indignation kind of turns me on."

"You might actually be worse than Vice."

"I take that as a compliment."

"You would." He got to his feet just as she did. He circled her, leaving enough space between them that she couldn't just reach out and go all ninja wolf on his ass, but he'd once again forgotten about the sick speed she could use even within short distances. His head spun as she was suddenly grabbing him from behind and pulling him to the ground and he couldn't even make a damned dent in her hold.

This was going to kill his rep. He could only pray that Jez—or Vice—holy hell Vice—never, ever saw this shit. . . .

"Did you just get taken down by a girl?" Vice's voice rang over him as Gillian effectively trapped his arms behind his back so he was eating dirt. "Holy shit—Jinx just got spanked by a girl."

"I'm a wolf, thank you very much," Gillian said as coolly as she could. And then she giggled. Yeah, she was having way too much fun with this.

"Perhaps you could let me up?" he asked and she relented, but slowly. He rolled over and she was towering above him holding out her hand to help him up. And Vice was literally on the ground laughing so hard tears were coming out of his eyes.

"Dude, I am so putting this in the next newsletter."

"We don't have a newsletter," Jinx said through gritted teeth.

"I'm making one, because this shit is that good," Vice declared. And then he suddenly got completely serious and said, "Wait a minute—Gillian's got an ability? An honest to Odin ability?"

"Looks like it," Jinx said.

"That means she's—"

"Fast and strong, yes," Jinx finished for him with a hard look for Vice to shut up and ix-nay the immortality thing. Too much, too soon and Jinx had barely finished explaining the Dire and Were thing.

To let someone know they were never, ever going to die wasn't something you spilled out. And Vice understood that better than anyone, nodded sincerely and said, "I'm still doing a newsletter. Or at least a long Christmas card. 'This year, we learned that Jinx can be felled by a girl and ridden like a pony.' Has a nice ring to it, don't you think?"

Jinx jumped him before the wolf could say another word and soon the two of them were slamming into trees and tussling like old times, like they didn't have a care in the world.

Chapter 24

"**S**he's got an ability. That's why she was given away," Stray said from his spot in the trees. They hadn't meant to spy but hell, wolf hearing made it nearly impossible to keep secrets. It didn't help that Vice was gleeful about the whole Jinx-getting-beaten-by-a-female thing.

Stray had to admit that made him laugh, the first real one in days.

"Maybe the Elders didn't see that coming," Killian offered.

"Oh, come the hell on, they know everything, remember?" Stray slammed the lid of his laptop down. "It's the only reason that pack was allowed to live and breed. We're the enforcers, so clearly they have to spawn Dires with abilities every once in a while for the amusement of the Elders."

"Does Rifter know?"

"You really think Vice can keep a secret?" Stray asked.

"Gillian could make a lot of money on the underground ultimate fighting circuit," Killian said thoughtfully. "I could even manage her."

"This entire place has lost its mind," Stray moaned, his head in his hands.

"Relax, brother. I don't think she'd go for it anyway. Doesn't mean I won't ask though."

Jinx watched Gillian cavort in the lake, splashing happily. Free. And what had been just a nagging feeling in his gut was sure.

She was a warrior. And not only in the way that Dires were. No, she was stronger. Faster. It wasn't Dire strength and speed, it was beyond.

It would take a strong man to submit to a warrior Dire like she was. And he would. He might say he was doing it for her but really, he was doing it for himself.

Finally, she seemed content enough to climb out of the water, shake off and shift. His wolf growled at her nakedness and he fought going over to her and taking her right then and there.

It helped that Rogue and Jez were waiting for him. They dressed and got back into the truck where Rogue and Jez waited.

"You ready? We need to go check on our charges," Rogue told him. "Just you and me. Leave Jez to watch over Gillian."

It was the right thing to do, but Jinx would rather walk barefoot over hot coals. "Maybe tomorrow night."

"I don't want to do this any more than you do. But I can't wait anymore. I'm connected to this. Those hounds didn't kill me because they recognized me as part of you," Rogue explained. "These markings make things call to me. I don't know if they're beacons . . . or if I'm being controlled by them."

"Jinx, let me go with you," Gillian said.

"Too dangerous—you can't see ghosts."

"I can see you."

He looked at her incredulously and she continued, "You saved me. I'm returning the favor."

He opened his mouth to tell her he didn't need saving, but the lie didn't come out. "You can't help me with the monsters."

"I can guard you while you're vulnerable."

"You want to be my bodyguard?"

"It's what the Dire female wolves are. We take care of our mates, especially the warrior women. You told me that, but I feel it, here. Let me take care of you."

How long had it been since anyone said that to him? His Dire brothers always would—that was a given. But Jinx was far more used to being the protection than the protected. Wasn't sure he even knew how to let himself be vulnerable.

"The best part is that no one will suspect it. They wouldn't know my strength or speed."

"You can't do anything in human form that will give you away."

"I'll have to be your secret superhero," she whispered into his neck before she nipped it.

"You two need a room in an apartment far from mine," Jez muttered from the front seat and Jinx ignored him.

"You can protect me," he said.

"That's a gift—I accept it with great honor."

"I'll watch both of you," Jez nodded. "Sorry, didn't mean to ruin the moment."

"And who'll watch you, deadhead?" Jinx asked and Rogue's voice answered, "Me," and then added, "This is becoming one big circle jerk."

"Rogue . . . you don't have to. . . ."

"Gotta know how bad it is. Better to jump in with both feet," Rogue said quietly.

"It's bad . . . and worse," Jinx told him as the truck made its way toward Pinewood Cemetery. They drove through the iron gates with guns loaded with rock salt. Holy water. Each of them held iron.

When they got out, Jinx made a salt circle around them and the truck; this way, they could get inside and stay there if things got bad enough.

"Tell me what you're thinking," Rogue told him.

"Besides the fact that I'm never letting you go back to hell . . . I keep thinking that we could use these fears to eradicate the trappers forever," Jinx admitted.

"And then what? The more these things feed, the more they want," Rogue pointed out.

"I know, you're right. We have to get them back inside. Locked up someplace tight."

"There are definitely places in hell they could go. Hell's expanded immensely since fears were created," Rogue told him.

"I don't think they'll just go if we ask." And they were right back at the beginning again.

"Something's here," Rogue said, his voice choked. The markings on his face glowed and he rubbed them almost absently as he moved around inside of the circle looking out into the night.

The ghosts moved around, waving to get Jinx's attention. "Do you see any of yours?"

"Nothing," his twin said hollowly as the hellhounds ran toward them, making the ground shake.

"What is that?" Gillian asked and then scented the air. "Hellhounds."

"Bingo," Jez said. "And here comes their charges."

The black and gray smoke twisted and rose from over the graves, racing toward the circle at alarming speed. They stopped right before them and hovered.

"I hate this part," Jez muttered.

Just then, Jinx dropped to his knees and Gillian dropped next to him.

"What is it, Jinx?" Gillian asked and when he spoke, his voice sounded hollow and odd, even to his own ears.

"The hellhounds aren't just to protect me," he told them. "They're to keep me from getting too close to the monsters released from purgatory. I'm locked out. And it's only a matter of time before the hellhounds rebel."

They'd gotten back in the truck and out of the cemetery after Jinx told the hellhounds to keep the fears under control. They seemed to still be obeying but how long that would last was any wolf's bet.

Now, they were up on the roof of the apartment building, with Rogue and Jez on one side and he and Gillian on the other.

"I'm so sorry, Jinx."

"Not your fault. My father tricked me. But because the Dire ghosts fought, he was laid to a peaceful rest. What do I get?"

"When I thought I was crazy, I would've done anything to get away from the disease. When you gave me a way out, I was relieved." She paused. "But you . . . you never get to walk away. You're hunted all the time."

He shrugged.

"You've got to find the good in it."

"I help humans. In return, they try to kill us," Jinx said, his voice tight. "I help ghosts. In return, they try to kill us."

"You helped me and I don't try to kill you," she pointed out.

"Because you can't," he said and snorted in spite of himself. "Speaking of . . . there's something I haven't told you yet. I was waiting. Didn't want to overwhelm you."

"And now, after we know that hellhounds are protecting monsters and will eventually turn against the world, it seems like a good time?"

"Actually, yes." He took her chin in his hand. "Your speed and strength—you know it's not normal for a Dire. You know it's called an ability."

"Yep. You told me that." He'd also listed all the other Dires' abilities as well.

"There's something that comes with abilities. At least it has for all of us." He stared at her. "I told you we mated for life. But I never told you how long that life would be."

She blinked, tilted her head. "I know you're old. I assumed . . . a lot of years?"

"I'm immortal, Gilly. And if I'm right, so are you."

"Immortal as in . . . I'm never going to die?" She tried to breathe but couldn't.

"And this is why I waited to tell you."

"If someone tries to kill me, what happens exactly?"

"You kind of die. And then you come back to life pretty quickly. It's not painless, but it's never permanent."

"I gather you've tested the theory."

"Unfortunately, yes."

She wondered if there was ever the possibility of a Dire with abilities not being immortal. But finding out would be akin to playing Russian roulette and she wasn't ready to do that, not after promising Jinx she would stay safe. "I'm okay. It's just . . . the concept of *never* is hard to wrap my mind around."

"Tell me about it after you've lived for centuries."

"You lived for centuries . . . with no one to love," she murmured.

"You were worth the wait. Well worth it."

Chapter 25

Vice heard the yelling in his sleep, assumed it was someone having good sex and ignored it. After ten minutes, he realized it was distress and that it was coming from the basement rooms where Max was being held.

Gwen checked on her several times a day, typically with Rifter. Vice seemed to set her off too much and, as he wanted nothing to do with her, that was fine by him.

But tonight, it seemed like he was the only one home. Maybe Gwen was out running with Rifter—Vice had come in early, mainly to sleep so he could forget about brooding and worrying, because there was so much shit going on he couldn't control or help with.

He missed Jinx. And Rogue. And Eydis. Had no idea how the hell they were going to deal with all of them. Was worried about Liam and the responsibilities the young king faced and, hell, Vice was charged with helping him.

When the hell had anyone decided putting him in charge of helping someone was a good idea?

Yeah, so much for sleeping off the worry. He definitely regretted coming home when he looked into the double-paned glass and saw Max doubled over. Between her legs was a puddle of water with some blood mixed in, so no, this wasn't her faking to try to escape. This was the real thing, weeks overdue.

He stood there, watching for a few minutes. She hadn't seen him, wasn't really yelling for anyone in particular. She was just yelling because of the pain. Then she'd pace and double over again as another contraction hit her.

Having this baby signed her death warrant. He tried to muster up sympathy for her and failed. He'd save it all for the pup she carried.

And, it was for that pup that he unlocked the door and went to help her.

"Vice, the baby's coming."

"No shit."

She ignored that, grabbed his arm and proceeded to attempt to crush it as she went through another contraction. When she finished, he managed to get her onto the bed, covered her up and noted that Gwen had already gotten a few things together for the baby.

He pulled out his phone and left Gwen a message. And Rifter. Stray and Killian too, for good measure, and the twins. Figured he'd keep Liam out of that loop, for obvious reasons.

"You're going to have to hold out until Gwen gets here," he told Max, who glared at him.

"This might be my first baby, but you and I both know you don't tell a baby to stay inside."

She looked tired. Defeated. She'd been locked in here for weeks, knowing there was no way out. She'd betrayed Liam in the worst way possible, and she'd have to pay.

"I came to terms with what's going to happen to me weeks ago," she told him now. "Please, just let me have the baby and then Liam can have his honor back."

That was damned important to Vice for sure. But still, delivering a baby was not on his list of priorities or his bucket list. Ever.

"Baby!" Vice yelled in the loudest voice he could—Marine voice—but no one heard him. And Max was clawing at his arm, yelling her head off as well. "Wolves know how to do this instinctively, you know."

"I'm not a wolf," she bit out.

"No, you're a traitor." One Vice would never forgive for hurting Liam. This baby wasn't Liam's, would never be in line to be king. It might never even be accepted into a pack, forced to live out its days as a lone Were.

But he wouldn't think about that now. Not when Max was delivering the goddamned baby as he watched. She'd gotten onto the floor, with towels under her and one over her legs. He guessed she was pretty much naked underneath and she lifted herself on her elbows and pushed. Vice had no choice but to throw the covers off her and see what was going on down there. And it wasn't pretty.

"Holy hell—this could scar me for life," he muttered. "I want to look away, but I can't. This is just not right."

"Bite me," she spat.

"Not a goddamned chance."

She screamed and then she pushed and Vice had no idea if that was the right thing or the wrong thing. He yelled for Gwen, for anyone, but no one came to help.

"I really need a smoke." Desperately. He grabbed for a blanket and looked back again and saw that there was a baby coming out. Right now. No waiting.

"I'll pay you to go back in until Gwen comes," he told the head and Max glared at him. And obviously, the kid was ignoring his bribe and already refusing to obey and Vice sighed and then swore and resigned himself to this task.

Buck up, Marine.

He spread a blanket under her legs, called for Gwen again and was met with deafening silence.

"Okay, look, I have no idea what the hell I'm doing. I'm just going to catch it when it comes out," he told her and she screamed and bore down, grabbing his hand and possibly breaking bones as he put his other hand out to catch whatever came out.

But it wasn't happening like that.

"Doesn't this just kind of pop out?" he asked.

"No, that is not how this works," Max said, near tears but obviously refusing to cry. He had to give her some credit—just a little—for what she was going through. "You have to guide him out or he won't make it."

Vice nodded, settled himself and when she pushed again, the kid's shoulders were out and Vice was able to gently pull and help finish the birth.

"You have to clear his mouth," Max said, showed him something she called an aspirator and told him how it worked. He did so and after a few seconds the kid yelled his head off. As he did so, Max cut the cord herself—she'd been prepared for this.

"This kid needs a bath," Vice declared as he held it up to the light for further examination. The kid stopped yelling and just . . . watched him.

"Take him," she said harshly. "I don't want to see him. Take the goddamned thing out of here."

It was similar to what his mother had told the servants when he was six, the first time his abilities had really come into play. Without another word, he cobbled the baby into the blanket, tucked it against him and walked out of the room.

It was hours of running in the woods but finally, Gwen seemed to have gotten Rifter to calm down to the point where he didn't look like he wanted to kill everything in his path. Which was good for him, Vice supposed, as he remained on the couch, holding the sleeping baby.

He'd fed it. Changed it. Rocked it. And now he felt like a goddamned woman. Even checked a few times to make sure his dick was there.

"Something you want to tell us?" Rifter asked as Gwen said, "Max!"

"She's downstairs, locked back up. I took the baby and left," he explained but Gwen was already going to check on Max, calling, "I'll be right back up to look at the baby."

Because if Max died before Liam got to perform the ritual, it would mar his kingship. Many of the packs were waiting to give him their final approval to see how he dealt with this.

"Is it . . . healthy?" Rifter asked.

"Seems it to me." Vice looked down at the sleeping bundle. "This place is getting crowded."

"So you delivered this baby?" Rifter asked.

"Yeah, yeah, make your jokes," Vice growled, but realized Rifter wasn't making fun of him. Instead, the king looked at him with respect in his eyes. He swallowed hard and kept his eyes on the kid because he didn't know what to say. He'd been the last person he'd thought who'd care for this kid, but hell, someone had to. For now.

Gwen came back in with another bottle of formula, said, "I gave her something to make her sleep. She'd cleaned herself up and she's not talking."

"She's preparing to die," Vice said. "That's part of the ritual for the Weres. Twenty-four hours before it happens, you stop talking."

"I'm going to have to check him out, okay?" Gwen asked.

"I think that's best," he told her, took the sleeping kid off his chest and gingerly handed him to her. But the second it lost contact with Vice, it howled. Turned purple and, dude, that was so not a good color on a pup. She handed it back to Vice and it stopped immediately.

"Oh, come on. You're kidding me, right? I'm not the type for babies. I'm too X-rated."

No one could deny that, but it was apparent none of them would sleep at all if that baby got moved from Vice's arms.

He sighed in defeat for the second time that night and crawled into his bed, the kid like Velcro against him.

"You should probably name it," she said. "It is a boy, right?"

"Definite boy parts," Vice agreed. Hell, the kid was cute for sure. And the truth was, Liam wouldn't name it, and they couldn't let Max. It would actually be too cruel for her, and Vice had done the right thing by taking the baby away.

Max hadn't wanted to see or hear him.

"I'll think about it," he said. Because it had to be the right name.

"I'll put the crib in your room," Rifter offered.

"Seriously? You're serious," he said as Rifter went down to the basement. Gwen added, "I'll bring up some bottles. I'll help with the night feedings. . . ."

"Night feedings?" Vice grumbled. "I'm owed big-time for this one."

Chapter 26

Liam hadn't been able to bring himself to visit the baby. Cyd told him that Vice—Vice—had delivered him and was currently caring for the kid who screamed if anyone else touched him.

Liam had to fight his smile at that, because, although Vice wouldn't ever see it himself, Liam could understand why that was. In the short time he'd been under the wolf's tutelage, Vice had become a father to him. And an X-rated older brother, all at the same time. The best of all possible worlds.

And now, he just wanted to make his mentor proud of him. Get his pack behind him.

He'd seen Max only once since she'd been here, and that conversation burned in his mind.

"I'd kill myself, but that would be another dishonor to you," Max told him. "I want to give you the honor back."

"I don't want anything from you," he told her. Wondered how he'd once loved her, considered her a mate.

Humans are weak. Foolish. Vice had been teaching him that, the same way his father had been trying to drill that into his skull for years. But he'd learned firsthand, and in the most painful way possible. He hated Max for her betrayal for the past month, had burned with the desire for revenge in his gut.

And then, just as suddenly as the hatred had come, it was gone, replaced by a sense of duty and responsibility for the bigger picture. The pack. His pack.

For the kid's honor, he had to do what pack law demanded. And that pup deserved a shot, no matter what his parents had done. If Liam had learned anything from living with the Dires, it had been that fact.

If he didn't kill her, he would never be able to get the pack under control and that was dangerous to all their existence.

He knew from Gwen that Max had been silent for twenty-four hours since the birth, as was expected. She was following pack law out of respect for the wolves. For him or Teague, he didn't know, but suspected it was for the baby most of all.

Still, she was allowed to talk when Liam gave her the opportunity. A chance for her to share her dying request. And as she knelt before him, she couldn't even look him in the eye, not until he told her, "Speak, Max, and tell me what's on your mind."

"You can't let that child pay for my mistakes," she blurted out, her voice unwavering but the emotion showed in the tear that ran down her cheek. "You have to show mercy. That's the kind of king you are, Liam. The kind of wolf you always were."

He wanted to tell her that she never really knew him, but that wasn't true at all. "I promise you that."

"Thank you." She stood, moved forward toward him. She was dressed in a simple white robe, as tradition called for. Cyd had made the arrangements with Gwen, and now Max followed him out through the tunnels and into the field. She remained silent. Stoic. That was the Max he'd once known.

Cyd, Cain and other Weres were standing guard against outlaw attacks. This matter was always done in private, and Liam held the sword, the handle smooth and the metal heavy in his palm.

She turned to face him, chin up.

"I'm not doing this out of anger, Max," he told her. "It's for the pack. I've forgiven you. Your child will have a chance."

"Thank you."

The night was silent. Somber. He did his duty quickly, not allowing her to suffer. As per tradition, he turned and walked away once Max crumbled to the ground. Cyd and Cain would take care of her burial. He smelled the blood and went into his room and into the shower and stayed there for as long as he could stand the hot water on his skin. Stayed until the smell was gone and his body stopped wracking with sobs and he could stand

tall and say he'd done what a king was supposed
to do.

He toweled off, put on sweats and a T-shirt and
walked out to find Rifter waiting for him with a
bottle of whiskey and two glasses, already poured.
Rifter handed one to him wordlessly, clinked his
glass to Liam's and the men drank. Liam appreciated the hot burn down his gullet and Rifter refilled
the glass for him several times in a short span.

Rifter didn't expect him to speak at all, he realized. He was simply offering support from one
king to another. And when Liam had enough to
drink, only realizing that when the room spun,
Rifter got him into bed and left Cyd and Cain to
watch over him. Liam kicked them out of the
room after half an hour, too restless to have anyone staring at him. He opened the window for
some light and the moon's touch and found Violet
sitting about twenty feet away from the house she
couldn't see, facing the woods he often ran in.

He was still angry at himself for egging her on
the other night, but for some unfathomable reason, he leaped out the window and stalked her.

Whether she knew he was coming or not, she
never turned. He gave her credit for that, more so
when she said, "Rough night?"

Instead of growling or pretending it didn't happen, he sat next to her. "I'm never mating again,"
he told her, because if that was somehow her in-
tention with this whole beta thing . . .

"I've never planned on it," Violet agreed.
"Seems like a really good way to get screwed up."

"Yeah."

"Sorry. Didn't mean to rub salt in the wound." She actually looked abashed.

"It's all right."

"My mouth tends to get me in trouble."

"I know a few wolves like that." He paused. "I'm supposed to meet with the hunters tomorrow. Are they going to tell me anything about you that you'd rather tell me yourself?"

"How much time do you have?"

"Why did you leave the hunters?"

She stared straight ahead. "They kicked me out."

"Why?"

"They were scared of me. Said I was uncontrolled during a fight."

"You're young." He realized it just then.

"I'm nineteen, okay?"

Fuck, this was not okay. "Then you're still in moon craze."

"I fight it. I didn't lose control when you fought me," she pointed out.

"Did your pack kick you out?"

"Yes. The hunters took me in. They think I'm twenty-three."

She looked it, but for Weres, there was a big difference between nineteen and twenty-one, which was exactly why she lied to the hunters about being well past moon craze. "Betas need to—"

"Keep the peace? Don't give me that bullshit. That's what omegas are for. Betas are to back you up. To keep a cool head if you're fighting. To make sure your alphas, like Cyd, are where they need to be."

She was right.

"I admire you for what you did, both with Max and the outlaws," she continued. "You're a true king."

There was no sarcasm in her tone, only reverence. And he did need a beta. He needed as many people on his side as possible and his gut told him that Violet was a good choice. Because, even before she'd told him what happened, he'd already known, thanks to his meeting with the head of the hunters. "How about a trial run as my beta?" he asked.

When she looked at him, her eyes glowed. "No mating—that's my rule. You can never force me or say it's for the good of the pack."

"I can accept that."

"What can I do to help you?"

"Let me sleep. Stand guard. Wake me if I have a nightmare." He didn't wait for an answer, just lay back under the moon and drifted off. He wasn't sure how long he slept, but when he woke, Violet was standing near him, gun drawn and canines elongated, guarding him with her life.

Chapter 27

As dangerous as it was, there wasn't anything the Dires could do about a newly shifted wolf's need to run. It was imperative that Gillian be allowed to do so, and separating and bringing her to a different locale wouldn't do much good. If anything, her pictures were plastered even more places now.

Jinx told her they weren't able to stop the pictures from getting out, assured her they were using extra security and running in a more secluded portion of the woods, one that humans found harder to get around because of fallen trees and lots of twisted brush and the like. It was dark and coarse and Gillian loved it from the moment they'd arrived.

"This is perfect . . . it's how I picture the old country when you talk about it—the dark woods where the Dires ruled the night," she said, her voice hushed. Even though he'd told her that the Dires' old days weren't always wonderful, she'd made him tell her some good things about her heritage. He understood why that would be important to her.

So he'd told her about the moon ceremonies, the parties they had still to honor that. How men and women danced and drank and cavorted freely, with no worries about their primal needs. About how many Dires fought side by side with humans through great battles, selflessly giving their lives to help their community. How they never betrayed who they were.

"I want to train in the warrior ways," she'd told him earlier.

"I think you've somehow imbibed the tradition." He'd meant it. With the speed and strength, that was half the battle.

"Teach me to fight."

"I can do that." Needed to. It was an art form, and for her, a necessary one. "Sister Wolf doesn't need training, but your other form does."

"So show me," she teased, her arms outstretched and fingers wiggling for him to come closer. And she was naked, which made him want to come very damned close.

But the mating . . . it meant no sex. Not until she was through all this and ready to make a permanent decision about spending the rest of eternity together. He was mulling over eternity with Gillian and liking the feeling when Brother growled in his head.

He turned to her. "The weretrappers are back."

She clung to his side as she shifted. He bent

down to look at her wolf. "Sister, you run. Don't look back, don't shift back. Go as fast as you can toward the house—I'll be right behind you. But you'll get there faster. Go get help."

Sister Wolf listened, took off at a dead run in the direction of the house while he ran behind her. He needed to be able to fight and if the weretrappers tried to tranq him, it would be far worse on him if he was in wolf form when they did so. They had drugs that they experimented with that were rumored to keep wolves in wolf form forever, and for Jinx, the idea of Brother living like that was too much.

He caught sight of Gillian far ahead of him as the tranq darts whizzed by him. There must also be trappers stationed ahead of them, prepared to drive them back into the woods. He passed several drugged Weres—the ones who were supposed to be helping guard the Dires—before he felt the hits.

Gillian was still moving. Her new wolf's metabolism was running high and she was able to do as he asked. He was hit three times to her single time, and the last thing he remembered was seeing her continuing to run as he collapsed.

Don't come back for me was his last thought.

She'd been hit. She'd been prepared to remain in wolf form, as Jinx had told her, but she felt her wolf's fear of the drugs. She shifted as she ran, turning around to catch Jinx's eye.

It was only then she realized that Jinx was no

longer behind her. Naked, dazed, drugged, she turned to look for him, knowing better than to yell his name. It was at that moment a hood went over her face and tightened around her neck. Instinctively, she grabbed to loosen it, to pull it off but her hands were yanked behind her.

"It's definitely Gillian," she heard and that's when she began to kick and yell in earnest. Even the police finding her would be better than this.

"Relax, Gillian—we work for your parents. We're going to bring you back someplace safe."

No. She bucked and kicked, felt another tranquilizer being injected, taking with her the last of her resistance. From what she'd learned about wolf metabolism, the drugs would metabolize out fast enough. She should remain still, even after they wore off, and she could give a surprise attack.

But if she'd already been taken away, locked up where no one could find her . . . what if she had to shift again?

Don't panic. You're strong, just like Jinx said. She went limp for a long moment, even though she knew it would be hard for her to pull herself back up. She heard the man carrying her curse and nearly drop her and she let him bring her close to him before slamming her head back and knocking him in what she assumed was his face with the back of her head. She heard a crack and a cry and she was dropped. She heard yells, a scuffle and she assumed it was from what she'd done. She managed to shove the hood off her face in time to see a tall, handsome man wrap his hand around one of her abductor's necks. There was a snap and the man dropped to the ground.

And then the tall human came toward her. The last thing she remembered before she passed out was an attempt to punch him in the face and then him picking her up and carrying her away from the van.

Jinx woke. Blinked. And attacked. Unfortunately, the wolf on the other end of the attack was Vice, who cursed viciously and returned the punches, even when Jinx pulled back.

"Fuck, Vice, come on."

"You started it."

Jinx weaved backward, the drugs still wreaking havoc with his system. Vice moved forward grudgingly to catch him before he embarrassed himself by falling on his ass on the floor. "Thanks. Gillian—"

"She's okay. Well, drugged and unconscious, but she'll be okay, according to Gwen," Vice admitted. "She's right next door."

Jinx pushed away to try to head that way but Vice held him fast. "Do you think you could maybe sit down for half a fucking second and get yourself together before you race away? Don't you fucking trust me anymore?"

"Of course I do." Jinx's tone came out with astonishment, especially when he realized Vice was serious. "Shit, Vice, I didn't mean . . ."

"Yeah, I know." Vice studied his face. "She's yours. I get it. And you're going through shit and

Jez is helping you. I'm helping Rogue. But you and me, are we cool?"

"We're cool."

"You're keeping shit from me. I don't like it."

"I know." Jinx stared at his bare feet, not able to say anything more.

"You're going to have to tell me what it is. All of us. You need us to get you through it."

"I can't, Vice. Trust me on this. I really can't. But I'll make it all right."

Vice shrugged. "If that's the best you can do—"

"Thank you for rescuing her."

"I didn't. Not exactly. She came to when I got there, told me that some guy rescued her from men trying to shove her into a van. She didn't remember anything, came to next to you."

Jinx raised his brows. "Find that guy."

"The twins are already on it. They wanted to wait to make sure you were okay, but I convinced them they'd do more good for you that way."

"They know who it was?"

Vice shrugged, then admitted, "Cain thinks it was a hunter. And we know the hunters can't protect her forever."

"They shouldn't be protecting her at all—that's my job," Jinx growled.

"Our job," Vice corrected. "And we can use all the help we can get. One of your twins trusts one of them—it's that fed, Angus."

Jinx muttered something and ran his hands through his hair. "Gillian wants to know her heritage—why she was given away or taken."

"Not an immediate goal."

Just then, Stray and Kill entered the room, with Stray turning on the TV.

"News conference," he said, his voice tight with anger as the screen flashed the Blackwells and a man named Joe Hinze.

The crawl under the screen showed he was a former Green Beret working in conjunction with the family on the search. In reality, the man was a leader of the East Coast trappers—and he was no doubt behind the tranq attack of Gillian.

"It has come to our attention that Gillian was spotted in upstate New York. She was with several men who grabbed her when she tried to come in with myself and the men helping to aid in the search," Joe said.

"Bullshit," Vice muttered.

"Agreed. And I think it's time to start checking into Gillian's background more seriously," Killian said. "Stray and I overheard you guys in the woods—we know she's got an ability."

Jinx shrugged. With wolf hearing, it was hard to keep anything a secret and the door had been open. "I wasn't going to hide it."

"They also know you were beaten by a girl," Vice interjected and Jinx shoved him.

"Could be a reason they gave her away," Stray said, but he didn't seem convinced either. "But I don't think they would've known that—not that early. And unless the Elders hid a prophecy from us . . ."

"The Elders, screw us over? Say it isn't so,"

Killian muttered sarcastically. "Look, the Greenland pack believes in that twin curse."

Jinx had dealt with the fallout from that twin curse bullshit for his first twenty-one years. "So I think that's the more likely scenario," Killian continued. "She was hit with the double whammy—being a twin and having an ability. Which means both probably have abilities."

"Two sides of the same coin, like me and Rogue," Jinx murmured.

"Who's going to tell her?" Vice asked and they all looked at Jinx. "Dude, I so totally nominate you."

"Dude, *why* did the eighties have to happen?" Jinx groaned. "Can't you move past it—come at least up to the nineties and I'll buy you some nice flannel and Nirvana's greatest hits."

"Don't you make fun of the eighties," Vice sniffed. "And Stray likes his hair bands."

Stray shrugged, because it was the truth. "Way better than grunge. And I nominate Vice to go talk to the lawyer who did the adoption for the Blackwells."

"Why's that?"

"Guy's a former Marine."

"*Semper fi,*" Vice said seriously.

There was no noise. The air even stilled and Angus simply froze in place as instinct took over. *Good human,* Cain thought to himself as he padded silently toward the man's back.

In seconds, Cain rolled him to the ground, his

canines sharp and hovering over Angus's neck. At least he'd had the sense to bare his neck in that show of submission that made Cain sing with pleasure, but he'd have to do this with every goddamned Were who attacked him. And, as a hunter, they would be lining up to take a shot. Killing hunters was weresport in more circles than he cared to think about.

"Good to see you too, Cain," Angus managed without moving a muscle. Cain leaned in, let a tooth scrape Angus's soft flesh and he felt the man's cock jump. He did it twice more, then licked where he'd scraped and heard the grunted intake of breath.

Yeah, can your boyfriend do that to you? I don't fucking think so.

"Are you this easy for all the Weres or am I special?" he asked finally.

"Fuck you, Cain," Angus said, but his voice was soft, not angry. Cain pushed off him, sat back on his heels and watched Angus not bother to try to compose himself or hide how turned on he was. Instead, he propped up lazily on his elbows and stared at him, his eyelids deceptively heavy lidded and lazy-looking.

There was nothing lazy about this man—he was the human form of a predator, and Cain wouldn't take any chances.

"Did you bring backup this time?" Cain asked and Angus shook his head.

"We're all alone. Unless you have Weres stalking me in the bushes."

"I do my own dirty work. Always have."

"So do I, Cain. Those men with me . . . we were working, but I would never bring anyone with me if I thought I'd see you." Angus stared at him unflinchingly and Cain felt a tug in his gut.

Cain decided to get right to the heart of the matter. "You're really a goddamned hunter?"

"Yeah, I really am."

"What the hell? Hunters are—"

"Crazy." Angus paused. "Like trappers and wolves. We formed to keep the peace. We look out for humans and wolves."

"Spare me the PR. They only accepted you because of your scars."

"So what? I've been there—on the receiving end of a Were attack. I never said all Weres were bad. But I know how this world works now, and I can't go back to the way things were for me. I have to do something."

"Like avenging whoever the hunters tell you to?"

"What the hell do you want from me?" Angus demanded, pushing off his elbows and in seconds, they were on their feet, facing one another.

Angus was getting riled again. Good. Cain wanted him angry and pissed off and uncomfortable. Anything but indifferent. That would kill Cain. "I didn't save you so you can get yourself killed."

Angus laughed then, looked up at the sky and muttered, "How is locking me up saving me?"

"You know why I did it."

Angus's stance softened slightly. "You don't

have to worry about me anymore. I'm trained. And I have backup."

"Wolves don't follow your rules."

"They don't have to follow any rules and when they lose it, we stop them."

"I'm glad you think surviving one Were attack makes you invincible," Cain muttered. "Why did you save her?"

Angus wasn't surprised that Cain had figured out who had helped Gillian. "That's what I do."

"A real do-gooder. Nothing to do with grabbing her to collect the five-million reward and getting caught by the weretrappers before you could bring her to her parents."

"I found her being shoved into a van by the weretrappers. I grabbed her and brought her straight to Jinx."

"Jinx doesn't remember seeing a van."

"Because he was drugged and lying on the ground. I know how to make people disappear, Cain. If I had Gillian and wanted her, why would I give her back?"

"I stopped wondering what was on your mind when you left."

That was like a knife, straight through Angus's heart. "She was minding her own business. She was with Jinx—I'm assuming she's not as dangerous as they say if the Dires are protecting her," Angus offered.

"You've really come a long way, Angus."

This proximity to the man was killing him. Cain's wolf wanted to smell him, lick him, taste him. Mount him, right here in the woods and he didn't think Angus would mind. "You're still playing with fire, Angus. Haven't learned your damned lesson."

"Maybe you should teach me," Angus said.

"You had your chance." It made him ache to say that. Obviously, the fed had saved Gillian—and Jinx, in the process. "We can't be seen together, for your sake. Just stay the hell away from the Dires and you'll live. Take care of yourself, human."

He pulled himself away from Angus, who looked angry and disappointed. Cain was equally so, but he wouldn't allow it to cloud his judgment.

He ghosted into the woods and still managed to feel Angus's eyes on him the entire way back to the mansion.

Chapter 28

Stray found a gold mine by sending Killian to break in to the Blackwells' safety-deposit boxes. He'd gotten the name of the adoption attorney and tracked him down in a nursing home in Ohio and Vice had left several days after Jinx and Gillian were attacked, wanting to make sure that they weren't going to need to defend themselves against an all-out trapper attack.

Thankfully, the trappers seemed to have no clue that Gillian was a Dire—or a wolf at all, for that matter. That was the word on the street anyway, according to Cyd.

Now, Vice had used his Marine background to get into the man's room, claiming that he'd been trained under him. No one here batted an eye about the age difference because no one really gave a shit. Not that they expected a wolf to come in seeking information from an almost ninety-year-old man.

Vice said he was a Marine who'd been assigned

to visit vets in nursing homes and slipped the man named Walter some good scotch and a cigar. They talked about the Marines and the like, both having coincidentally served in the same battalion, just years apart. Vice didn't bother telling Walter that he'd actually served first. Guy was confused enough by Vice's appearance.

But finally, Vice confessed the real reason he was there. "I'm in the PI business these days and I'm trying to help out a friend. She's pretty desperate to find her birth mother. She needs to know about a certain medical condition. She doesn't want to mess up the chick's life or invade in any way. But medical records are pretty important. She was adopted by the Blackwells twenty-one years ago."

Walter agreed. "That's a tough one, I know. But it was a private adoption, so the records are sealed. I don't know how difficult of a time your friend will have with the courts. They're more open about it today."

"So you remember the girl?"

"My last case." Walter stared off into space, like a dog hearing something in the distance and Vice bit back his impatience and sat as still as possible. Kill and Stray weren't right for this job because they didn't want to risk influencing an old man whose memories were in and out, depending on the day.

Vice hoped it was a really good day.

Finally, he snapped his fingers and Walter looked back at him like it was the first time he'd seen him. "Son, you wear more jewelry than my wife used to."

Vice spread his hands in a what-are-you-going-to-do posture as Walter continued, "And all those tattoos? How are you ever going to get a respectable job looking like that, Marine?"

"Heard it all before, old man. Can we move this conversation along?"

Walter stared at him and then broke into a smile. "I like you. You're not like those sycophant grandkids of mine who'll say anything to get my money."

"Not interested in your money. Interested in an adoption you brokered twenty-one years ago, remember?"

"Right. The twins."

Twins? Yeah, Stray and Killian had good instincts. "I'm talking about one girl—she went to the Blackwells. You're saying she had a sister?"

"Right, the rich folks. And one of the girls went there. The mother didn't want them going to the same family. I couldn't understand why—the Blackwells would've been able to take them on, no problem. But she insisted."

"What was her name and where is the other girl now?" he asked.

"Ah, Vice did you say your name was? My files are all locked up in storage. Can't fit them all here."

"Names, Walter. Think. Anything—first, last. City and State."

The old man scrunched up his face and then

shook his head. "I can give you a key to the storage boxes but I can't remember where they are."

"Yeah, I'll take it. I'll bring it back tomorrow." He palmed the key and tried again. "Where's the storage facility?"

Walter scrunched his face up again. Ah shit. "Walter, what hospital were they born in?"

"Not in this state."

"She had to bring you birth certificates, right?"

"She brought enough money for me to make them," Walter told him. "I had six kids to feed."

"Yeah, I get it. I'll get this key back to you."

"And some whiskey," Walter whispered. "They won't give me any in here."

"Bastards," Vice whispered conspiratorially. Left his cell number on the pad on Walter's nightstand and headed out.

On his way out of the lot, he called Stray. "I've got news. Not sure if any of it's good or not."

"Way to sell it, Vice."

Three long weeks had passed. Gillian had shifted back from Sister Wolf successfully, but the tranquilizer was wreaking havoc with her system. It was made strong enough for a Dire wolf, the way the trappers always made their darts, just in case they ever got the opportunity to grab a Dire again. Gwen was keeping Gillian as calm as possible inside the mansion while trying to flush the long-lasting drug from her system.

Gillian slept through most of the first two weeks anyway, and Jinx hadn't left her side, spending most of the time in Brother Wolf form on a stretcher right next to her so she could reach out and touch him for comfort.

She did so, often. She dreamed, too, mainly about running—with Jinx. Sister Wolf calmed her, though, and she slept and healed and finally, she woke.

Jinx was next to her on one side, curled up in wolf form. Her hand was buried in the fur in Brother's neck and she didn't want to wake him.

"Hey, Gillian."

Vice's voice. She turned to find him on the other side of her.

"You're guarding me too?" He shrugged and flushed a little, and she realized Vice was watching over both her and Jinx. "Thanks, Vice."

"Just glad you're okay."

"Is Jinx okay?"

"He'll be better now."

"Rifter was okay with him—with me—staying here?" she asked, her voice hushed.

"He wouldn't've had it any other way."

She looked over at Jinx and then back at Vice. "Do you think that things between me and Jinx are okay?"

"What do you mean, okay?"

"Like, is he with me here because he . . . pities me?"

"Gillian, is this like a girl moment? Because in case you didn't notice . . ." He stared down between his legs and back up at her and she fought a laugh.

"You're the only one who'll tell me." She gnawed on her bottom lip for a second and then went for it. "It's about sex."

"Jinx will be mad if you have sex with me, yes."

"Vice, be serious."

"That is me being serious." He paused. "Okay, keep going. But no more propositioning me."

"It's embarrassing, but I think you're the right person to talk to about it."

"That's me, a regular Dire Dr. Ruth." And he wasn't being sarcastic about it in the least. "Come on, hit me, Gillian. Nothing you ask is gonna shock me."

"Jinx doesn't want to sleep with me."

Vice narrowed his eyes. "When you say sleep, you mean . . ."

"Sex."

"Can we define the term?"

"How is that important?"

"You'd be surprised."

"Intercourse. We had it twice but it's like . . . he avoids it purposely. We do other things . . . and I like it . . ."

Vice hummed at that and she shook her head and continued, "But I feel like, maybe I'm bad at the sex thing. And I don't want to ask him because . . ." She looked at Brother Wolf and hoped the wolf wasn't relaying this to Jinx somehow.

"Ah, okay. Jinx definitely wants to have sex with you. Why he's not has to do with the mating."

"The mating."

"Yeah, it's a Dire thing. An Elder rule." He rolled his eyes. "It's one of the old ways, designed to keep us from screwing everything that moves and never actually doing a full monogamous mating. Sex for us . . . hurts. During orgasm. And we're not supposed to be with the same person more than twice. It's a way of making sure we're serious about mating."

"So it wouldn't affect me as much? Because I'm not feeling bad when I . . . you know . . ."

"Come?" he asked bluntly and smiled. His eyes glowed a little and he said, "It wouldn't be pleasant, but it definitely is more of a guy thing. Trust me, Jinx would like to nail you in every—"

She held up a hand. "I get the picture. Thanks, Vice."

She sat up and hugged him and his body stiffened, like he wasn't used to being hugged, or at least not touched gently. But then he put an arm around her, hugged her back and growled, "Don't do shit like that to me. You're going to ruin my reputation."

She wanted to tell him that the baby blanket hanging over his shoulder already kind of did him in, but she refrained. And she was far happier than she'd been ten minutes ago.

"By the way, mating involves a ritual. With chains."

"He'll have to chain me up?"

"Other way around, sweetheart."

"Ah." Now, she had to convince Jinx that it was the right time to mate. Maybe she'd just drag some kind of chains into his room . . . not subtle, but she'd bet it would be effective.

Gillian purposely waited until Jinx woke and went out hunting with Rogue and Vice before she asked Gwen if she could talk to Rifter.

"I need to see him alone," she said. "I've got something important to tell him."

"I can do that," Gwen told her and ten minutes later, she brought the big, dark-haired wolf king back to see her.

Gillian had gotten up and dressed in that short time span, and she was sitting in one of the chairs next to the bed when he came in. She started to stand but he shook his head and told her, "It's okay, Gillian. Mind if I close the door?" he asked, his voice low and she nodded.

Rifter made her nervous and she knew she owed him an apology.

As if he'd read her mind, he started with, "I don't hold any grudge against you sticking up for Jinx. You're young. New. And the mating bond is a hard instinct to deal with on top of all you've been through."

"Thank you. For that—for all your help. For letting me stay here with Jinx while I was healing." She looked into his eyes and noticed for the first time that there was a lot of kindness there—and hurt. He didn't like what he'd had to do to Jinx. Not at all. "I know Jinx got kicked out—and I know why he did it. He wasn't out of control—not really. He had to get himself kicked out."

"You're saying he got me angry on purpose?" Rifter asked and she nodded. She didn't say anything else though, and he pulled up a chair and sat next to her. "It's not betraying him by telling me. I need to know if he's in trouble. It's my job, my responsibility to help him. I also want to help him. He's my brother."

That last part softened her completely, especially because it was the truth. She could see it in his eyes. He was hurting as much as Jinx was, and that was her sole motivation in telling him what she'd learned.

"He doesn't know I'm telling you. But it's time." She swallowed hard and confessed, "During the time of the Dire ghost army, Jinx accidentally opened purgatory. He was tricked by his father. So that's why he did it. It wasn't his fault."

Rifter stared at her, stunned. "He didn't want us to know."

"Can you blame him? He's been trying to fix it. Rogue's been trying to help—and Jez, but there's a lot of . . . things—monsters—that don't want to go back."

Rifter just sat there, openmouthed and okay, it was a pretty big deal and a lot to take in. Opening purgatory didn't happen every day. In fact, had it ever actually been opened before?

"Rifter, purgatory's completely closed—"

"Okay, that's good," he breathed.

"But some things did manage to escape and they're pretty horrible and threatening to wipe out humankind," she finished.

"And that's really, really bad. I need to see Jinx. And Rogue. And Jez. You're going to have to ask them to come here and don't tell them what you've told me."

"You're not going to sell me out?" she asked.

"No. I'm going to get it out of them and get you off the hook. Jinx has enough going on and he's already trying to alienate himself from you because of all of that. It makes sense now. And I can't let him push away the best thing that's ever happened to him," Rifter told her. "But Gillian, your face is still on wanted posters across the country. . . ."

"You think the Greenland pack will be coming for me."

"I have no doubt someone's been keeping up on this news," he agreed. "They'll be worried about exposure—that we'll tell the Elders what they've done."

"The Elders didn't care what happened to Stray and Killian."

"That was prophecy. This was something different. Unexpected." He paused. "Anything else you need to share?"

"You might know this already but I have an ability. I asked Jinx if I could be the one to tell you and he agreed. It's my speed and strength. And I have no way of knowing if that influenced the Greenland pack's decision to give me away. . . ."

"But in light of what happened with Stray and Killian, I'm guessing it was more than enough of a reason," he said tightly.

"I don't want to run, but I also don't want to bring trouble onto your pack. Or Jinx. I want to mate with him. Plan to—in the ritual chains way," she added and Rifter smiled.

"We'll talk to the Elders about your ceremony once we figure the rest out. For now, you need to lay low and let us figure out the best way to help you."

"I'll do anything, Rifter. Just don't take me away from Jinx. He needs me, especially in light of what's going on with him."

Rogue was staring out the window, listening to the hellhounds circling the house. Guarding him. His head throbbed along the side where the glyphs were, and he rubbed the tender skin and wondered how this would all end.

"Gillian told me about Jinx," Rifter said from behind him. And although Rogue really wished she hadn't, it was probably for the best.

"And I'm sure you promised her you wouldn't tell me it was her."

"Yes. You'd know it was her anyway, and I know you won't hold a grudge against her."

That was true. Finally, he turned to face his king. "So now you know."

"Why didn't he tell me, Rogue? We've been through everything together." Rifter looked genuinely upset. "I've always been a brother—a friend—not just a king."

It was true—but since mating, Rifter had undergone a significant change. A necessary one. They needed a leader.

"Seeing ghosts always got us in trouble with our father," Rogue explained. "We learned not to tell anyone when bad things were happening in the spirit world. We just fixed it."

"How are you planning on fixing this?"

"Don't you get it? This was never your battle. This is mine and Jinx's. And Jez's, as it turns out. We keep you out of it—and we keep you safe." Rogue was getting angry. "Jinx can do this. You depend on him for everything. And then you don't give him the benefit of the doubt."

"That was never what this was about," Rifter said. "We've always trusted him. No matter what Kate felt. He challenged me." He paused. "Now I realize he did it to keep us safe."

"Yes," Rogue agreed.

"What can we do?"

"Keep Gwen safe. Let us finish what's been put into motion."

"Rogue, this is so dangerous."

"And that's why we were spared the Extinction—to help humankind. It's what we do, right?"

Rifter nodded. "It's what we do."

Chapter 29

Cain stayed at the apartment that night instead of the Dire mansion. Something drew him there and even though he knew what—who—it was, and even though it was dangerous as anything, he still did it.

He roamed the place restlessly. Paced the floors. Threw the windows open and let the scent come to him.

When it did, he nearly went to his knees. Time stilled and he waited impatiently, stalking the door.

When the knock finally came, his body heated as if on fire. He scented Angus through the door and opened it quickly, yanking the man inside before he was spotted.

"I wasn't followed," he said defensively.

"That you know of," Cain shot back. "You're good, human, but you are human. And why are you here, after I warned you to stay away?"

"You told me to stay away from the Dires, not from you."

"Semantics," Cain told him.

Angus yanked him closer. The move made Cain growl, his canines elongated and his eyes flickered between wolf and man.

"Don't," he told Angus.

"Trust me, it's the stupidest thing I've done," Angus muttered before he brought his mouth down on Cain's. The electricity jolted between them as he wound his fingers in Angus's short hair and let his tongue play with Angus's. There wouldn't be a fight for dominance—Angus had already surrendered. He moaned against Cain's mouth, his body melted against Cain's and Cain would take advantage of this.

Fighting it had proven worthless. Kissing Angus was right. Had been from the first. Now, Angus didn't seem worried—but Cain still was.

Worried about hurting Angus. Worried about the trappers hurting him. The hunters hurting him. At least they were semi-protected in this apartment. This was when wolves and hunters ran wild in the night and Cain would keep the man here until dawn, at the least.

All for his protection.

Angus pulled back then, sank to his knees in front of Cain. Cain held his breath as Angus unbuttoned his jeans and yanked them down. Cain stripped off his shirt and Angus sat back on his heels and just stared up at him.

"You're so fucking beautiful, Cain. Can't stop thinking about you."

Cain growled deep in his throat and he dove for the man, tackling him to the side, rolling him underneath him, pinning him there. Angus drew in a surprised gasp and then grabbed the back of Cain's head, drawing him down for another kiss. They ground their bodies together, all the desire they'd been building up over the past weeks boiling over. There would be no stopping this time, even if the building came down around them.

"Lock me in, Cain," Angus rasped.

"So you can say this was against your will? No fucking way."

"Lock me in and tie me down," Angus said, his tone a beg that went straight to Cain's cock. "Not because of what you're thinking."

Cain looked down at him for a long moment and then he realized, "You're scared. Of me."

"Not you, no." Angus shook his head, then stared up at the ceiling. "The attack . . ."

The attack he'd survived had been massive. The fact that Cain was the same species, could kill him in a second, was something they'd both have to live with.

"Please. I don't want to run away from this. Just get me through it."

Cain's expression was unreadable and Angus held his breath and prayed the wolf would consider his request.

"I don't mind the fear. But the thought of running from you . . . I wouldn't be running from *you*. I've always wanted to run toward you," Angus finally told him when the silence became too excruciating. Cain swallowed, hard. His expression softened and he pressed his lips gently to the scars on the side of Angus's neck.

Angus blew out a soft breath, because he felt the promise in that gesture. No matter what else happened next, he would remember that. And then Cain got up, pulling Angus with him, leading him to the bedroom.

"Strip and lie down," he said, and he watched as Angus did so, stared at him head to toe, his eyes glowing. Angus saw the outline of Cain's cock straining his pants and he lay down on the mattress, put his head on the pillows and tried to simply breathe, which was a lot harder than it should've been.

Cain moved after a few long minutes. Grabbed a pair of heavy chains that Angus had seen in the apartment the last time he'd been there and dragged them up next to Angus.

"Put your hands up over your head," Cain told him, his voice raw and gruff.

Angus needed him so badly. He did what the wolf asked and Cain chained his wrists together and wound them around the bedpost, effectively immobilizing him.

His breaths were fast and he shook a little, even as Cain placed a flat palm on his abdomen and the wolf's touch was hot as fire. And Angus wanted more but Cain still looked unsure.

"What are these for?" he asked as he tugged on the chains, mainly to get the wolf to talk to him.

"Moon craze," Cain said, an odd glow in his eyes. "I used to have to chain Cyd here so he wouldn't go out hunting. Do you want to talk—or fuck?"

"Fuck. Definitely." He'd spoken without hesitation, but Cain still leaned forward and unchained his wrists. Angus wanted to cry out the word "no." But he held back as he watched Cain nudge him over and then strip out of his clothes. And then the wolf handed Angus a key—the key—to the cuffs he proceeded to chain himself to.

He winced as the silver hit his skin and Angus did say, "No," this time but Cain managed, "It's fine."

"Why?"

"Better this way," Cain said simply. "You're safe, Angus."

"I always was with you, dammit." He brought his mouth down on Cain's, their tongues dueling, and soon Angus had crawled on top of him, bringing their naked bodies together. The fear was gone—and Angus didn't think the chains had anything to do with it but he would be forever grateful to Cain for thinking of this.

Next time, no chains, he thought and then wondered if there would be a next time.

He took Cain into his mouth and Cain bucked his hips up with an intensity that might've frightened Angus had he not looked into the wolf's eyes. His cock tasted salty, sweet—Angus sucked, ran his tongue along the fat head as Cain howled his approval softly. Whimpered. His eyes had changed and he was doing that glowing thing again and Angus wanted to tell the wolf that he'd loved him probably since the first day he'd seen him.

But he held his tongue on the words, used it to drive Cain crazy, until he forced the orgasm from him.

It seemed to go on for hours. Angus watched in amazement as the thick ropes of come decorated Cain's chest. He licked at it—it tasted like nothing he'd ever tasted before. Loved the way Cain groaned and growled and writhed. It made him feel strong.

Finally, he crawled next to Cain, whose eyes were closed but who definitely wasn't sleeping.

"That was worth waiting for," Cain told him, his voice husky and when he opened his eyes, they were back to normal. That helped Angus relax and he reached for the chains but Cain shook his head. "Not yet."

"Okay."

"You know what I'd do to you if I wasn't chained?" Cain asked and Angus shook his head. "My fingers would be inside of you, opening you up, readying you for me," the Were said, his voice a perfect melody of gruffness and growl. "You'd be moaning for me. Mouth hanging open. Taking everything I give you."

"Yeah," Angus agreed, closed his eyes and pictured it.

"It's okay that you can't let that happen, Angus." Cain's words were soft and when he opened his eyes, Angus saw the soft lighted glow around both of them.

"Next time, I want you to be able to hold me," Angus said honestly and Cain flushed.

"Move closer."

Angus did, lay on top of Cain, his ear to the wolf's chest, listening to the fast heartbeat. He held the key in his palm, but he was glad Cain didn't ask to be unchained because he didn't want to let the wolf go. What would happen after this . . .

What the hell did you think could happen?

Cain could sense the human's mind going a hundred miles an hour before Angus finally blurted out, "I'll get the weretrappers off Gillian's trail."

"Angus, they'll kill you. And you can't go back to the hunters either. Not now anyway."

"I can trust them."

"You've known them less than a month."

"Some of them I've known a lot longer." There were many retired FBI and CIA agents who were hunters. Lots of former military guys too—all of them who'd had the supernatural curtain drawn back for them.

"Why were you really there that night?"

"Honestly? Because there were reports of monsters running through the woods."

"And you and your band of merry men are going to fight them?"

"People are getting killed, Cain."

"And you were almost one of them," Cain shot back. Figured Angus only escaped because the hounds saw he'd pulled Gillian to safety. He'd come close enough to death to make Cain weak and he hated being weak.

"When I was with Shimmin, I heard about the hunters. Met with them in secret. Found my old FBI partner. I thought he was dead." Angus closed his eyes, curled a fist on his chest. "He joined the hunters years ago and he told me there was a place for me in the group now that I knew things. He said I'd never be able to go back to my normal life again—I could try, but nothing would ever be the same. And when you locked me in here, I knew."

"Knew what?"

"That no matter what I did, you wouldn't trust me. Wouldn't accept me fully."

Cain considered that for a moment. "But you think the Weres who are hunters do?"

"They're in it for the common good, many on loan from their packs for just that purpose."

That was true. "Packs make their own laws."

"So do the trappers. How's that working for you?"

"Why here, Angus? Why come back here?" Cain asked.

"This is where they assigned me."

A lie, but Cain let it go. "Yeah, okay. Good thing you were here."

Angus glared at him. "Actually, it is. But Gillian

is in danger. Why are the Dires so hell-bent on protecting her?"

"They're do-gooders too," Cain offered. "You're really staying with this group?"

"I see no reason not to. But I'd like us to work in conjunction with you."

"I'll be moving to Manhattan with Liam," he said carefully and felt Angus's body still.

"Is that what you want?" the man asked slowly.

"It's an honor."

"That's not an answer."

Cain didn't want to consider why he couldn't give a more definitive answer. As an omega, his guard would always need to be up. He could be easily used and also be a prime target for kidnappers. Liam told him he thought Cain's omega status should remain hidden but it was only a matter of time before his healing power was discovered.

Plus, he had special mating specifications. According to werelore, an omega's mate found him, and that mate was preordained. His mate would be the one to see him glow and Cain had no other omegas to ask because they were literally under lock and key.

He thought about the beatings he'd endured, the endless whippings where the skin had been flayed and it took weeks to heal, because he didn't dare show what he was.

They thought he was moon-crazed. Had no idea what they'd let go. "You can undo the chains now."

He sensed Angus's disappointment but the

man didn't protest, just unlocked the heavy cuffs and Cain pushed them all to the ground.

"Who did this to you?" Angus asked as he traced the scars on Cain's back. Cain let him do so for a few seconds before turning back to face him.

"My first pack, before they kicked me out. Jinx took me and Cyd in and got us through the worst part of the moon craze."

"You were lucky."

"Very. You've been lucky too. How many lives do you think you have?"

"TBD."

"The Weres are going to smell me on you. A shower won't help."

"Don't you have some super secret trick, like your glowing thing?"

Angus was joking but there was something Cain could do. Of course, it was only supposed to work on his ma—

"What the hell did you say about the glowing thing?" Cain demanded.

"When you healed me, you glowed."

Cain forced himself to breathe as Angus added, "Shimmin said that meant I was your mate."

"I told you that you shouldn't get your information on the supernatural from trappers," Cain managed to say, but he turned away to stare out the window, his heart racing.

He'd have to attempt to protect Angus and see if there was any truth to this. "There's something I can try, for both our sakes."

"Then do it."

Chapter 30

Jinx moved Gillian back into the apartment with Jez a couple of nights later, and he'd left her with Jez while he ran with Rogue and Vice to let off some steam. Since Gillian was finally awake, he didn't want to keep what they'd discovered from her any longer. And so after he shifted, he took the stairs fast and slammed into the apartment, refreshed by the run. He found her in the living room, curled on the couch and it felt so right to see her here.

He'd missed it here. Missed Jez, although he'd never admit it. And while Rifter had told Jinx that he could stay as long as Gillian needed to recover, he didn't want to put any more strain on his relationship with his king.

Gillian beamed at him. "Next time you run, I'm going."

"I can't say no to you," he told her.

"Good." She paused for a minute and then said, "I know about the mating thing."

"Ah, okay."

She put her hands on each side of his neck. "You have to know that I fell in love with you. I may have been off the market for a while, but I lived before that. I know what my heart tells me."

"It's too soon—because of your shifts."

"Vice said after the third shift, I'd be pretty safe."

He blinked and was staring at a gorgeous wolf.

"You're killing me," he told her.

She howled in response, then shifted back. Her clothes were in tatters around her and he said, "I'm going to kill Vice."

"Vice is who you think about now?" she said, and then asked, "What is it you want to tell me? I don't think it has anything to do with mating."

"You're right."

She nodded, went to grab her clothes. He knew she suspected something. That was the problem with Dires—they were all suspicious, their hearing off the chart and they could smell deception on one another.

Gillian was developing these traits more rapidly than he'd thought possible. Taking to her new role easily. Reveling in it, actually. It reminded him how good it was to be a wolf. "We found something out about your background."

"About my family in Greenland? Because I don't think I want to know. I've had enough of parents and authority figures to last me a lifetime." She was serious—he knew that—but he also figured she'd want to know about what he'd learned.

"It's mostly about your sister," he said quietly and her eyes lit up.

"I have a sister?" she asked, her voice barely above a whisper.

"A twin."

She pressed her hands to her chest, crossed them and bent forward like she was in physical pain. He rubbed a hand on the back of her neck. "Breathe, Gillian. Please."

"Where is she?" Her voice was tight, her face pale. "Don't tell me she's there with those wolves in Greenland. What if she went through the same abuse Stray did?"

God, he hoped not. "Even if that's the case—and we don't know that—she's young. She'll heal."

"We have to go get her," she said, standing suddenly and he knew that if she started running now, she'd never stop. And they'd all have a hell of a time keeping up, or catching her.

"I know. But we can't let the Greenland pack near you. You are important to me—to us, Gillian. You have to know that. You have to let us help you."

She seemed to focus at his words. Blinked a few times and then said, "Okay. I understand. But can you tell me everything you know?"

He told her, and it wasn't much at all. Barely anything to go on beyond the word of a man with faded memories and a shifting sense of time.

She was skeptical, but knowing that Vice was convinced put it into perspective.

"He's pretty sharp," she admitted. "He wouldn't let himself be lied to."

"No, not about that. The guy was pretty specific . . . and your family's hard to forget."

"But the Blackwells have no knowledge of my twin?"

"None. And the lawyer confirms he never even told them." He spread his hands and shrugged. "Cyd's going to try to trace the scent on the storage locker for the guy's files, but it's a long shot."

Gillian was up, pacing now, her wolf restless. He wouldn't be surprised if she shifted right in the middle of the living room, but she held it together. Didn't ask to go outside, although at points, she stopped in front of the large picture window, raised her palms to press against the pane, put her cheek there as if feeling the sun through the glass.

Maybe that's what she did when she was at the psych hospital, he thought. She'd been held back for so long.

"Want to tell me what you're thinking?" he asked.

"She's out there, shifting for the first time. Alone. Scared . . ." Gillian put her hand to her throat and didn't finish the thought.

Jinx didn't know what to say, because she was right. Stray would probably have to check into unexplained animal maulings but that would be no comfort to know that, at this rate, they were more than likely to find her sister through a murder report.

"Shouldn't I feel her, the way you do Rogue?" she asked, just as Cain let himself into the house, carrying bags of food and some beer and soda.

"Who's the beer for?" Jinx asked Cain, who pointed to himself, and then Jinx answered her,

"We grew up together. Slept in the same bed as infants."

"But how does it happen? How do you call for him?" she persisted as Cain cracked the first can and chugged.

"It's just . . . I've never had to think about it before," he admitted, even as he cast a worried glance in Cain's direction and wondered what the hell was going on. "Rogue can tell if I'm in pain. If I'm upset, nervous, unhappy. It's not like a psychic prediction. I'll just feel it and I'll know it's his feeling."

"So say I'm happy and get an odd nervous feeling for no reason?" she asked the unfinished thought and he agreed. "Could be your twin. But it won't help you to locate her."

"Cyd and I can pass messages to each other in our minds," Cain offered, after a loud burp. "Sorry." But he continued chugging the beer, wiped his mouth on the back of his hand and, Christ, this was going to be another long night.

"Seriously? And you never thought to mention that you communicate telepathically?" Jinx asked.

"I thought you and Rogue could do it too," Cain explained and Jinx wondered if it had something to do with the omega thing. He rubbed his head, then instructed Cain to call both their brothers.

He thought about excusing himself from Gillian for a second but hell, she'd hear it anyway and it's not like they needed to hide things from another Dire.

"They're on their way in," Cain confirmed. "They were together anyway."

"Before they get here, want to discuss what's bothering the shit out of you?"

"No," Cain said pointedly and opened another beer. "Maybe I should call them and tell them to bring more beer."

"Or maybe you could answer my question." Jinx eyed him steadily.

"Angus Young saved Gillian."

"The guy from AC/DC was in the woods?" she asked, and Cain said, "I kind of love that you know who he is."

"Are you kidding? I love their music," she said with the first smile he'd seen all afternoon.

"Okay, hold up. Before you two bond over your love of classic rock, Cain's talking about an FBI agent."

"Former," Cain said. "He's a hunter now."

"And don't hunters hunt . . . us?" Gillian asked.

"It's really goddamned complicated," Cain told her as he went to fiddle with the incredibly complicated sound system Jez had installed in here before the opening strains of "Let There Be Rock" rang out overhead. "Want a beer?"

"Yes!" She accepted one and they knocked their cans together and he half expected them to break out lighters and sway together to the song.

But hey, it got her mind momentarily off the heaviness. Cain had a gift for shit like that and Jinx forgot how much he appreciated it. Realized how much he missed that, missed him and Cyd too.

"Cain, do you want to explain . . . about Angus?" he called over the music and Cain called back, "No goddamned way!" as Jez came in and stared at the two dancing wolves for a long moment.

And then the vampire broke into a smile, announced, "I have Guitar Hero," and Jinx groaned and sank down on the couch because there was no way out of this. If he brought Harm out, this would be an eighties party extraordinaire.

He simply crossed his arms and watched them, especially Gillian, her movements fluid, graceful, her eyes glowing.

He was never letting her out of his sight again.

When Rogue and Cyd came in, they simply stared as Cain, Gillian and Jez danced around making devil horns at the sound system and singing at the top of their lungs. Then Cyd, of course, jumped right into the action and Rogue sat down next to him.

"This is what happens when you fate twenty-one-year-olds, old man," Rogue told him.

"You're only six minutes older than I am," Jinx reminded him.

"I guess that's why my knees ache," Rogue said seriously, bent down to rub them with his palms. "Did you call us here for the concert?"

"She wants to know about our twin thing," Jinx said. "How we . . . feel one another."

"You make it sound so dirty."

Jinx laughed and looked out at the group. "It's nice that she can have some fun. She's been through . . ."

"Hell?"

"I didn't say it."

Rogue shrugged. "Hell is whatever you think it is. I'm not one to lord it over everyone just because I've really been there."

"Yeah, you are."

"Of course I am," Rogue agreed.

"We're going to look into your background more thoroughly," Stray explained. "And we didn't want to go behind your back. So now that it's all out in the open, we wanted you to be . . . involved."

"Thanks for that," she said. The music blared still and the others were listening and the heavy feelings she'd managed to shed for a little while came back. She supposed that was how it would be from now on, until she found her twin. "Go ahead and talk. I'm okay with it."

Killian jumped in first. "The Arrow line . . . shit, I mean, there were three daughters around our ages, from what I remember, but Gillian could be a grandkid of theirs at the rate they breed."

"It's not like they keep any kind of birth records," Stray added.

"How about checking psych hospitals?" Gillian suggested quietly.

"All across the country?" Kill asked but Stray was already typing.

"If I set up some search parameters, I might get a hit," he said.

"Might want to check prisons too," Vice offered and ignored Stray and Jinx's glares. "Come on, man. Be realistic. If she's strong and exhibiting signs of violence like . . ." He jerked his head toward Gillian and made the universal sign for crazy by his ear.

"You're aware that I can see and hear you, right, Vice?" she asked.

"Of course he is," Stray grumbled.

"Part of his charm," Killian tacked on.

"Least someone appreciates me," Vice huffed.

"Do you have the key Walter gave you?" Stray asked and Vice nodded. "Think Cyd could track the scent?"

"This thing's passed through many hands."

"Recently, yours, Walter's and the man who owns the storage facility. That's three," Stray said and Vice shot him the finger.

"Fine, worth a try, I guess. But let's try New York, otherwise it's a wild-goose chase," Vice said.

"Maybe both twins were placed in New York," Killian said hopefully.

"Why so close to us, though?" Vice mused.

"My parents moved to New York when I was five," Gillian said suddenly. "Before that, we lived in Texas. From before I was born, my parents lived there."

"Guess Cyd and I will get our cowboy boots on," Vice said and Cyd did a loud yeehaw that turned into a howl. "We'll work on that. Come on, Were, let's go pack for our trip."

"I'm totally hanging my head out the window the entire time," Cyd said as they left the apartment.

"Do you think they got freaked out over the prophecy?" Stray asked Killian.

"It said brothers," Jinx pointed out.

"I never said the pack was smart," Killian snapped. "I guess they didn't want to take any chances."

"I wonder if they're identical?" Stray mused and Gillian left them to their searches and speculation in favor of sitting with Rogue and Cain and finding out more about this twin bond they seemed to have.

"Even with Cyd gone, I can feel him. Hear him, actually, if need be," Cain told her. "It's been that way for as long as I can remember. Close your eyes. Concentrate."

"Might be tough for her because of Jinx—that bond they have might interfere," Rogue pointed out and she was glad he'd said that. Because every time she closed her eyes, she saw Jinx's face. Not a bad thing by any means—just not what she was going for at the moment.

Still, she gamely tried everything they said. They even went up to the roof, because she felt more open there. And still, nothing.

"Just keep concentrating. Keep trying," Cain told her.

"What if she doesn't know she's got a twin?"

"But what if she does?" Rogue asked.

"Do you always play devil's advocate?" she asked and Rogue gave a wry smile and said, "Unfortunately, I have no choice."

He left her and Cain together, and Cain sat next to her as they dangled their feet off the rooftop and looked out over the buildings.

"She's out there somewhere," she said, wrapping her arms around herself.

"And we'll find her. Cyd's a great tracker. If he can't find it . . ."

"It doesn't exist," she finished and he sighed and nodded. "You know, the missing part . . . I thought it was just family. But even after meeting all of you, and Jinx, especially, I was so happy. But something still nagged at me. But she's what I'm missing."

"Sounds like it," Cain said.

"Would I know if she was . . . dead?"

"Yes," Cain said seriously.

"But if I'm immortal . . ."

"I don't know if she is. I don't know how these Dire abilities get parsed out. It would stand to reason she'd have an ability as well," Cain said. "Maybe you could appeal to the Elders?"

"Jinx forbade me to do that. And I understand why—I want nothing to do with them." She practically spat the words and Cain smiled a little. "What?"

"You're such a goddamned Dire."

"I'm hoping that's a compliment."

"It is," Cain assured her.

"And you're in love with Angus Young, by the way," she said softly.

"The guy from AC/DC?" he asked and she smiled a little.

"I hope he loves you back."

"Me too," he muttered.

Chapter 31

Cain and Vice walked out of the penthouse together after Jinx had come for Gillian. Cain was drained after his discussion with her, but helping the Dire was necessary.

"You were good with her," Vice said.

"I like her."

"Don't say that in front of Jinx," Vice warned. "You need a ride home?"

"No."

"You shouldn't be running alone, wolf."

"I'm staying in the apartment tonight," he admitted. "I just figured I'd walk you out."

"My bodyguard," Vice said sarcastically. "I guess we're going to your apartment to talk."

"I actually was going to call Jinx about this."

"Is this a twin thing?"

"It's a mate thing."

"I know a little something about that." The Dire wouldn't take no for an answer so Cain didn't bother trying. Angus was meeting him later, but if the human walked in while they were there . . .

Turned out he didn't have to tell Vice shit. Even though Cain was able to hide his scent on Angus, he could do nothing about Angus's scent in the apartment.

"It's on you, too. Faint, but it's there," Vice told him as he sprawled out on the couch and Cain locked the door behind them. "I figured it was just from when you spoke to him in the woods. Turns out, I was wrong."

"He's been here, yes."

"You've been playing with fire, wolf." Vice's eyes glowed.

"That might be why it's been so good."

Vice gave a soft laugh and Cain hung his head. "He's my mate, Vice."

"Get the hell outta town."

"Yeah, that too. I'm supposed to, with Liam."

Vice sat down next to him, handed him a silver flask and lit himself a hand roll, which Cain took from his hand and inhaled. Strong shit. He took another toke and then a few long swallows of the strong whiskey that burned going down.

"You're sure about the mate thing?"

"He told me I goddamned glow."

"I hate to say this, Cain, but he's a hunter. Maybe he heard the lore—"

"How would he know what I was? He saw me glow long before he was a hunter. He's got nothing to gain with that shit. Makes it even worse for him."

"Did you protect him?"

"I had to."

"You did. You're right." Vice lay down onto his back, blew smoke rings as he considered the situation. "Jinx would come talk to you if you called him. You know that, true?"

Cain did. But Jinx appeared to have more than enough problems. "I haven't even told Cyd any of this. I tell him everything. But this was all kinds of sacred."

"So you decided I was the right person for sacred?" He and Vice both laughed at the Dire's words, but the truth was, in some odd way, Vice was sacred.

"Vice, what am I going to do? I'm mated to a human."

"One you happen to have fallen hard for." Vice stared at him. "And dude, I'm the last one you should be asking for advice on your love life."

Cain decided he needed to tell Angus before he did anything else. After Vice left, he paced again with the window wide open until he scented the human. And blood. He had the irrepressible urge to lock the man in the apartment again and never let him out.

Because that went over so well the first time . . .

He practically dragged Angus into the apartment, stripping him down to check him as Angus said over and over, "It's not my blood, Cain—I'm fine."

"I'll be the judge of that." His mating instincts were in full force. They wouldn't be as bad as

Rifter's . . . but they'd be tough to handle for a human.

He's tough enough.

He'd have to be. He stared for a long moment at the handsome brown-haired man who was a couple of inches taller than he was and then dragged his eyes along the lanky chest, nearly growling at the old scars. His wolf wanted to scar Angus, but in the good way.

Get ahold of yourself.

Once he had Angus naked and was convinced that no part of him was bleeding, Cain threw the clothing in the washing machine and dragged the man into the showers. "Don't want you smelling like anyone but me."

Angus didn't say anything, but his stance was calm. He stroked his hands through Cain's hair as they stood under the spray, Cain still fully clothed. He didn't protest when Cain spun him around and barked, "Hands on the tile."

The human shuddered a little but he did as requested. Cain soaped his hands and spread them along Angus's back and shoulders, watched as the tension bled out of him at the gentle touch. He moved a little closer and soaped the man's chest, then moved lower to circle his cock with a soapy hand.

Angus jumped and Cain asked, "Want me to stop? I will."

"I know. And no, don't." Angus's eyes were screwed shut and his breath came fast and Cain knew it wouldn't take long. The man was rock hard.

He stroked gently even as he kept his body from touching Angus, so the man wouldn't feel boxed in. There was just Cain's hand and Angus's soft moans and he cried out Cain's name as he spilled onto Cain's fingers.

He pressed his forehead to the tile and Cain released him. The man shook and Cain realized it was in relief, not panic.

"Come on, Angus—let me finish," he said quietly, his wolf calmer now. Angus let him wash him down completely and then dry him. He wore a pair of Cain's sweats and Cain stripped off his wet clothes, which landed with a heavy thump on the tiled floor, before drying and dressing himself in a similar fashion.

Angus looked relaxed, like he could fall asleep. He also deserved an explanation. "Come on—I've got to talk to you."

"Okay." Angus let Cain tug him out to the couch, where he sat calmly, but Cain smelled the fear rising again. And fuck it all, he was nervous too. "If this is bad news—"

"It's not. Not exactly. Fuck." He slid a hand through his hair. "I don't think it is. But it's . . . unexpected."

"Cain, if you don't start telling me what it is—"

Cain held up a hand. "Okay, look, the other night you mentioned the glowing thing. And the mating thing."

"And you told me I had the wrong information."

"What if I told you that you didn't?"

Angus blinked. "I was right?"

"Yeah."

"But that means . . ."

"Yeah," Cain said softly. This was worse than an out-of-control roller coaster—too fast, too many twists and turns and he wasn't sure if he could handle the trip down. But he was balanced at the top and all it would take was one little push. . . .

Angus moved next to him, took his face in his hands. "Good."

And then the man kissed him and Cain roared down the tracks at a hundred miles an hour. He forced himself to tamp it all down, to wait for the mating instead of doing this now and possibly scaring Angus more. Because the human still *was* scared, no matter how much of a show he was putting on.

He also loves you. Cain knew that, even though Angus hadn't voiced it yet. And he let Angus kiss him, reveling in the fact that the human wasn't asking for chains or trembling. Maybe it was the bond he'd put on him the other night to cover his own scent or maybe he was just trusting Cain to control himself.

Which was why Cain would. Slowly, reluctantly, he pulled away from the kiss, kept his hand on Angus's thigh.

"Is that why . . . the smell, the shower?" Angus said, his sentences as jerky as his breathing.

"It's the wolf. He's really possessive. He's been that way since the beginning. He knew before I did, I think."

"And that's why you locked me in here."

"That's one explanation. I want you safe, Angus. If you can't figure that out by now . . ."

"I can."

"Good. Ask your questions."

"What makes you think I have any?"

"Okay, FBI."

Angus shoved him. "Fine. With this mate thing . . . even if I didn't like you—"

"You liked me from day one."

"You were a murder suspect."

"Maybe that turned you on," Cain said with a smirk. "You said yourself that you're addicted to danger."

Angus grew serious. "Are you only with me because we're mates?"

"That's not how it works. There has to be an attraction there for fated mates to even be an option," Cain explained.

"There definitely was."

"You were letting that guy touch you on purpose?" Cain demanded and Angus shrugged. "You'll pay for that."

"That's kind of what I was hoping."

Cain led him to the bedroom, where he chained himself to the bedposts again. He wanted Angus comfortable and the man had already received enough information tonight to make his head spin. And when he rutted against Cain, making the men come nearly at the same time by jerking them off together, his palm hot and sure against Cain's cock, Cain did howl, a low, harsh sound.

And that made Angus come again immediately, his body jackknifing, the look of surprise on his face making Cain flush with pride. It took several minutes before he got his breathing under control and Cain wanted to rip the damned cuffs off and hold the man.

As if Angus knew, he finally pushed himself up on his elbows and used the key. Cain brought his hands down around the man's shoulders. "Is this okay?"

"Holy mother of God," Angus muttered in response.

"I'll take that as a yes. But what would the nuns you grew up with say?"

"Probably that I was going to hell," Angus admitted. "And right now, I could give two shits. I mean, what was that?"

Cain nuzzled his neck. "The wolf's pull is strong. Just means your body's accepting it. Submitting to it."

"I've never considered myself submissive."

"You're not going to have a choice with this."

Angus stared up at him. "Somehow, I don't think I'm going to mind much. Are you doing that protection thing again?"

"For now, I have to do it every time we're together." His mate was protected, but still so damned vulnerable until the true mating happened. "I don't want to rush you, but I can't have the normal human courtship, Angus. There's too much at stake. Too much danger," he explained. "Wolves work fast. When an omega finds his mate, he usually claims him within twenty-four hours. That's why my wolf's getting controlling and impatient. I can't hold it off much longer."

"How does it all work?"

"I mark you as mine. It protects you, but it also could make you a target."

"What happens when . . ." Angus shook his head like he didn't want to go there.

"When you die?" Cain asked and Angus nodded. "I only get one mate. I mate for life."

"But you'll live longer than me. How is that fair to you?"

"Already trying to hook me up with someone else?"

"No," Angus said so quietly the word almost didn't register.

"What happened tonight?"

"The blood was another hunter. He got into it with a trapper at a bar. No big battle or anything. I just played medic."

Cain nodded. "You're marked as a hunter now, but you know, that will have to end."

"I never said I was giving that up. You can't ask me to do that."

"The fuck I can't," Cain roared, pinning Angus to the bed. The ex-fed struggled, put up a better fight than most, but he was no match for the wolf.

"Is this how every fight between us is going to end?" Angus asked as he looked into Cain's lupine eyes.

"You are fucking lucky you're cute."

"Cute?" Angus huffed. Tried to ignore his raging hard-on as Cain traced the scars that ran along his neck to his shoulder, then along the bite marks on his chest made by a wolf named Jamie, who'd risked his life to help Angus and the Dires. Not a bad reminder of where they'd been.

Cain had a feeling Angus had brushed over this marking thing too quickly, and although he was reluctant to bring it up, he figured he'd put all his cards on the table and see how badly Angus reacted. "There's a little more to this mating thing."

"I'm not wearing a dress but I'd consider running around naked under the moon."

"I'll take you up on the second one," Cain said.

"Look, I know," Angus said.

"What do you mean?"

"After Shimmin told me, I explored the lore a bit." He swallowed a little harder than normal.

"And you're freaked the fuck out."

"Some. But I trust you."

"You still have nightmares about what happened. Every night," Cain said. "Don't lie."

Angus remained silent and Cain touched his arm. "I try to stop them before they start—that's why I wake you."

"I thought that was for sex."

"Well, that's kind of a bonus."

"Thanks." Angus paused. "When you bite me, you link your life span to mine, right?"

"Or in this case, yours to mine." Cain said somberly. "But I'm hard to kill. And you won't age. You'll heal faster."

"But I won't turn into a wolf."

"No. But I'll still love you."

Angus grinned. "Where do you have to bite me?"

"Wherever I want," Cain said. "Gotta leave a visible scar so you're marked."

"And then everyone who sees it will know I'm yours."

"Yes," Cain answered absently. He was still trying to decide if Angus was better served with a public mark or a private one.

"When does this happen?"

"Soon. I just have to get permission first."

"Permission to mate?"

"Permission to stay here, with you."

"You're giving up your place in Liam's pack."

"It's not safe for you there," Cain said.

"You can't keep me in a bubble forever."

"I can try, human. I can try."

Chapter 32

After everyone left the apartment and Jez went to the roof, Jinx turned to Gillian.

"You need to run."

"I need more than that, but we can start there," she said honestly.

He made a call to Vice, who promised to have wereguards posted and they got onto Jinx's Harley and headed for the protected woods. He was surprised she'd waited this long without asking.

Despite all the danger hanging over them, this was another oddly playful run. She'd barely been able to contain herself, cut loose as soon as she got into the woods.

He followed her scent, deeply arousing, and he thought maybe he should turn around because there was no way he'd be able to resist her. But Brother Wolf drove him forward like they were on autopilot, unable to resist Gillian any more than he could a siren's song.

When he got to the place where her scent was

strongest, he couldn't find her immediately. He hadn't shifted yet, and he spun around looking for her, reluctant to call out and break the silence.

He sensed nothing nefarious, but he would always worry. Being what they were was fraught with peril. Nothing would change in this lifetime.

But mating with Gillian would make it worth it, no matter how much the thought made him pulse with fear.

"Gilly, come out and play," he called quietly and she jumped him from behind. She flipped him. Straddled him. And her hand went to his throat again, a makeshift mating collar. His stomach tightened at the thought of that—at the thought that she still wanted that, despite everything she'd learned.

She was holding him down. He bucked up but it didn't come close to throwing her off. She smiled a little, gripped his wrists and held them above his head.

"Now you're just showing off," he muttered.

"But I think you like it." She ground against his erection and he bit back a groan. "I want to tie you up. Hold you down. Take you."

"Gillian . . ." Why bother protesting? He let the tension go out of his arms and she slunk forward and began to kiss him, hard and sweet and, oh yeah, he could get used to this. Because, oddly enough, the ghosts that usually hovered had gone silent during this. And while they usually did leave him alone during intimate times, they'd gone away long before the intimacy had started.

But caring about the ghosts became of little importance when Gillian reached between their bodies and unzipped his jeans.

"I'm so glad you go commando," she whispered.

So was he. And apparently, she'd taken to going the same route, because when she slid out of her shorts, her bare sex brushed his cock. Her shirt was long enough to cover them, which he preferred, because even though they were deep enough into the woods, he didn't like the idea of anyone seeing her but him.

Jealous alpha male much?

"You know the rules, Gillian," he told her. They couldn't have sex this third time without bringing the wrath of the Elders on their heads. The third time had to be a true mating or they'd risk not being allowed to mate at all. And he didn't see any of the mating chains out here, although he'd run to the house to get them, if she asked.

She didn't, but continued to rub against him, kiss him, hold him down and he was arching against her, a howl rising inside his head.

"Got to let me protect you, Jinx," she murmured against his cheek as she stroked against him.

"This isn't fair."

"I know. Never said I had to fight fair."

Why was he even fighting this? She had the strength, speed . . . he knew she had the mental fortitude. "Why do you want to do this for me?" he asked finally and she stopped, looked surprised.

"Because I love you, wolf. And you love me."
She said it so simply and easily, it awed him.
"That's what it's all about, right? I'll protect you
because I love you. You'd do the same to me. You
have done the same for me."

"You're twenty-one. I'm like—"

"Old. You're old," she teased. And then she
bent down again and kissed him, released his
wrists and his hands went around her.

"I want to mate with you," he said against her
mouth.

"Yes," she told him.

"You don't understand—I want to mate with
you—right here and now."

"Oh." Her eyes widened. "Then my answer is
still yes."

"Good." He rolled her to the side and stood.
"Wait here. Don't move."

"Try to stop me," she told him.

He backed away because he didn't want to take
his eyes off her and he called for Vice who came
running like a shot, his white wolf coming to a
complete stop directly in front of Jinx. He shifted,
asked, "Where's the fire?"

"It's ah . . ." In my fucking pants. "Can you
keep the others away?"

"Because you don't want them to know you've
been beaten by a female again?"

"Because I'm going to mate with her, despite
everything. If she'll have me."

Vice cocked a brow. "I'm the first to know?"

"Yeah."

Vice smiled and tossed him a pair of handcuffs, because Vice wouldn't be Vice without always carrying something of the sort. "Go get 'em, wolf."

When Jinx came back minutes later, Gillian expected to see him dragging the heavy mating chains with him. Instead, he had a lone pair of handcuffs already attached to a wrist.

He leaped onto her and then rolled himself easily back under her. He was so graceful when he moved. She loved that he was strong enough to handle her. Because he was, no matter who won the wrestling match. He had the strength exactly where it counted.

"You didn't change your mind, did you?" he asked.

"No. But I thought we needed chains. Special ones."

"Fuck traditions. We'll make our own, and Odin help anyone who tries to tell me that I'm not your mate," Jinx growled, his eyes going lupine. "Go ahead and give me everything you've got."

Jinx's words were an immediate aphrodisiac—a dare, a promise, and she kissed him. His tongue lapped against hers, dueling for the last vestiges of domination he'd have tonight. And he was willing to be submissive for this—for her.

They were already both naked, needy and willing. His cock lay heavy and rigid against his belly and he reached down and stroked it a few times while watching her.

She liked that, especially because he used the

hand that had the cuff around it. "I could get used to having you bound."

He stared at her. "So could I."

The rumble of his voice was enough to make her blood boil. She leaned forward and he continued stroking himself while he took her nipple into his mouth and sucked hard, enough to make her cry out in pleasure. She felt more wild than ever—completely free, uninhibited.

Jinx would be hers and she his, forever. She'd wanted this from nearly the moment she'd seen him. And she'd never felt anything more right in her entire life. "I love you, Jinx."

He smiled up at her, his eyes heavy lidded. "I love you, Gillian. I'm ready to mate with you. To face whatever comes next together."

With that he let go of his cock and she put both his arms over his head, cuffing them together, a concession to tradition. The rest of the bindings would be symbolic, but no less meaningful.

And then, as had happened before, a hand went to his throat and Jinx bared it for her to get a better grip.

"This is . . . during mating, this happens," she whispered. Vice had told her about the chains, but not their placement. Still, she suddenly knew exactly where one of them was meant to go.

He nodded. "I'd wear a collar. And I like this one very much."

She'd been making this unconscious gesture from the first time they'd been together. She kept her hand there as she used the other to stroke his already hard cock before bringing herself down on it, inch by inch.

"Don't worry about hurting me, Gilly. You wouldn't. I know that," he managed and she was a little worried, because of her strength and her newness at being a wolf. She didn't always have the control she would've liked. But Jinx trusted her.

She pushed herself all the way down so he was completely buried inside of her. Her womb ached with need but she remained still for a long moment, wanting to never forget this feeling, this moment in time.

Jinx was slightly more impatient. He groaned, arched his back so his hips jutted up, filling her. She held to him tighter, instructed him not to move.

He smiled, did as he was told. She loved this power, the way he trusted her not to hurt him. She knew she had to have an uncontrolled shift for this to work . . . and he would remain still so as not to spook Sister Wolf.

Don't worry, Sister told her.

And she didn't, rocked against him as pleasure seared her body. She moved faster and faster, closed her eyes, unaware of anything but her harsh breaths and Jinx's groans. She leaned forward and held his arms down, even though he hadn't moved them at all.

"Harder—take me harder," Jinx growled, and that alone made her come as though he'd commanded it.

When she opened her eyes, she was Sister Wolf, standing next to him, raking his shoulder with her claws. Jinx growled, his eyes lupine but he remained still as she marked him, stalked him, jumped on him and huffed.

Finally, she shifted back, in a daze. Jinx's arms were around her, his blood on her chest as he hugged her, turned her and fucked her on all fours while she cried out. Her moans rose, the air around them sticky and sweet. When she climaxed, wet and hot against him, he went over the edge as well, calling out her name.

It was done. They were mated. And there was no separating them now.

Chapter 33

Liam came upon the skirmish that Cyd called about, with a group of outlaw Weres who weren't getting with the new program. Cyd had gone to lay down the law, but it was turning into a fight.

Liam needed to be on-scene. He drove the big, bulletproof truck through the darkened streets, his blood thrumming with the need to fight. Everything for him was amped up these days, almost as if he was a newly shifted wolf. The adrenaline churned in his gut and his hands ached from fisting them along the steering wheel.

He'd gotten used to fighting, to defending his honor, and he liked it. He didn't know if his father's first days as king had been like this, but Linus had taken the kingship away by challenging their old, corrupt packmaster. Liam had heard stories of that fight hundreds of times.

Your father would be proud of you, Vice assured him hundreds of times over the past months. He'd never expected the ferocious Dire to deal with his neediness, but he'd learned a lot about that wolf. Never wanted to be his enemy or meet him in a dark alley, but with Vice on his side to teach him, Liam knew he could lead this pack long before he was supposed to be ready to do so.

And now, Vice was taking care of the baby.

He shoved those thoughts out of his mind as he came across the small battle. Cyd was fighting three Weres and apparently he'd already killed several more.

He wasn't the only one fighting, though. Violet was there. This time, with a red bra underneath the white shirt, army green cammie and high black boots she was kicking ass with, and his reaction was visceral. His body tightened, his dick on auto-drive and he could take her now, make her his and he had no fucking idea why or how.

His wolf liked the idea so much that he found himself walking toward her, to help her. When she tore the outlaw Were's throat out and stepped back, he realized she didn't need help at all.

She still bore bruises from their fight and it didn't seem to bother her. "What the hell are you doing here?"

"Fighting. I'll prove my worth to you if it kills me," she told him. He hadn't seen her since she'd watched over him that night, but apparently, she'd been working with Cyd.

You gave your approval. "Today, it might kill you."

"Better to die on your feet, right, king?" she asked, but there wasn't a trace of sarcasm in her tone. She jumped then and he went for her, but she was over his head in seconds.

When he turned, he saw she'd taken out an outlaw Were with her hands on its neck before wheeling around to defend Liam again.

No *way* was he letting a female fucking save him.

But you just did.

It couldn't be put off any longer. Vice escorted Cain inside to see Rifter and Liam, filling the role that would normally be Jinx's.

Vice also carried the baby strapped to his chest in some kind of papoose thing, but Cain didn't say a word. Because Vice actually seemed calmer. Happier.

Just then, Jinx walked through the living room. "Sorry I'm late—I didn't miss it, did I?"

Cain looked at Vice, who shrugged. "Figured you need all the support you can get."

"Silent support, in my case," Jinx said. "Safer for all of us."

Cain nodded and took a few steps farther to where Rifter and Liam waited in the kitchen for him. Cain had asked both wolves for this face-to-face meeting and now, he almost chickened out. Vice pushed him forward gently and Cain was grateful for that, more so when he saw the look of concern on both Liam's and Rifter's faces.

"Thank you both for seeing me," Cain started. "I have something of great importance to share with you both."

"Report," Liam said and Cain nodded in deference to both kings.

"Angus Black is . . . back."

"Back in black," Vice sang. "Come on, you're telling me you could resist that?"

Rifter ignored him, Liam bit back a grin at his mentor and Cain's heart beat so loudly he knew the entire room could hear it.

"Wolf, sit," Rifter ordered and Cain did so as the dizziness swept him.

"Cain, what's wrong?" Liam—friend, protector, king—looked so concerned that Cain felt even more guilty.

"He's . . . he saved Gillian. He's a hunter," Cain said.

"We know that," Rifter said.

"And he's my brother's mate," Cyd added. Cain cursed under his breath, hadn't heard his twin enter. "I'm expecting that not to be a problem."

There was dead silence as both wolves blinked at Cain.

"It's true. I didn't know it until a few days ago. I had to be sure."

"And it's not a problem, right?" Cyd pushed. Rifter growled and stood, the chair slamming back behind him.

"It's not," Liam said without further hesitation as he also stood, seemingly to calm Rifter from Cyd's prodding.

"Cyd is protective of his twin," Laim said to Rifter. "He doesn't mean any disrespect."

"It's the only reason he's not flattened under my boot," Rifter said.

"Cain, I know your mate's chosen for you," Liam continued.

"The attraction's been there from before I knew," Cain admitted.

"The fates know what they're doing," Rifter said. "An omega's never mated without love. Omegas die without true fate."

Cain was grateful for the understanding. But there was more to his mating with Angus before it became complete and he didn't know how the hunter would react.

"I'd like Cain to stay here, with us," Jinx said. "Safer for him and his mate, although I know he'll be missed in New York."

Jinx, coming through in the clutch. "That's what I was thinking, Liam. I'd still be honored to be your omega, if you'll have me."

"It's an excellent plan, for the good of the pack," Liam said. "I'd like to take Cyd."

"You need him," Cain agreed.

"You have to tell Angus everything," Jinx told him and Vice broke in with, "I'll tell him."

A chorus of No's in unison answered him.

"Explaining mating to Gillian was enough," Jinx growled.

"And you're *welcome*," Vice said with a smile.

Chapter 34

That next night after Jinx and Gillian's mating, he and Rogue needed to go hunting. Gillian stayed home reluctantly, because pictures of her were circulating and there was even more interest in the case because of a rumored press conference being held the next day by the Blackwells.

The newscasters speculated they were going to up the reward. The whole thing made her sick to her stomach.

Jez was here with her, but for the last half an hour, he seemed . . . distracted. More than that, actually—he seemed downright out of it. He was on the phone, pacing. Whispering. And then he went into his bedroom and closed the door and she decided there was no time like the present.

She'd gotten herself into this mess—she'd have to be the one to get herself out. She wasn't hiding forever, wasn't getting shipped off to some strange pack. And she wasn't going to get cut out of Jinx's life that easily.

She didn't exactly sneak out—Jez was yelling now and no one stopped her as she walked out the door and went down the stairs. She took one of the two Harleys she found in their parking spaces, using a helmet only because of the risk of being seen.

The Harley she'd grabbed the keys for was Jez's—it was sleek and smooth, not at all like Jinx's noisy one. She felt like a predator on Jez's bike, had to make sure not to go over the speed limit. But oh, it was tempting. She promised herself a ride on this tonight, when the risks were smaller.

Already, she felt freer, even though her heart was beating wildly from nerves. She parked the Harley at the edge of the property, in the woods, before the security camera line, left the helmet behind. Hopped the fence and walked up the driveway, knowing there were silent alarms going on all around her.

She was still wearing Gwen's clothing, but it fit her well. All black, a cute T-shirt and jeans, flip-flops, all things the Blackwells did not like. They still dressed for dinner nightly, while she stripped and shifted under a full moon. Different strokes.

She stared at the mansion and tried to decide what was so different about it from the Dire mansion. The proportions were similar from the outside, although her parents' house was cozy in comparison to the massive rooms and ceilings hidden inside the Dires' house. But still, she felt a thousand times more comfortable there than she ever had in Blackwell Manor.

She'd been most comfortable at Jinx's place, but

she pushed down that emotion. One thing at a time. If she freed herself from this, took the bounty off her head, she wouldn't have to go into hiding.

She was tired of hearing about the Greenland pack. Maybe she'd meet them one day, on her own terms, but she'd be damned if she'd be pushed into their arms. Paws. Whatever.

The cameras would pick her up by the time she was halfway up the driveway. She was surprised no one had come out to greet—or grab—her but she had the feeling she was being watched. No doubt, they were closing a circle of people around her, ready to entrap her.

"Do you not see me walking willingly to the door," she muttered under her breath as she spotted two men in the bushes to her right. They were aiming something at her—probably tranquilizer guns and she did not relish the thought of being drugged again. Ever.

She quickly rang the bell, knocked a few times and her father opened the door. So yes, if he'd done that instead of the staff, he'd definitely been tracking her movements by camera.

"Hi, Dad," she said with a small wave. His face contorted a little and then he regained his composure.

"Gillian, you've come home."

"I've come here to talk to you," she corrected. "Can I come inside?"

"Of course. Gilly, this is your home."

No, not anymore, but she bit her lip to keep from saying so as she stepped into the parlor. It all looked the same—pretty, polished. Lifeless. She turned midway through the hallway but her father urged her onward to the main living room.

Her mother waited there, pacing anxiously. It was the most movement she remembered seeing from her mother, a small, frail woman who was always in bed with a headache or some other ailment. When she did entertain, it seemed to suck every bit of life out of her, and she always sat like the queen in the middle of the event, letting people come to her.

Very effective.

"Mother, hello," Gillian said now, keeping her voice low.

"Oh, Gillian, I'm so glad you came to your senses."

Well, yes, that too. She sat down on the couch across from her parents. A woman dressed in a starched black uniform brought the ever-present tea set and poured her a cup. Gillian mixed more cream and sugar than she normally would have, caught her mother wincing.

"Sorry," she muttered, took a sip and put the cup down so they wouldn't notice her shaking hands. God, she was nervous, and the rustling in her ears wasn't helping.

Sister Wolf hated it here, and she was making her opinion known.

"Look, I'm sorry I caused you worry when I left the hospital. I didn't mean to. I just had to . . . find myself. And really, I did. I'm better. I'm twenty-one now. I'm ready to be on my own."

"Oh, Gillian," her mother said with a sad shake of her head, like, "Oh, Gillian, you're so deluded it's not even funny." And her father added, "We're not supporting you."

"No, I don't expect you to at all. I'm okay. I've got a place to live. A job." Technically that was true as the Dires were tasked with helping humans. A nonpaying job but none of the Dires had asked her to contribute. She had the feeling they were quite comfortable in the money department. "I'm happy. I came here because I want you to know that. I'm not . . . sick. I can't explain it, but everything that happened over the past years . . . well, it's all okay now. I'm fine. And I just wanted you to know that. I'll be okay—I am okay. So I'd like you to call off the dogs. I'll stay out of the media and just live a quiet life."

"Gillian, that can't happen," her father said sternly.

"But it is happening. You can't put me back in a hospital without my consent."

"We can ask a hospital to hold you for forty-eight hours until a doctor assesses you."

"Do I seem like there's something wrong?" Gillian asked calmly. "I wish you'd believe me."

"I want you to move back in here, not the hospital," her father said and for a minute, she thought they really believed she was better. But his next words proved that was the farthest thing from the truth. "You'll have your own doctor, round the clock. You're sick—you just don't realize it."

She hadn't thought it would be easy. She'd

never win this argument—she just hoped to come out unscathed. "I need you to respect the fact that I've made this decision."

"You don't have a choice, Gillian," her mother said sadly, and at those words, her anger rose. She swallowed her temper, not wanting to prove them right about anything.

In her calmest voice, she asked, "Where did you find me?"

"What are you talking about, honey?" Her mother wrung her hands together, urgency in her voice. "Dave, tell her she's sick."

"I know I'm not your biological child." She stared between them, looking for any kind of tell, but there wasn't one. They were good. But why the big secret? Plenty of people were adopted. There was no shame in that.

Although, with the Blackwells, continuing the line was important. Hiding her and her faults, more so. But using her to front their philanthropic efforts . . .

"You need to get back on your medication, Gillian. You'll feel much more like your old self," her father explained with a logic she used to believe in.

When had she begun to see through the act? There was the normal parental rebellion for sure, but she'd taken it further. The more they disapproved, the more she'd pushed. Until . . .

"Your temper caused the death of your classmates."

"Dave, we promised we'd never tell her," her mother cried out.

"She has to know the consequences for what she did. What could've happened to her if we'd told the truth."

She was shaking her head, standing and backing away from them like that would make what they'd said disappear. Out of sight, out of mind.

"Gillian, please. We promised the judge and the doctors—the families of the victims—that you'd forever remain in custody, watched by a doctor. If you don't, we have to put you in prison."

"Prison," she repeated. "I don't understand any of this."

"Because you didn't remember what you did. Dave, it wasn't her fault—it was the horrible mental illness," her mother said.

"I don't know what you're talking about—why you're lying about everything!" she yelled, right before she felt the prick of a needle in her neck. She whirled around and drop-kicked the man who'd stuck her with the tranquilizer, threw him across the room without thinking. Sister Wolf was enraged, gearing up to be uncontrollable, which Jinx and the others had warned her about and, yes, this had all been a huge mistake.

And there was no turning back from it.

She fought as long as she could, the hallway leading to the front door seeming to stretch out as she ran toward it, a never-ending kind of hall as she ran on jelly legs.

They'd used the same amount of drugs they did at the hospital—the dose was enough to take her and her wolf down, no matter how hard she fought.

Gillian woke up slowly. Her head throbbed, her face was sticky and when she touched it, she realized she'd been bleeding. She ripped a piece off the bottom of the T-shirt she wore and held it to the cut to staunch the bleeding, because there was nothing else in this literal cell that would help.

A mattress on the floor. A small window she couldn't escape from—and it was barred anyway—and cold, hard cement floor and walls. A door that looked solid. She stood and tried it anyway. The doorknobs bent under her touch and she frowned at that. Why would someone bother to make a prison like this and use shoddy equipment?

She tried the handle again and only succeeded in ripping it off, which was no help to her. She crushed it in her hand, the metal cutting her. But it seemed to heal quickly. Just like her head. She felt for the cut that had reopened and there was nothing.

Only then did she realize that the knob wasn't the issue—she was. She'd never translated her strength into being able to do things like this, but she was getting stronger on an hourly basis, it seemed. And none too soon.

She stepped back and readied herself, gave the door a hard kick with the bottom of her bare foot and waited for the pain.

There was none. Instead, the door flew open

and she realized she hadn't needed to kick that hard. She walked out and found herself in a maze of hallways. It was only when she reached a staircase that she knew exactly where she was.

She was home.

There were running footsteps above her head. She waited, crouched in the dark corner, because in order to get out of here, she would have to get upstairs.

The door opened with a creak and she heard lots of talking. They must have hidden cameras upstairs, watching her every move.

She heard, "She's out . . . door's off . . . impossible."

Impossible.

"It's the sickness. I've heard mental illness makes people do things they normally couldn't do."

Her mother's voice. They had no idea Gillian was a wolf. That in and of itself actually made her feel better. If they'd known all this time . . . if they'd been using her . . . well, that was worse than locking her up because they didn't know how to deal with a perceived illness. Not by much, granted, but still.

"There were marks on the side of the van . . . looked like they'd been made by animals," her father was saying. "One of the men swore he heard barking."

She smelled them now. The hellhounds. They were protecting her because she was Jinx's.

And they would kill anyone who they thought was hurting her.

She had to get out of here, lead them away from this house, her parents, or there would be a bloodbath. And as she moved to walk up, prepared to leap past her parents, when they met her halfway up the stairs, she simply froze at the fear in their faces.

"You can't leave, Gillian," her father said in a tone of voice she'd never heard him use before. "You're violent. You've hurt people."

"I didn't do what you're saying. It was a car accident." She wanted to believe it—she did believe it—but she couldn't remember anything about the night in question.

"There was no car accident. We told you that."

"My legs were broken."

"You were tied down after it all happened, for your safety and everyone else's. Look at the pictures." Her father shoved them at her angrily. He looked at her as though he'd never seen her before, like she wasn't even his.

Because she wasn't. But they wouldn't—couldn't admit that. They could only pretend to take care of her because they loved her.

She slid the pictures out of the folder, glanced down at the first one on the pile and nearly vomited. It showed dismembered people. She forced herself to stare at them. She recognized the faces of the dead . . . three of her classmates. She saw deep claw marks and bites on their flesh.

"You did this. You scratched and clawed at them. You strangled them first. And then you did horrible, inhuman things to them. You were like an animal," her father told her as her mother sobbed behind him.

"I didn't do this. I couldn't have."

"You're violent. You attacked people at the hospital."

She had. She couldn't deny that, but never anything close to this. It looked like the work of a wolf, but she hadn't been one until days earlier. She hadn't done this. But who had? "Where did they find me?" she demanded.

"In the corner, crying. You were covered in blood but there were no marks on you. The doctor said you had some kind of psychotic break."

That's what had happened. It wasn't the car accident. . . .

What she'd witnessed must've been so terrible that she blocked it from her memory to this day. Although she felt horror at the pictures, she honestly couldn't remember those people, that night, at all. "Everyone really thinks I did this? You both think I was capable of this?" she whispered.

"We didn't want to. But you did it, Gillian. We have to take responsibility because we adopted you without knowing your background. You have to take responsibility by living under the conditions we all agreed to, for the safety of others. You're a danger. You need to be locked up," her father said, and Gillian's shoulders sagged.

Someone had set her up. How and why were the biggest questions and would remain unanswered for as long as she remained on lockdown here.

If she broke out, the bounty on her head would intensify. They would hunt her down. This story of what really happened that night might leak out, no matter how carefully her parents had buried it. "It wasn't me."

"Gillian, you don't know how badly I want to believe that," her father said sadly.

"I'm going to prove it to you, Father, if it's the last thing I do," she whispered as she felt the air move behind her. There were men approaching her. She smelled the drugs they carried, couldn't let that happen again.

It was either go through her parents or fight and get drugged.

"Please move. I don't want to hurt you."

Her mother gave a soft gasp. Her father said, "You couldn't possibly hurt us any more than you already have."

She jumped onto the railing, balancing herself and her parents jumped away in surprise, leaving her just enough clearance to move by them. Sister Wolf was struggling to get out, but she couldn't let her. Not here.

"Hold on, hold on, hold on," she kept repeating as soon as she ran through the hall. There was security at the door. With guns.

She veered left and leaped out the plate glass window closest to the woods that backed up the estate. She did it how she'd seen Jinx jump, limbs and head tucked to hopefully prevent glass from cutting anything major. She hit the ground still tucked in a ball with a hard thud and then, ignoring the pain, she went on, speeding through the night.

She was leaving a blood trail. She shifted, knowing Sister Wolf would heal faster. The blood would also get caught on the fur and leave behind less of a trail. Her wolf led her deep into the woods, circling as she went in an attempt to lose the men.

They're going to send the dogs after me. And then the dogs from hell that protected her would go into damage control. She needed help, and fast.

She threw her head back and howled.

Jinx recognized the howl instantly. It was as distinctive as Gillian herself.

"She's trapped," he told Jez, who he'd met in the woods behind the Blackwells' house. Jez had called him, frantic that Gillian had escaped. He'd trailed her here and Jinx couldn't be angry at the vampire because he'd never seen Jez this distraught.

"I was distracted," he muttered. "I know better."

"She's out, Jez. We'll get to her," Jinx said and then a howl came up and they both froze.

"We'd best do it before the hellhounds decide to help her," Jez said in a slightly strangled tone of voice just as Gillian broke through the small clearing, shifting from Sister Wolf as she did so. She was obviously much faster than the men shooting at her through the trees, but they were still coming. He moved to grab for her as Jez said, "They're surrounding us from all sides."

"Gilly."

"I'm okay," she told him. But she was bleeding and covered in glass and obviously distraught. And she smelled as though they'd drugged her, which explained a lot. "I can't see anything, but I feel it. The same thing I felt the other night." She moved closer to Jinx and he stared at the circle of hellhounds that sat around them, at the ready.

"I think trappers are coming to the aid of the Blackwell security team," Jez said. "Rogue's getting the truck as close as he can."

For the first time in his life, Jinx hoped to hell the trappers backed off.

"Jinx, what are you going to do?" Jez asked.

"Whatever we need to," Jinx said. Fighting would give them away. So would shifting. They were trapped and the hellhounds knew it. He whispered, "You leave them alone," but this time, they weren't listening.

One minute they were there and the next, gone. He couldn't see them anymore, only the men coming at them with UZIs and the trappers coming along the other side. But then came the bloodcurdling screams and the men all stopped in their tracks.

Rather, they were stopped.

To the average eye, it looked incredibly violent but oddly so. Humans were getting slashed, ripped apart by something invisible. Gillian moved away from the bloodbath, hid against a large tree, pressing her face into her palms as though that could make all of this go away.

Jinx wished it could be that easy. Calling off the hounds now wouldn't make a damned bit of difference. He'd been in danger and so had Gillian. They were pledging their loyalty.

Trappers weren't exactly innocents, but surely, no one deserved to die like this.

"We need to run, Gilly," he managed and together, they ran through the blood and gore, Jez flying along with them into the night.

Chapter 35

This time, Gillian made sure to keep pace with Jinx, refusing to leave him behind. Jez was somewhere above them and finally, in the distance, she saw Rogue's truck waiting for them. The back doors popped open and she went in first, followed by Jinx. His door wasn't fully closed before Cain took off. Rogue rode shotgun and he turned to check on them.

"We're okay," Jinx managed and he was lying, but she understood why. They were all three shaken to the core by what they'd seen. The hellhounds were no longer taking any kind of direction from Jinx. She supposed she should be grateful that they hadn't turned on them.

Or maybe we just got away in time.

She shuddered at that thought and Jinx put a firm hand on her thigh. "It's going to be all right."

"You're angry I turned myself over to them. But I had to give them one last chance." And they'd let her down again. "What they believed me capable of . . ."

"They aren't . . . they don't know wolf. They saw the signs, misinterpreted them." Jinx flailed for an explanation. "Fuck, family can let you down sometimes."

She reached out, traced the scratch marks on his neck, half-hidden by the collar on his jacket. "Is this from family?"

"Yeah. I asked for it. I deserved it," he muttered. "Where are we going?"

"To the mansion," Rogue answered.

"No argument," Jinx said.

"I think the vampire's on the roof," Cain told them, but he drove fast anyway. "I'm assuming he's good at hanging on."

Jez was, jumped off unscathed in the Dire's garage and helped Rogue get the couple out of the truck. Gwen was waiting for them, led Gillian into one of the examining rooms and started by getting the glass out of Gillian's skin. It was an excruciatingly long process but Gwen did it expertly, carefully digging out the smaller bits that had been embedded.

She'd forced herself to start to heal fast. But her skin had healed over the bulletproofed, double-paned glass, which made the removal process worse than it had to be. Gwen told her that so she could keep it in mind for next time. Because, for the Dires, there was always a next time.

"I was worried they'd track the blood," she explained. "I thought the glass would push out."

"It's all right. You did good, Gillian. And you're safe," Gwen assured her. But she looked over at Jinx and Jez and Rogue, knowing they all heard the not-so-gentle hum of the hellhounds vibrating the house.

Whether they were protecting them or waiting to attack was anyone's guess.

"I'm almost done," Gwen said. If she heard them, she didn't acknowledge it, but she was in deep concentration mode. "There. You're good. I'll just put on ointment and they'll be healed up before morning."

Morning was the only thing that would get rid of the hellhounds. At least that was the way it worked in the past and Gillian had never been more grateful for a sunrise in her life. After Gwen dressed her wounds and helped her sponge off and dress, again in Gwen's clothes, which was getting to be habit, the female Dires joined the males up in the kitchen.

They were all there, and Jez as well, gathered around the table, sitting on counters. There was coffee and breakfast and Vice was holding the baby and looked perfectly comfortable doing so. The dichotomy wasn't something Gillian thought she'd ever get used to.

"I owe you all an apology, especially Jinx," she started and all eyes turned to her. "I went to try to get my parents to stop running the stories. I thought if they saw that I was all right, they'd back off. But now I know why they're so anxious to keep me locked up."

Her voice broke a little and Jinx was by her side, his arm around her shoulder. She could do this. "I don't know if it's true, but I don't remember it."

"Tell us, Gillian," Rifter said and she nodded, told Stray, "Look up this date."

She rattled it off and Stray typed fast into the ever-present laptop in front of him.

"There's nothing," he said with a shake of his head.

"It's buried. A small article, nowhere near the front page."

"I found it," Stray said. "It's pretty innocuous, just mentions a few teenagers killed in a home invasion. But it doesn't give names or anything."

"I can give you names," she said, and she did, listing the three teens savaged that night. "I was there. My parents think I killed them. And I saw the pictures . . . the damage was done by a wolf. A Dire wolf."

They all stared at her, stunned. She continued, "I must've blacked out. Blocked it out. I still can't remember what happened. All I know is that the police found me and my parents told them I was in shock and then made up some story about drunk driving to me. I agreed to let them put me in the hospital, to get better, but they'd planned on locking me up and throwing away the key so what really happened would never leak out. I was the only witness. The kids who were killed were from prominent families."

"There's still an active investigation on for the killer," Stray told her. "You're mentioned as being traumatized and unable to remember anything."

"I want to see those pictures," Rifter said.

"I'm on it," Stray said. He left the room with his

phone and Jinx urged Gillian to sit down at the table. Even though her nerves were on overdrive, her stomach growled and she couldn't deny the need to eat. She had to keep her strength up, be prepared for anything.

Gwen passed her hot food and coffee and they all ate in relative silence, save for the baby's cooing.

"We don't think you did it, Gillian. Just for the record," Killian said finally and the others nodded in agreement.

"How can you be so sure when I'm not?" she asked.

"We've got pretty good instincts," Jinx told her.

"I don't even think you would've been capable of what you're describing," Gwen added.

"She'd have to have been shifted," Rifter agreed, just as Stray came back into the kitchen. After a few taps on his laptop, he turned it over to Rifter. "Good thing someone owed me a favor— this shit was buried by the Blackwells."

"These markings were definitely made by a shifted Dire. There's no way she did this," Rifter confirmed and Stray agreed as everyone but Gillian had a look over Rifter's shoulder. "But a wolf definitely did."

"And it left me alive. Which meant . . . it knew what I was," Gillian murmured. "A wolf tried to frame me."

"A Dire," Rifter said. "Which means the Greenland pack knows where you are. They have known."

They all let the enormity of that—and the implications—settle in.

Finally, Gillian said, "If I had nothing to do with it, why did I just sit there and let it happen?"

"You were in shock. Or maybe the drinks were drugged. There's nothing you could've done." Gwen's voice was gentle.

"I need to remember that night, Gwen. Can you help me?"

"I don't know how to use hypnosis. That would be the only way I can think of, and I don't even know if it would work on a Dire," Gwen explained.

"I can do that. It's not exactly hypnosis, but if you invite me in, I can find the memory," Jez offered. She'd almost forgotten he was here, sitting quietly in the corner.

"Like a dreamwalk," Rifter said, turning toward him.

"Similar. But I don't think you can walk into a memory she's not having," Jez told him. "She'll actually be telling the story as she relives it. But she still won't remember it. And I think that's best in this case. So are we going to do this?"

"Yes." She was putting her mind in the hands of a vampire.

And you're a wolf, don't forget that.

Yes, nothing was ever going to be the same.

"I can only do this because you're a young Dire," Jez admitted, as though he didn't like giving away his secrets. "I'll zone you out. You'll go to sleep and you'll wake up fine when I bring you out of it."

She nodded and Jez walked over and touched his palm to her forehead. Her eyes closed automatically. She was aware of sleeping, practically on her feet, but that sensation was overshadowed quickly by the flickering of memories—everything flashed through her mind, like she was flipping through a photo book . . . until she got to that night and she walked into the memory.

She was warm. A sticky August night, a small party at a friend's house before they went out to a club.

"I was grounded, so I had to sneak out the window," she said, heard herself talking even as she watched herself walk out the window of the Blackwell Estate, sneak through the woods and into a waiting car.

"It's Jory. He's waiting for me in his convertible. We drive alone with the top down, music blasting." She felt her hair blowing in the breeze, smelled the smoke from Jory's cigarette. When they pulled up, she said, "It's Julie's house."

Julie McFadden, heir to McFadden Enterprises. Her parents, like Gillian's, were rarely home. This night was no exception. She knew all the others there, said their names out loud as she looked at each of them.

"I started drinking right away. Shots. Some champagne." She tasted it. "I took a few hits from Jory's bong. We put on some music. It's all casual and fun and relaxed."

It was the kind of night where you'd never expect anything to go wrong.

She reached out to grab Jory's hand when it all went to hell. She didn't know if she was actually holding Jez's hand or not, but she wasn't letting go.

Not until Jory was ripped away from her. Her hand, arm ached from being jerked from his grasp.

What was it? She didn't look. Couldn't. She slid down the wall, buried her face in her knees. She couldn't block out the screaming. All she could do was wait for her turn.

Look up, look up. . . .

But she hadn't. She stayed curled up until the screaming stopped and hours had passed. Until day turned to night and the day staff came. And then there was more screaming.

She didn't know who was lifting her, taking her away, the smell of blood in her nostrils.

"Gillian, come back to me." Jinx's voice, a seductive whisper. Her bad-boy wolf.

She opened her eyes. "I want to take a ride on the back of your bike."

Jinx nodded in agreement. Gathered her in his arms and walked past everyone to the garage. She climbed on behind him, wrapped her arms around his broad chest, tucked her head against his back and welcomed the blast of cold air.

Jinx drove fast, like he was trying to outrun both their demons. The harder he pushed the bike, the more it vibrated between her legs, revving her up. She let everything fall away into the wind. And when he stopped, she opened her eyes. They were in the middle of the woods, and as much as she wanted to run, she wanted Jinx more.

Rifter was furious, but he'd managed to hold back until Gillian left with Jinx so as not to scare her. "I want the leader of the Greenland pack. I want to fight him. I want his head on a stick."

"And then what happens? You take over their pack?" Gwen asked.

"Yeah," Rogue said. "They'd be under his kingship. Which, technically, they should be anyway."

"I guess the Elders forgot to mention that," Stray said. "We'll help with anything you need, Rifter. But we've got to figure out why they'd set up one of their own like this. She was a baby—she couldn't have done anything. And why frame her? Why not kill her?"

Rifter stilled. "Because she can't be killed."

"Which meant they knew about her ability from before she was born. We all had ours from birth, but they didn't manifest until we were a couple of years old," Kill pointed out. "But you're right—it's the only thing that makes sense."

"There's a hidden ability that her family would've known would come out. So they tried to hide her in the human world. It's entirely possible the Blackwells had no idea what she is," Gwen said.

"Killian can make a list of families," Stray started.

"Or we can find out more from the Blackwells," Kill finished with a look at his brother. "We can make them want to tell us."

Together, the brothers could. "We have to know what they know," Stray agreed. Kate was near him, slipped her hand inside his. "I'll go with you."

"I have to think about that," Rifter told them. "It's a risky move."

"He's right," Killian said. "It's an ingrained memory—a horrible one."

"Just give us a moment," Rifter said and they all left him alone with Gwen. "What's wrong?"

She was fisting her hands on the table in front of her. He saw the tears blurring her eyes. "I can't help all of you."

"You've helped, Gwen. And as years pass and people come and go, you'll be able to walk more freely."

"If Jinx tells the hellhounds to kill our enemies, no one would ever know. I can't be used against you."

He stroked her hair tenderly. "You know as well as I do how wrong that would be."

"I know. But it's tempting."

"That's why we have to get rid of them." He tugged her so she was standing, pulled her close. "Never forget that you saved us, Gwen. You saved me. You made me a real king."

"I feel like that's broken up the family," she confessed.

"Growing pains. We're all going to be fine." Whether or not he believed it, he would do everything in his power to make Gwen believe it.

Jinx took Gillian back to the apartment, found Rogue and Jez there waiting for them.

"You guys okay?" Rogue asked.

Jinx nodded, but Gillian stayed silent, sat down at the table next to them as Rogue continued with, "We can't stay here."

Jinx told him, "There is nowhere to go that she won't be recognized. If we refuse to run now, if we stand our ground . . ."

"One of us will get captured," Rogue finished.

"No way. I will never let that happen," Jinx said fiercely.

"Who are you kidding? You'd sacrifice yourself—I know you would, brother, so don't try to deny it," Rogue shouted back and Jez was nodding in agreement. "Even the vamp thinks so."

"But the vamp also doesn't think we should run," Jez said.

"Then what?"

"If we can prove to the Blackwells that Gillian had no part in the murders . . ."

"They'll take away the reward and let her live her life," Jinx finished.

"That sounds like a plan," Rogue said, a heavy dose of sarcasm in his voice. "We'll get right on figuring that one out."

Gillian looked dejected and Jinx shot his brother a look.

"Shit, I'm sorry, Gillian. I just think—look, we know you didn't do it and you know you didn't. You can't change the Blackwells' feelings about it. I say we just disable their campaign."

"The families who lost their kids think I'm guilty. I'll have to live with that," she said. "I guess it brings them peace. And it all happened because of me, anyway. It really was my fault—my parents weren't far off at all."

"You cannot take on that responsibility. That

was a sick wolf who did that. You never would've killed like that."

"On a shift, maybe?"

"You did shift. You weren't violent, were you? Did you have an urge to kill innocents?"

No, she hadn't. "Do you think it was my real mother or father who could've done that to frame me?"

"I don't know. But I'm going to find out. I can promise you that." He paused. "Did they hurt you?"

"Not physically," she told him. "I'm sorry I put your family in danger."

"Your family," he interrupted. "You thought you were helping the situation."

"I didn't mention you at all. Just in case. They're not going to drop it, though."

"Not without a major incentive," Jinx agreed. "I know just how to give it to them."

"They didn't care about me. It was all about their reputation."

Jinx put an arm around her. "I'm sorry, Gillian. I know what it's like when family lets you down."

"You mean Rifter?"

"No. I've let him down. I mean, my parents. Rogue and I went through a hell of our own growing up. It was a long time ago, but I think it's possibly the worst betrayal. If you can weather that, you can weather anything."

"I don't have a choice."

"Always a choice," he told her.

Chapter 36

When Rogue left, Gillian was nearly dead on her feet, so Jinx insisted she get some sleep.

"Nothing you can do right now. Everyone's working on something," he told her. "The best thing you can do is stay alert."

Finally, she agreed and after he made sure she didn't need anything—and she didn't, since she was asleep literally seconds after she put her head down—he walked back out into the living room to find Jez on Skype with someone. Several someones, by the sound of it. He waved to Jinx as he spoke to the screen.

"Yes, it's a relatively new development. Yes, the cell phones as well. Everything's changed. Privacy is nearly a thing of the past. You must be very, very careful," the vampire was explaining. "And no, you shouldn't post videos to that thing called YouTube. A very big mistake."

There was more talking through the speakers and Jez shook his head and looked upward before saying, "No, I don't think any of you need a Twitter or Facebook account."

More talking and then, "Yes, I'm aware that I'm no fun."

And then Jez went silent, as did the screen and he looked up at Jinx.

"Whoever that was sounds like they know you well," Jinx said. "They got the no-fun part."

"I *am* the party, wolf, and you know it." Jez leaned back and closed the computer's lid carefully, ran his fingers across the smooth metal, looking very much like he wanted to say something more. So Jinx sat at the table across from him, staring at the Chinese take-out menu he'd practically memorized and he waited patiently. Because if the vamp needed to talk, well, he'd listened to Jinx more times than he could count.

"Those were my brothers," Jez finally said and Jinx raised his brows. "They're the reason I fucked up so badly tonight with Gillian. I hope you can forgive me, but hearing from them was quite . . . unexpected. Wonderful as well."

"Are those the others you mentioned to me—the ones that were waiting in the wings to help the Dires when needed?"

"Yes," Jez told him. "That's them. There are eleven of them. I'm the twelfth, the youngest."

"Explains a lot."

"Shut up." Jez managed a smile and then he grew serious again. "My brothers were gone—lost to me for thirty years."

"That's when you started following me. That's

when you moved here," Jinx said. "You said it was ordained."

"I might've stretched the truth on that. You opening purgatory, that was ordained. I would've done that even if . . ." He took a deep breath and said, "My brothers were released from purgatory when it opened. They'd been wrongly imprisoned there and I had no way to get them out on my own. But I knew you'd be opening purgatory and so I was able to watch you. To help you."

"You knew your brothers would be imprisoned in purgatory and you couldn't stop it from happening?"

"We didn't know when it would happen—or how. Just that, thirty years later a great wolf would free them and we would owe him everything." He stared at Jinx. "I was supposed to be locked in purgatory with them. It was a stroke of . . . luck, shall we say, that I escaped. Although there've been many times over the years I wished it otherwise. But no matter what, I owe you a great debt. We all do."

"Where were you when they were taken?"

"I was resting in a different nest when the spell was cast by a powerful warlock. I knew where they were . . . and I knew about the prophecy. So I'm in your debt."

"And these deadheads I freed?"

"They're cool."

"They're from purgatory."

"Because they're undead. All vampires don't go to hell, you know."

"Sounds like hell is preferable. Did you use me?" Jinx demanded.

"No, wolf. I knew what was going to happen and I was sent to protect you, regardless of what happened with my kind in purgatory. I couldn't do anything to aid them—once you opened the door, it was up to them to claw their way out."

"And they did?"

"And they did," Jez confirmed. "They're now dabbling in social media and buying up cell phones. And, as I told you, I'm indebted to you, as are they."

"No one needs to be in my debt."

"Everyone needs a favor now and again. Consider us your twelve favors," Jez said. "Like your kind, we have certain burdens to bear for being what we are. Gifts are given, but they always come at a price. We knew this from the start, we accepted our fate."

"You had a choice?" Jinx asked.

"In the beginning, yes," Jez said quietly. "I can't tell you more. Not now, wolf. It would put you in danger. And I wish I could've told you about this earlier, but I didn't know if everything would come to pass at this time. Things could've gone wrong."

"I thought they did," Jinx muttered.

"You'll meet them one day. I think you'll like them."

"As much as I like you?" he asked and Jez looked as if he was waiting for the punch line. But there was none, and when both wolf and vampire realized that, there were small smiles of understanding.

"You're not a half-bad roommate, wolf," Jez told him. "But the sex on the roof is cramping my nighttime style."

"Do you think they can help with this other situation?"

"Maybe."

For the first time since it happened, Jinx allowed himself to think on it. To relive it. He'd hear the screams in his ears for a long time to come. "I didn't tell anyone. Not even Rogue."

"I'm sure he knows," Jez said quietly. "You're not responsible. I know what you're thinking, but don't. You may think you have some level of control over these beasts, but no one truly ever could."

Jinx looked down at his hands. "I should've tried harder. Done something sooner."

"We knew that the monsters were getting antsy, but we weren't seeing anything crazy on the radar. Small possessions, yes. I guess they were testing their limits. They don't like being put on a leash. Pretty soon, they're going to want to inflict terrible pain and when they do, it's going to be hell on earth. Brother turning on brother. We're talking irreversible damage if you can't get this shit under control."

"Do you have a plan?"

"It's in the beginning stages, but yes," Jez assured him. "I think, tomorrow night, we'll have to try to send them into hell."

"I'm not letting Rogue do that," Jinx said fiercely.

Jez looked odd as he agreed just as fiercely, "Rogue isn't going anywhere near hell again. I'll make sure of it."

Jinx didn't push the vampire further, but something told him that they would all be sorry long after this was over.

Kate, Stray and Killian had FBI badges, thanks to Jinx. The wolf was good at supplying them, although he'd never tell where he got them.

"I'll take point on this," Killian said.

"Wouldn't have it any other way, brother," Stray said, attempting a joke that came out more hollow than he'd hoped.

"Brother, it's going to be all right. I'm not going to let you face this Greenland shit alone," Killian told him. "Your life's different now."

"You've got us," Kate added and Stray felt himself relax a bit.

"I know. Let's get this over with." He pushed the doorbell, heard the low clang. A member of the staff, dressed in butler clothing, answered the door and guided them into a dark paneled study.

"This place is huge," Kate whispered.

"Our house is bigger," Stray scoffed and she smiled.

"Yes, honey, yours is definitely bigger."

"Funny," he said as Mr. and Mrs. Blackwell walked in, Mr. Blackwell leading his wife with a hand on the small of her back. She looked whippet thin and ready to fall over at any moment, although her handshake was surprisingly strong. "Mr. and Mrs. Blackwell, I'm special agent Garcia, and these are agents Weir and Lesh. We're here to ask you some questions about your daughter."

Mrs. Blackwell motioned for them to sit and she did so on the leather couch across from the chairs the butler had moved so they were all facing one another. Mr. Blackwell poured himself a scotch before joining his wife on the couch, and Stray was surprised when he handed it to his wife, who downed it.

"The FBI was here the other day. I told them everything I know. They said the reward was a bad idea, but I don't give a damn."

"I understand that you want her back," Kate started, but he waved a hand at her.

"No, you don't understand. She's dangerous. She's going to hurt someone." Mr. Blackwell put a hand over his wife's. "It's imperative that you find her."

"We're here to ask you some other questions," Kill told them. "I think you want to answer everything we ask you honestly."

"I want to answer everything you ask honestly," Mr. Blackwell repeated and his wife nodded her agreement.

"Gillian's adopted, correct?"

"Yes. We got her when she was four days old," Mrs. Blackwell said. "We were so happy. We got the call and we picked her up and went to our house in Texas and stayed there for a while. Told everyone that she was ours, that I'd given birth while I was away on our year-long cruise of the world."

"Who called you?"

"Our lawyer said someone contacted him. We never knew who it was," Mr. Blackwell said. "I can give you his name."

"Please do."

"The thing is, you know Gillian isn't dangerous," Killian said.

"She's not dangerous," Mrs. Blackwell agreed.

"She doesn't need any drugs or hospitals. I think you can let her live her own life. Call off the search. Take down the reward money," Killian told them. Stray read their minds and saw that Killian's ideas had taken root. The problem was, neither wolf knew if the change would stick permanently. The longer the original memory had existed, the harder it was to replace.

Chapter 37

Cain was waiting in his truck when Angus came to his apartment. Angus got in the passenger's side.

"I'm hungry. Mind if we grab food at the diner?"

"Works for me," Angus said. He smelled like Cain, and Cain realized he was wearing one of his T-shirts.

His wolf definitely approved—Angus could tell by the glow in the Were's eyes. Cain reached out and slung a hand possessively over Angus's thigh as they drove and Angus wondered if the wolf would always be like this—or if his possessiveness would get worse.

Angus wouldn't mind that, he realized.

"You're nervous," Angus said suddenly.

"Little bit. I talked to Liam and Rifter."

"Let me guess—they want to kill me."

"Maybe. But they won't."

"Great reassurance," Angus said with a snort.

"Listen, there's a lot of chatter from the trappers about Gillian. About why the Dires are protecting her."

Cain nodded, but didn't offer up any *Gillian's a wolf* explanations. He supposed plausible deniability would be effective that way.

"Are they circling the wagons?"

"They're staking out the woods at night, more heavily than normal," he admitted. "They need that reward money."

"Jinx said that the weretrappers lost a lot of ground—and a lot of money," Cain explained. "That money would help them a lot."

"She can't hide forever, unless she goes deeper underground." He'd worked with enough witnesses and some U.S. Marshals to know. "I could make some calls, try to get her help if she needs it."

"It's under control, but thanks." Cain parked and looked at him. "You know I'll tell you more when I can. This is more about you—the less intel you have . . ."

"The less valuable I am," Angus finished. "If they believe me."

Cain frowned and then he did that thing with his hand on Angus's bare chest. The scenting protection thing, even though he obviously wasn't worried that they'd be out in public together. And then he said, "We're here."

Angus finally looked out the windshield of the truck up into the blinking sign that said MO's. "Never been here."

"It's a little more out of the way," Cain agreed as they got out of the truck. Angus froze when his feet hit the pavement. "What's wrong?"

"There are snipers on the roof," Angus said without moving his lips or looking at the roof. Because it took a sniper to know one.

"Yes. Mo's is a family-owned diner."

"Family of weresnipers?"

"Something like that. And they're for your protection as much as theirs." Cain motioned him to follow, led him inside and toward the back. They ordered and Angus had just finished his meal and Cain was starting in on his third when Angus realized the real reason he'd been brought here.

The man walking toward him was a rock star in every sense of the word. His career spanned centuries, Angus knew that now, but this most recent incarnation had garnered Harm fame and fortune in the band Knives n' Tulips.

It made sense now as to why he was moody and his concerts started so late.

He stood and met the six-foot-seven-plus wolf face to . . . neck. Stuck out his hand and Harm shook it without hesitation, said, "I didn't kill any of those women."

Harm was the reason Angus had come to this town. He'd been tracking the rock star for years, since he was a suspect in a long string of murders. Turned out that the murders had happened for hundreds of years, which is what led to Angus's interest in the supernatural to begin with.

And now, he was face-to-face with the man—

wolf—he'd hunted for so long. "I believe you're innocent, especially after the evidence Cain gave me."

"I'd like to see all your evidence. I'll share mine. I need to find this wolf. You're not the only one investigating me," Harm said.

Ellen came over, took his massive order. Cain just shrugged and finished his fourth burger.

"We can compare. I need help with this. It's what hunters do, right?" Harm asked and yeah, Cain was going to find Angus jobs within the hunter realm that kept him close to home. Well played, wolf.

Cain's eyes glowed for a minute, like he'd read his mind, and the soft glow around his body circled around him as well. Angus's heart filled.

"Okay, yes, I'll help you, Harm."

"For a human, you're not that big of an asshole," Harm said.

Angus could only hope that was a compliment.

Chapter 38

When they pulled up to Pinewood, there were several other parked cars hidden along the side of the road toward the woods. Jinx looked back at Gillian and Rogue, who rode in the backseat, and they both shrugged.

He turned to look at Jez, but the vampire was already out of the car, walking toward Rifter, who was with Stray, Killian and Kate. Jez shook Rifter's hands and then turned to Jinx and said, "We need to talk."

"What's going on?"

"I have a plan. It's going to work, and we need to execute it now," Jez said. When they'd first left the house, Jez told them they were simply coming here to test a theory.

Jinx let the lie go, said, "Okay, so tell me."

Jez straightened, stuck his chin out. "I'm going to lead the monsters to hell."

"And you waited to tell me until right now?" Jinx demanded.

"Yes. Because if you had time, you'd insist on a viable alternative."

"What's wrong with that?"

"There's not one," Jez said sadly. "I'm the viable alternative to your brother doing this. After what happened the other night, things are only going to get worse. Fast. Once I get the hellhounds and monsters to follow me, they'll be gone—no more haunting for you, except your ghosts, of course." He paused. "I don't think it will help Rogue's hell problem, though."

"Why would you do this? Did you always know, the way you knew I'd open purgatory?"

"Yes. I'd hoped there was another way but I was prepared for there not to be."

Jinx couldn't blame him.

"You have to let Gillian help you. Let her ease some of your burden. She wants to. It's what her wolf is telling her to do. Don't protect her so much that you smother her," Jez told him.

"What are you, the Oprah of vampires?"

"I prefer Dr. Phil. He looks . . . tasty."

"For the love of Odin—TMI," Jinx muttered.

"Listen to me, wolf—"

"I've spent my life listening. Doing the right thing. Doing what I was born to do. Guess what? What I was born to do was open purgatory."

"And free my brothers. My family," Jez pointed out.

"And that's a good thing?"

"Yes, it is," Jez said quietly. "Rebellion isn't always wrong. Rebellion brings change. But you can't change the fact that you see ghosts any more than you can stop your love for Gillian. If it's freedom you're looking for, well, maybe Rifter will give it to you without the snarling and the snapping."

"I don't snap. Poodles snap," Jinx huffed. "Jez, you just got your family back."

"They sacrificed. They paid. And they'll help you while I'm gone. Your legacy was to lead the monsters out of purgatory and free my brothers and mine was to lead the monsters back into hell."

"Why didn't you say something earlier?"

"I wanted there to be another way," Jez admitted.

"Jez, there has to be."

"You've got to promise you're not going to try to get me out. You have to promise me."

"I can't do that."

"I can't let you fuck with it. Not you or Rogue. You're too tied to it—too many things can go terribly wrong." Jez touched his shoulder. "I appreciate you wanting to do that, especially when you wanted to kill me a few short weeks ago."

"Not kill. Maybe maim a little." Jinx forced a smile. "We have to find another way."

"I haven't seen a way around this from day one. I'm not sure how much longer we can let those things roam."

Jinx knew he was right. But to have to give the undead that kind of death sentence was unthinkable to him. Jez was stoic, but not exactly happy.

"Rifter knows about this—I went to him first, out of respect for your kind," Jez explained.

"Please go to him. Make peace while I'm still here to see it. It will give me comfort to know you're with your pack again."

Jinx pushed the tears back and nodded. Reached out and embraced the vampire, who hugged him back and then pulled away fast, as if afraid he'd never let go.

"Go, Jinx," he urged and Jinx went to Rifter.

"Rifter, I'm—"

Rifter shook his head and reached out to trace the scars he'd left along the bottom of Jinx's neck. "*I'm* sorry."

"Ah, Rift." The wolves embraced and it was like they were young wolves again, surviving the Extinction.

When they pulled apart, Rifter said, "Please come back to the mansion. You and Gillian. I realize you've mated and might want to spend time alone and that's fine. But I'd like the mansion to always be open to you."

"I'd like that," Jinx said and Gillian was next to him, her hand in his. The other wolves looked relieved but troubled at what was about to happen to Jez. They'd all grown fond of the vampire.

"I can't believe . . . he's watched out for me and now . . ." He trailed off and Rifter said, "Let Jez have his honor."

Jinx could only nod.

"It's time, Jinx," Jez told him. Jinx turned to see that the vampire's fangs had elongated, his eyes black as polished marble and he walked backward, watching them all.

Jinx swore he noted a slight tremble in the vamp's body, but then Jez straightened and whistled. The hellhounds shook the ground as Jez circled them.

"Dammit," Rogue swore from behind him.

"I know. There's no other way," Jinx said, his voice breaking. He looked behind him and saw that the other Dires were there—for solidarity. He and Rogue and Jez were the keys here. Kate had sprinkled a heavy salt circle around them and they all stood inside of it and watched.

Gillian gripped his hand tightly and Jez walked into the middle of the cemetery and called for the hellhounds. They came at a rapid pace and the monsters followed as well.

"He's got a job for you—listen to him," Jinx forced himself to call out. The words nearly died in his throat but the look Jez gave him made him play his role.

Once he'd said it, Jez gave a smile, almost angelic and that was something to see on a vampire.

From the safety of the circle, Jinx and Rogue joined hands and began to chant the ancient prayer Jez had given them. They'd memorized it in case the wind picked up and ripped it out of their hands. At first, getting the words out was hard, because it seemed as though there was an outside force working against them. But they persevered and repeated it three times, and halfway through the fourth time, it began to happen.

Jez fell to the ground, as did the hellhounds. The smoke seemed to scream into the night and everyone covered their ears against the sound. The ground beneath their feet shook like a great earthquake had come, and then there was a blast of blinding red light. Jez screamed then, like he was burning alive and the smoke attacked him.

Jinx moved to leave the circle, to help his friend, but Rogue held him back. "No, Jinx. Don't you dare."

Jinx struggled as Jez continued to yell. In a matter of seconds, all of it—the smoke, the hellhounds, the vampire, were absorbed into the hot flashes of light and then there was nothing at all.

Chapter 39

Vice scented Liam before he saw him. Vice was in the living room, lying in a daze on the couch because the kid seemed to work on little to no sleep and still wouldn't stay with anyone for long periods of time without fussing. Now, he was asleep on Vice's bare chest as Vice flicked through the millions of channels and found nothing to watch.

"He's asleep," Vice offered when Liam edged in, hands stuffed in the pockets of his cargo pants. Liam nodded and slid into a seat that let him look at Vice but not get any closer. Vice pulled the blanket over the kid a little higher. "I know this is hard as hell for you."

"Yeah." Liam looked lost.

"You need my help with something? I can call Gwen."

"I need your help, but you don't need to call Gwen." Liam clenched his jaw and said, "I know I can't ask this, that I've asked too much already.

But if I keep him . . . I don't know if I can ever fully accept him into my pack. But if he's yours, Vice . . . if he's yours . . ."

"You will accept him." Vice stared down at the innocent charge on his chest and maybe for once in his long life, he was speechless. It was the last thing he'd expected to hear from the young king, the Were he'd saved months earlier, the one he'd been training nearly nonstop.

The one who'd been through some of the worst personal pain, dealing with the loss of his father and his mate.

"Yes," Liam managed. "I've been wrestling with this, Vice. I didn't know the right thing to do, but after hearing about the baby having bonded with you . . . I knew the right thing, for both of you."

Vice blinked and cradled the babe in his arms. Wanted to say, *I can't be trusted with a half-human, half-Were life, not with my general fuckedupitness*. But Liam was looking at him like he could. And hell, he'd been put in change of making Liam a king.

The wolf before him was nearly there. Would be, once Vice agreed and so he did. "I'll keep the Were and raise him as mine. When he comes of age, he can choose to pack with the Weres or the Dires. No matter what, he'll always have a home with us."

"Thank you, Vice. I can never repay you."

"Good thing you don't need to try."

It was done. How hard could raising a babe be, after all? Couldn't be any worse than a Were's teenage shifting years, right? And he'd made it through Cyd and Cain's general insanity.

The baby woke then; his eyes were shining bright and a laugh emerged from his throat as he stared at Vice. And just then, Vice knew exactly what his name should be.

Chapter 40

It had been forty-eight hours since Jez walked the hellhounds and dragged the monsters kicking and screaming into that hole in the earth. Gillian still couldn't get the image out of her mind, and she knew Jinx and Rogue weren't faring much better.

"Do we have to contact his brothers?" she asked now. Jinx had told her and Rogue and the others about the other eleven vampires.

"I tried his computer but it was wiped clean. He said if we needed them, they would come," Jinx said. "Maybe they just sense us?"

"According to Jez, they all knew what he needed to do on his end," Rifter reminded him. "I'm sure it's a blow to them as well."

Rogue had his head on the table, was staring into space. "We have to get him out of there."

"I know." Jinx put a hand on his twin's arm and Gillian's stomach twisted as she thought of her own twin out there, confused and alone.

"As much as I hate to say it, we still have a

pressing problem," Stray reminded them. The TV was on mute behind them and Gillian knew if she turned around, she'd find news of her parents upping the ante on the reward. They'd gone into overdrive since her escape but from what she'd seen, they hadn't mentioned having her in their grasp. The thoughts Kill tried to plant hadn't worked exactly as they'd hoped, since her parents were now saying things like, "She's been seen in the vicinity of this house. We think she may be trying to hurt us."

She would make them believe she was innocent. Had to. She put her fingers on her temples and massaged them now, thinking about everything that had happened. The memory Jez had triggered was still there, and she could access it over and over, although it was still like watching a TV show. It was still as if it hadn't happened to her.

Huddled against the wall, refusing to get up. Whatever the wolf had planned, he wouldn't just stop, right? The Greenland pack had to have been following her—or that wolf had, at least.

Was he out in the woods looking for her? Surely the Dires wouldn't have given a thought to scenting another Dire in the woods. But how else would he get to her?

"My parents," she breathed.

It was so obvious, she didn't know how she hadn't seen it sooner. Gillian knew she had to go back to the Blackwell mansion, had to go to her parents to try to warn them. Jinx and Vice were with her in the woods; the others were in the area, waiting for the signal.

She wasn't sure what she would say to the Blackwells, but Killian and Stray promised they could change her parents' memories if things got bad and they discovered she was a wolf. Since that would be a new memory, it could be easily discarded.

Now, in the woods, she could still smell the blood. The hellhounds must've completely obliterated the bodies, because as far as Stray could see, there had been no reports of any of that.

There was no real plan of how she was going to tell them. Gwen had suggested using the phrase, *serial killer stalking* and Gillian rolled that on her tongue, trying to make it all sound plausible.

She would not bring up wolves.

"Killian and Stray took care of the press for now," Jinx told her. They'd been camped outside the gates ever since the reward got upped—she was now worth ten million dollars.

"Suppose they don't believe me?" she asked.

"We'll make them," Jinx promised.

"I like believing you."

"You always should, mate."

"I like that too." She flung her arms around him, nuzzled against his neck. Neither one knew if the mating would be accepted officially by the Elders, but in her heart, it had been official from almost the first time she'd laid eyes on her warrior.

"You just keep yourself safe, Gilly. No matter what—you keep yourself safe."

*   *   *

Hours into the stakeout outside the Blackwells' mansion, Sister Wolf smelled the danger and Gillian took off at a dead run toward the house. The other Dires were behind her and she jumped onto the front staircase between the columns, lunged over the dead security guards. The smell of blood lay thickly metallic in her mouth and she broke through the locked front door like it was butter.

"We've been waiting for you," the man said. Not man—Dire. Like her. Just like her.

His eyes were the same unmistakable aqua blue. He had a gun to her mother's head. Both parents were side by side, tied to chairs. Neither was gagged but her mother appeared frozen with fear.

Did they remember what they thought Gillian had done? Even with Killian's help, she couldn't imagine that this wouldn't trigger some memories. But her parents weren't looking at her with hatred in their eyes. Come to think of it, they never had.

And this time, the fear they had wasn't directed at her.

She glared at the wolf holding them hostage and fought the urge to run at him. It went against everything she wanted to do by simply standing there, but she did. She would take her opportunity when it arose, and it would.

"Gillian, have a seat."

"Who are you?"

He jammed the gun hard against the side of her mother's head. "Sit. Down."

She complied, tucking her hands underneath

her. Hopefully, the others wouldn't slam in here the way she had.

"I'm your uncle. Call me Uncle Sam." He pointed to her parents. "You knew you were adopted."

"I did."

"You don't look happy to meet your biological family," he said, almost mournfully. "Didn't you want to search us out?"

"No," she said honestly. "I'm happy with the family I have."

Her father gave a tenuous smile in her direction and her uncle growled.

"Ungrateful. Just like your mother."

"Where is she?"

"I killed her maybe a month after she gave you and your twin away. Abominations, both of you," he spat. "She was told to put you down when she discovered there were two of you in there. And if she didn't, we were to put her down. She didn't listen. She ran—hid. And now, look where we are."

Her heart ached for the woman who'd carried her, who'd cared enough about her to give up her babies so they'd be born in freedom. "We're here because of you," she told him. "If you hadn't gotten involved, everything would still be fine."

"Really? It's fine to let abominations walk the earth? The Elders may deem it so, but our pack follows the old traditions," he sneered. "By doing my job, I'll be paying my debt to the warriors of old."

"Why didn't you take me when you killed my friends?" she demanded.

"We don't want you near us. We tried that once, with Steele. We don't want twins, abilities or not. My pack figured they'd lock you up and throw away the key. Drug you. Keep the shift at bay. And if you had abilities, the other Dires would find you. That was fine with the rest of my pack but I couldn't let it end there."

Her father's eyes widened at the admission and a tear ran down her mother's face—they only understood part of what the older wolf was saying, but it was enough.

"Why not just give me to the other Dires to begin with?" she asked.

"We don't help them. They're the reason our kind is nearly extinct."

"I'm not locked up anymore."

"You will be when they find you here, your parents dead in the same way your friends were killed and you, guilt ridden, mentally ill and shot by your own hand. I wanted you to be here to watch them die. Abominations deserve pain—you reap what you sow."

He thinks you can die. And she really didn't know for sure that she couldn't, or how fast she'd recover. She could only hope that Jinx rescued the Blackwells in time.

Let him go to report back to the pack that she was dead. He was obsessed with the twin curse, knew nothing of the ability.

I could trail him to find my twin.

She freed her hands from under her thighs and Uncle Sam told her not to move.

She stood anyway, moved threateningly toward him, aware that Sister Wolf was ready to take the reins. Her canines were already elongated and she was never more sure of anything than this.

The bullets ripped through her chest and she crumpled after taking a few more steps. Her breath grew harsh, her eyes hazy and the last thing she saw were the Blackwells' faces before she closed her eyes.

Her final thought was of Jinx and then everything went black.

Gwen had to fight Rifter to be allowed to come on this stakeout. Now that the Dires surrounding her began to drop, she was so grateful she'd followed her instincts.

"Gillian," Jinx cried out. "She's been shot."

Gillian's death didn't fell the other Dires immediately, but they all stopped moving within moments, their bodies pained. It had happened before, many times over the years and it always hurt like hell, but this time, Jinx wasn't upset.

It meant he'd been right—Gillian was immortal. Of course, he'd kill her later when he talked to her about what a chance she'd taken.

"What now? If she's dead, there's no one to protect her parents," Kate said as they stared into the window at the scene in front of them.

"She wouldn't know that when she's killed, the others die too and they recover together," Gwen said. "Kate, stay here with them—Liam, come with me."

Gwen's wolf was eager to come out but she didn't

want the Blackwells to see a wolf coming at them. Instead, she slammed through the bulletproof glass with her foot, then leaped through the rest, not stopping for a second, moving over furniture to pin the man down seconds before he shot the Blackwells.

Liam was shouting, grabbing the gun, and Gwen raked her claws across the wolf's left cheek so he'd be easy to find—and then she let him run.

"Tell Cyd to stay close to him. If he gets and keeps his scent, maybe he can lead us to Gillian's twin," she instructed and Liam called Cyd and did just that.

She moved to where the Blackwells were passed out, but alive. She smelled the chloroform he'd used and wondered why he hadn't killed them on the spot.

"I hope Kill comes to soon, because he's got to plant some new memories," Liam mumbled.

"Or maybe not," Gwen said. "Maybe they have a right to know."

"And maybe you've gone crazy." But he was smiling as he said it.

Cain tore through the woods behind Cyd. Keeping up with the Dire wasn't easy, but the strong scent of his fear certainly helped. And suddenly, Cyd stopped on a dime, Cain skidding to a stop behind his twin.

Cyd shifted fast, as did Cain and they watched the Dire pull out a long sword from behind one of the trees. He'd done this purposely, known someone would try to track him.

"I failed," he said to no one in particular.

"We've got to stop him," Cyd said, leaped over the brush to get to the Dire before he ran the sword through his heart. Cain watched as his twin got there just in time, surprising the Dire just enough so the sword flew. But Cyd was no match for the Dire—hell, both Cyd and Cain combined weren't. And holding the sword to him wasn't much incentive, because the Dire wanted to die.

"Where's Gillian's twin?" Cain demanded. The Dire smiled.

"Wouldn't you like to know?" were his last words before he ran straight to Cain. The force of his body hitting the sword slammed Cain into the tree behind him. He watched helplessly as the wolf died in front of him.

Gillian woke slowly, painfully. Gwen was standing over her, putting cool water on her face and Gillian sat up. Too fast, because the room spun.

"Gillian, it's okay. Your parents are safe. Cyd's tracking the Dire. Everything's okay," Gwen assured her and Gillian gripped the doctor wolf's hand.

"Thank you."

"You started it."

"And you finished it," Gillian said. "Where are the others?"

"Here," Jinx said, limping in.

"What happened?" Gillian asked, confused as all the Dires walked in behind him like the centurions they were.

"When you die, they all . . . die," Gwen explained.

"Shit, I had no idea," Gillian said.

"Maybe next time, explain things thoroughly, Jinx?" Vice said. "And you wonder why I told her about the mating."

With Gwen's help, Gillian got off the floor and went to hug Jinx. Gwen told her that her parents were in the other room, resting.

"I have to see them," she said and Jinx held her hand as they walked in. They looked all right, but shaken.

"Baby girl, can you ever forgive us?" her father asked. She hugged him first, then her mother.

"I already have. And I'm sorry I scared you all these years."

"I don't understand why that woman's family would do such a thing to her," her father said.

"The less you know, the safer you'll be. Just please, get the search for me called off. Clear me. Get my face wiped from the news."

"You can say this was a robbery gone bad," Jinx said. "You've been on the news so much and everyone knows how much money you're offering. I'm sure the police will be here soon, so let's get the story straight."

Which meant they needed to leave. Gillian hugged her parents again and her mother said, "Will you visit? Both of you . . ."

Jinx nodded and Gillian embraced her mother again. The only one she'd known. It hadn't been perfect but it had been hard on them too. "We'd like that."

Chapter 41

Cain dialed the phone over and over, hitting the buttons more frantically each time. No answer. Mailbox full.

It didn't make sense.

Panic raced through him and, for the first time since his original moon craze, he couldn't control his wolf. He shifted in the middle of the Dire living room as all the other wolves around him growled and surrounded him. He was prepared to fight each and every one of them to the death if it meant getting outside.

He was desperate. Growling, frothing at the mouth and he shoved at Rifter, who shifted and rose on his hind legs.

Cyd lunged then, but at Rifter. And Cain took that opportunity to crash out the side window that hadn't yet been repaired, splintering wood as he went.

The scent was getting fainter than it had ever been. Why was that happening? He swore he could hear the man in his ear, but that was wishful thinking.

Angus, where are you?

He ran through the woods, searching every corner and crevice frantically, did so for hours, barely aware that the other wolves were following him. But they weren't interfering.

Finally, he hit on a spot and he sniffed and dug . . . and then he found it. His wolf howled uncontrollably and he wanted to stop, to make calls, to be sure. But until Vice's hands touched him, didn't let go even when Cain bit his hand deeply, he couldn't calm down.

Vice's ability was his extremes of emotions. He was worried too, but he managed to push himself in the other direction and the pendulum swing of calm forced Cain to be so as well. In a matter of minutes, he was able to shift, and when he did, he bit out, "Angus is gone."

"What do you mean, *he's gone*?" Vice asked, still calm so Cain could be. The other wolves shifted and moved around him.

"Someone dragged him out of here. He's not answering his phone—and it's here—crushed." He pointed and they all looked at the destroyed cell, covered in Angus's blood.

Cyd had an arm around him. "We'll find him, brother. If it's the last thing I do."

Cain could only nod, because he was reeling.

"How protected is he?" Vice asked.

"A little. But we didn't mate, yet. We were waiting until . . . tonight." His voice broke on that word and the last thing he remembered hearing was Vice cursing as Cain shifted uncontrollably into the wolf again. And then he ran.

He might never stop. Not until he found Angus.

Angus woke in the back of what he assumed to be a van. He was hogtied, but not gagged, and he wasn't alone. He turned and let his eyes adjust to the light so he could see Bobby, his old partner. And try as he might, Angus had no memory of why they were together in this van.

"Bobby, what the hell?" he asked and Bobby opened his eyes and stared at Angus in the darkness.

"I thought you'd never wake up," Bobby said. "It's the trappers."

"Trappers? What are you talking about?"

"Weretrappers got us, Angus. Two up front, probably four more in the car following. I only got a quick look before they bashed my head in."

Maybe trappers were a new gang? Angus shook his head, trying to clear it, but that was a mistake. The dizziness overtook him and he gagged, trying not to throw up.

"Dammit," Bobby cursed. "They hit you hard. You've got a concussion. You need to stay awake, Angus."

But it would be so much easier to just close his eyes and sleep. "Were we on a case? Did you let our sup know where we'd be so he could send backup?"

"Angus, you're not in the FBI anymore."

"What do you mean, Bobby? Have you lost your mind?"

"Don't you remember? We were in the woods, hunting Weres. Wolves."

"I never liked hunting."

"Shit. Don't you remember Cain? Do you think he might be able to help us?"

"Is Cain an informant?" Everything was swimming in a jumbled mess in his mind. He felt fear now, and at the same time, he began to shiver. The motion of the van was making him seasick and he got onto his knees, tucked himself into a small ball like he was trying to disappear.

If he was lucky, maybe he would.

Chapter 42

The Dires gathered in the woods, along with Liam, Cyd and Cain, who still wore silver chains to stop him from erratically shifting. The past weeks, days, had been so hard on all of them, but they were out here under the moon, bruised and a little worse for wear, with big worries hanging over their heads.

But, as Rifter pointed out, with great sorrow must come great joy. He told them it would be irresponsible not to celebrate. That it would be a slap in the face to Dire tradition, and to the traditions that they'd created together.

"We're going to make more of our own," Rifter promised now. "It's time. We have to break away from the old enough to let in some of the new."

The baby on Vice's shoulder made a cooing sound, as if in total agreement with the king. Jinx put his arm around Gillian's shoulders and let the goodness of that sound seep into his soul.

This naming ceremony would also be a mating

blessing. The Elders were called for, but none came.

"What does that mean?" Gillian asked him.

Vice wanted to say that it meant the Elders were assholes, but Harm spoke first.

"We're here. And we're the ones who count," Harm said, and his voice was sure and firm. "I'd take Rifter's rule over them any day."

Rifter nodded and moved in front of Jinx and Gillian. He blessed the union with a prayer in the old language as Gillian held tightly to Jinx's hand, her eyes sparkling. They kissed, everyone clapped.

They would run under the moon after blessing the baby.

"Dire, do you have a name for your son?" Rifter asked, and it was the first time anyone had called this baby Vice's son. He didn't bother to hide the tears, cleared his throat and said, "He will be called Niclass."

Rifter smiled. "You gave him a Dire name."

"He is, for all intents and purposes," Vice said. "We'll call him Nic."

"His name means victory of the people," Rifter explained to those who didn't know. And then they all chanted a prayer and protection blessing for the little one.

"Now, we run," Rifter proclaimed and they all headed deeper into the woods. Rifter and Gwen shifted first, and the others followed in quick succession. The last ones with Vice were Jinx and Gillian. Vice wanted to shift, but he wouldn't leave Nic.

Maybe he could come up with some kind of sling for Brother Wolf.

Now, Jinx and Gillian stood on either side of him.

"You two need to run," Vice told them.

"Maybe this is our new tradition," Jinx told him.

"I like it," Vice told them. He put the baby in Gillian's arms and Nic cooed. "He likes you."

"I like him, too."

"Gillian, don't ever give up your search, okay?" Vice told her. He hadn't, thousands of years later, still hadn't. Nic was in his arms and he knew this was the right thing to do.

Liam had come far in a short time span. Vice would take none of that credit. The fact that Nic would be with him through all his years . . . that was something that scared Vice. But he'd always liked a challenge.

Together with Nic, they walked farther into the woods as the shifted Dires cavorted around them. The moon shone above them, bathing them in all things good and warm. And no matter what would happen, what could, they were family.

Epilogue

Not all who wander are lost.

Eydis had read the *Lord of the Rings* books and watched the movies so many times, she knew many of the lines by heart.

That particular one struck her every single time. She was a living, breathing example of that wanderer. No matter how lost she wished she could be, it would never happen.

She could still scent Vice, had never stopped being able to, even when she was killed by her own Dire pack and ascended to the Elders. Many times, she'd wished she'd simply died, but she'd always been able to comfort herself by knowing she could watch over Vice.

The other Elders had always been able to torment her in turn by tormenting him. But this last favor she'd begged for the immortal Dires who walked the earth, and in order to have her promise granted, she'd done the proverbial put up or shut up. And now, she was back here, an immortal, unshifted Dire walking the earth.

Even if she was allowed to see Vice, how could she explain the choices she'd been forced to make?

The choices you did make. There was no going back, but there was no forgetting either. She'd accepted her punishment easily, knowing how lonely it would be.

If you go to the Dires, we'll make your life a living hell, the two remaining male Elders had promised.

Like it hadn't always been, she'd told them.

If you go to the Dires, we'll make their lives a living hell. We'll take away anyone and anything that's ever been important to them had been the final threat, the one that made her accept that being alone, for the rest of her immortal life, was the only path she could wander.

Don't miss the first book in Stephanie Tyler's
exciting new romantic suspense series.

SURRENDER
A Section 8 Novel

On sale now from Signet Eclipse
Please turn the page for a preview.

Prologue

Zaire, twenty years earlier

The explosion threw him forward hard, the heat searing his body, debris cutting into his back as he covered his face and stayed down. Darius didn't need to look back to know what had happened—the bridge had exploded. Simon had purposely cut off their last means of escape. It would force their hands, Darius's especially.

"Darius, you all right?" Simon shook him, yanked him to his feet and held him upright. His ears would continue to ring for months.

"How much ammo do you have?" he called over the din. Couldn't see the rebels yet, but he knew they were coming toward them through the jungle.

"Stop wasting time. You go." Simon jerked his head toward the LZ and the waiting chopper about thirty feet away, crammed full of important rescued American officials and the like. Already precariously over capacity. "Go now and I'll hold them off."

Simon had always had a sense of bravado and a temper no one wanted to deal with, but one against twenty-plus? Those odds were not in the man's favor. Darius shook his head hard, and it was already spinning from the explosion.

"You are no fucking help to me," Simon told him. "I can't watch your back this time, Darius."

"Fuck you."

"Leave. Me. Here."

"If I do that, I'll come back to just a body."

"You're never coming back here." Simon's teeth were bared, ready for battle—with the rebels, with Darius, if necessary.

"If we both fight, we've got a better shot," Darius told him.

"You would tell me to leave if things were reversed, Master Chief, sir." Simon stood straight and tall, hand to his forehead, and Darius growled, "Don't you dare salute me, son." Their old routine. Simon managed a small smile, one that was as rare as peace in this part of the world.

"Don't take this from me, Darius. Let me save your goddamned life. You have your son to think about—I won't take you away from Dare."

Dare was in middle school—his mother had already left them both, and pain shot through Darius at the thought of leaving his son without a parent.

Simon knew he had him, pressed on. "The team

will always need you, and me—well, you can always find someone who can fight."

"Not like you."

"No, not like me," he echoed. "You go and you don't ever return."

Darius didn't say anything, and for a long moment they were silent, listening to the rustling that was still a couple of miles away. The blood was running down his side, and if he stayed in this wet jungle much longer with a wound like that . . .

"There's one spot left for a ride home." Simon told him what he already knew. "That seat is yours."

"I'm half-dead already."

"You think I'm not?" Simon asked, and Darius flashed back to a younger version of the operative in front of him, walking along a dusty road two miles from Leavenworth.

Darius had gone from being a Navy SEAL, fresh from capture in an underground cell where he'd been held for twenty-two days, to a medical discharge, to a phone call inviting him to join a very different kind of team. The CIA was creating a group—Section 8. For operatives like him. They'd have a handler and all the resources they'd need. Their only rule: Complete the mission. The how, when and where were up to them.

He was maybe the sanest of the group, and that was saying something. Simon always had the look of a predator, occasionally replaced by a childlike wonder, usually when Adele was around. If you looked at the team members' old files, you'd see everything from disobeying orders to failing psych exams to setting fires.

But if you knew S8, you'd see the mastermind. The wetwork expert. The demolitions expert, the one who could handle escape and extractions with ease. They could lie and steal and hack. They could find any kind of transport, anytime, anywhere, anyhow, that could get them the hell out of Dodge.

In the beginning, they'd been nothing more than angry wild animals, circling, furious with one another and their circumstances. But once the trust grew, it was never broken.

Separately, they were good. Together, they were great.

And now, three years later, two S8 operatives stood near the wreckage of a bridge in Zaire and they were both about to die.

"If you could save fifteen people . . . or just one . . . ," Simon prodded.

"Don't you pull that trolley problem shit on me—I've been to more shrinks than you and I'm not leaving you behind like this," Darius said, his voice slightly vicious. But they both knew he'd relent. He'd done everything Simon had asked of him, and this was for the good of the rest of the team.

"They'll never recover without you," Simon told him. "You're the goddamned heart of the team."

"And you're my best goddamned friend," Darius growled. Simon's expression softened, just for a second.

"Just remember the promise," Simon warned.

We don't try to find out who's behind S8. No matter what.

Neither Darius nor Simon believed what happened today was a screwup their handler could've known about. But their promise referenced him specifically. They knew they'd been brought together by the CIA, but their handler picked the jobs, gave them orders and anything else they needed. Once they started distrusting him, it was all over.

"I'll remember," Darius told him now.

"Good. Go." This time, Simon's words were punctuated with a push. Darius barely caught himself, and when he turned, Simon was already running in the direction of the rebels, the crazy fucker confusing them with his contrary tactics. Because who the hell ran toward the bad guys?

Darius made his choice—he was a liability, so he made his way to the helo, pulled himself on board and shoved himself into the pilot's seat. Within minutes, the steel bird was grinding gears, rising above the heavy cover of jungle. As the chopper blades cut the air smoothly with their *whoompa-whoompa-tink*, Darius turned the helo and stared down at the man who'd left himself behind as Darius took the rescued civilians—aid workers, a diplomatic attaché and other Americans who'd been working in the area—away. He'd never take credit for the glory on this one, though. Simon could've sat in this pilot seat as easily as Darius did.

There was a chance Simon could fight them off. There was always a chance. And as he watched for that brief moment, he hoped beyond hope that Simon could win, fight his way out of the mass of humanity that was trying to kill him simply because he was American.

One last glance afforded Darius the view he didn't want—the mob surrounding Simon. It was like watching his friend—his teammate—sink into a manhole as they swarmed over him.

Section 8 had ended at that moment, at least for him. He'd later learn that their handler had agreed, and the group of seven men and one woman who'd been thrown together to work black ops missions around the globe with no supervision and very few, if any, rules, had been officially disbanded, the surviving members given large sums of money to buy their silence and thank them for their service.

He would have to explain to the team why he'd left Simon behind, although they'd know. They'd get it. They all prepared for that eventuality every single time they went out. It was part of the thrill.

There was no thrill now as he watched his best friend die. And he didn't turn away, stared at the spot until he couldn't see anything anymore, and knew he'd never get that image out of his mind.

Chapter 1

Twenty years later

Dare O'Rourke believed in ghosts because they visited him regularly.

He woke, covered in sweat, shaking, and immediately glanced at the clock. He'd slept for fifteen minutes straight before the nightmare. A record.

The screams—both those in the dream and those that tore from his own throat whenever he allowed himself the luxury of sleep—would stay with him as long as he lived, wrapping around his soul and squeezing until he wished he'd died that terrible night.

A part of him had, but what was left wasn't a phoenix rising from the ashes. No, Dare was broken bones and not of sound mind. Might never be again, according to the Navy docs, who said the trauma Dare had faced was too severe, that he wasn't fit for duty. He had no doubt those doctors were right, wasn't sure what kind of man he'd be if he *had* been able to go the business-as-usual route.

He'd never be the same.

The CIA felt differently. *You'll survive. You'll recover. You're needed.*

And even though he knew the world needed rough men like him, no matter how fiercely the government would deny his existence if it came down to brass tacks, he told them all to fuck off and went to live in the woods. He was no longer a SEAL, the thing that had defined him, the job he'd loved for ten years.

Dare had prayed for many things that night in the jungle, including death, but none had been answered. And so he'd stopped praying and holed up alone and just tried to sleep through the night.

Three hundred sixty-three days and counting and not an unbroken sleep among them.

Three hundred sixty-four was a couple of hours away, the day giving way to the dusk, and the car coming up the private road couldn't mean anything but trouble.

Three hundred sixty-three days and no visitors. He saw people only when he went into the small town monthly for supplies. Beyond that, he remained on his property. It was quiet. He could think, whether he wanted to or not.

As for healing . . . that would all be in the eye of the beholder.

He rolled out of bed, flexed the ache from his hands before pulling on jeans and a flannel shirt he left unbuttoned. Barefoot, he went out to greet his guest.

He met the car with his weapon drawn, put it away when the car got close enough for him to see the driver.

Adele. A member of the original Section 8—a black ops group of seven men and one woman recruited from various military branches and the CIA. All loose cannons, none of them taking command well. All of them the best at what they did. A real life A-Team, except the reality wasn't anything like it was portrayed on television.

Dare's father—Darius—had been a member, was MIA and presumed KIA on a mission last year. At least that's what Adele had told Dare.

All Dare knew was that S8 had officially disbanded when he was thirteen, and for years, its members worked black ops missions on their own steam. Until they'd gotten a call—that call—the remaining six members and one last job. Back into the jungle they'd sworn not to go back into. *A mistake to go*, Darius told him. *We're too old.* But they were still strong, with plenty of experience. And they went anyway.

Four men never returned. Adele and Darius did, but they were never the same. Refused to talk about it and went off on more unreachable missions until they'd both disappeared more than a year ago.

Dare had wanted to assume that the secrets of the group were all dead and buried with them.

Fucking assumptions would get him every

time. He knew better. His father and Adele had come back from the dead more than once.

Adele took her time getting out of the car. She was stately looking, at one time considered more handsome than pretty, with short hair and kind blue eyes, a thin frame that belied her strength. It was hard to believe she was as deadly as the men she'd worked with.

"I have a job for you," she said when she reached the porch he refused to leave. No preamble, all business. The only thing contradicting her deadliness was the frail frame she now carried.

She was sick—he could see it in her pale coloring, the darkness shading the skin under her eyes. His heart went out to her; she'd been the closest thing to a mother he'd ever had, even though she'd been far more like a mother wolf than a nurturer.

But it had been enough. "I can't."

"You're not broken, Dare." Adele sounded so damned sure, but why he wanted her reassurance, he had no idea.

He jerked his gaze to her and saw her own quiet pain that she carried, kept so close to the vest all these years. "It was all a setup."

Adele neither confirmed nor denied, but the truth of his own words haunted him.

It was a setup . . . and you were supposed to die.

A Ranger had received a dishonorable discharge for rescuing him against a direct order. Dare would never forget the soldier's face, and he doubted the soldier would ever stop seeing his.

Two men, bound by pain.

He closed his eyes briefly, thought about the way he'd been found, nearly hanging from his arms, up on a platform so he could watch the entire scene being played out in front of him.

The villagers. His guides. American peacekeepers. His team. All slaughtered in front of him.

The fire came closer now . . . and he welcomed it. Had prayed for it, even as his captors laughed at his predicament, spat in his face. Cut him with knives and ripped his nails off one by one. There was nothing he could offer them, nothing they would take from him.

He'd offered himself multiple times. They refused. He must've passed out—from pain, hunger, it didn't matter. He clawed at the wood, his wrists, forearms, fingers, all broken from trying so hard to escape chains not meant for humans to fight against. It hadn't stopped him—he'd been nearly off the platform, ripping the wood out piece by piece, when the worst of the rape happened in front of him.

It would've been too late.

Could've closed your eyes. Blocked it out. Let yourself pass out.

But if they were going to be tortured, the least he could do was not look away. And he hadn't, not even when they'd nailed his hands to the boards, not for twenty-four hours, until everyone was dead, the village was razed, the acrid smell of smoke burning his nose, his lungs. The sounds of the chopper brought him no relief, because he knew they'd save him before the fire reached him.

The group of Army Rangers had been going to

another mission, stumbled on the destruction by way of the fire. They'd come in without permission, the Ranger who'd saved him taking the brunt of the blame, or so Dare had heard later.

Dare hadn't gone to the hearing for that soldier who'd saved him. It wouldn't have helped either of them. In the next months, Dare was sure the soldier would be found dead under mysterious circumstances, another in a long line of men who'd interfered in something S8 related.

He turned his attention back to Adele, who waited with a carefully cultivated pretense of patience. "Why come now?"

She hadn't seen him since right before that last mission. Hadn't come to the hospital. Hadn't called or written. And while he'd told himself it didn't bother him, it had.

"Your sister's in trouble."

Half sister. One he'd never met before out of both necessity and her mother's insistence. He didn't even know if Avery Welsh knew he existed. "I thought she was well hidden."

"We did too."

"Where is she?"

"On her way to the federal penitentiary in New York—or a cemetery—if you don't hurry."

"Are you fucking shitting me?"

She twisted her mouth wryly. "I assure you, I'm not."

"What did she do?"

"She killed two men," Adele said calmly. "The police are coming for her—she's about forty-eight hours away from being sent to jail for life. Of course, there are other men after her too, and they make the police look like the better option."

So the men who were after her had tipped off the police. "She's what—twenty-two?" A goddamned baby.

Adele nodded. "You'll have a small window of opportunity to grab her in the morning at the apartment where she's been hiding."

"You want me to . . ." He stopped, turned, ran his hands through his hair and laughed in disbelief. Spoke to the sky. "She wants me to help a killer."

"Your sister," she corrected. "Is that a problem?"

He laughed again, a sound that was rusty from severe underuse.

Avery had been secreted away with her mother before she'd been born, the relationship between her mother and Darius brief once she found out what Darius's livelihood was. But after that last mission, everything S8 related seemed to die down. Until Darius went missing. Until Dare was almost killed.

Until Adele showed up on his doorstep, dragging the past with her like an anchor.

"She's a known fugitive and I'm supposed to hide her?" he asked now.

"She's family—and she needs your protection."

He turned swiftly, fighting the urge to pin her against a column of the porch with an arm across her neck. The animal inside him was always there, lurking barely below the surface, the wildness never easily contained. "What the hell is that supposed to mean?"

Adele hadn't moved. "Don't make me spell everything out for you, Dare. You know you're still wanted. Why wouldn't she be?"

"I can't do this. Find—"

"Someone else?" she finished, smiled wanly. "There's no one but me and you, and I'm about to buy the farm, as they say. Cancer. The doctors give me a month at best."

"I'm sorry, Adele, but—"

"I know what happened to you. But we protect our own."

"I didn't choose to be a part of your group."

"No, you were lucky enough to be born into it," she said calmly.

"Yeah, that's me. Lucky."

"You're alive, aren't you?"

He wanted to mutter, *Barely*, but didn't. "Where's my father, Adele?"

She simply shrugged. "He's gone."

"Yeah, gone." Darius had been doing that since Dare was six years old.

"They're all gone—the men, *their families*. All *gone* over the course of the last six years. Do you understand?"

He had known. Dare had kept an eye on the families left behind by S8 operatives. Even though Darius had growled at him to stay the hell out of it, he'd found a line of accidents and unexplained deaths. They were all spaced widely enough apart and made enough sense not to look suspicious to the average eye.

But he wasn't the average eye. This was an S8 clean-house order, an expunging, and Dare knew he was still on that list and there was no escaping it.

For Avery, he would have to come out of hiding.

"Hiding won't stop your connection with Section 8," Adele said, as if reading his mind.

"I'm not hiding," he ground out.

"Then go to Avery—show her this from Darius."

She handed him a CD—the cover was a photograph of Avery. He glanced at the picture of the woman, and yeah, she resembled her father—the same arctic-frost blue eyes—but her hair was light, not dark. She was really pretty. Too innocent looking to have committed murder, but he'd learned over the years that looks could never be trusted. "And then what? I'm no good for this."

"You're better than you think."

"Bullshit—I'm just the only one you've got."

She smiled, but it didn't reach her eyes.

He looked at the picture stuck into the clear CD case again, and something deep inside him ached for his lost childhood. He hoped Avery had had one. "I'll think about it."

With that, she walked away, turned to him when she was halfway to her car and stood stock-still in the driveway. The back of his neck prickled. "Best think fast, Dare."

It was part instinct, part the way Adele paused

as if posing. She gave a small smile, a nod, her shoulders squared.

He sprang into action, yelled, "No!" as he leaped toward her, Sig drawn, but it was too late.

The gunshot rang out and he jumped back to the safety of the house, cutting his losses. Adele collapsed to the ground, motionless. A clean kill. Sniper.

She'd made the ultimate sacrifice—going out like a warrior to force him to get off his ass and into action—ending a life that was almost over anyway. His father would've done the same.

Now there was nothing to be done here but get away and live. A hot extract involving just himself.

He shot off several warning rounds of his own to buy himself time. He took a quick picture of Adele with his cell phone camera and then went inside, grabbed his go bag and the guitar, then ignited the explosives he'd set up for a just-in-case scenario because, as a kid of a Section 8er, he was always a target.

That entire process took less than a minute, and then he took off in the old truck down the back road, the CD still in his hand.

Adele was too good not to know she'd been followed. She'd trapped him by bringing the trouble literally to his front door.

He cursed her, his father and everyone in that damned group as he motored down the highway, even as another part of his brain, hardwired for danger, made lists of what he'd need.

New wheels.

Guns.

New safe house with a wanted woman.

He threw the CD on the seat next to him and fingered the silver guitar pick he wore on a chain around his neck.

Goddammit, there was no escaping the past.

Also available from

Stephanie Tyler

SURRENDER
A Section 8 Novel

For former Navy SEAL Dare O'Rourke, Section 8 was
legendary. The son of one of its missing members, he
grew up in the shadow of its secrets. All he knew was that
it was a cabal of operatives discharged from branches of
the military and reassigned to dangerous, off-the-books
missions. And that their handler was as shrouded in
mystery as the missions themselves. Now the handler of
Section 8 has given orders to kill any remaining members,
along with their families. Dare must save his long-lost
half-sister, whom he was never meant to meet. They must
bring together for one last mission those who are in
danger—to avenge their families and to survive.

"No one writes a bad-boy hero like Tyler."
—*New York Times* **bestselling author Larissa Ione**

stephanietyler.com

Available wherever books are sold or at
penguin.com

facebook.com/LoveAlwaysBooks